A WHISPER IN THE DARK

U. S. A.

UNHOLY SLAYING AGENCY

BOOK ONE

GUY QUINTERO

Sinister Raven Publishing LLC

A WHISPER IN THE DARK

Book One of Unholy Slaying Agency Series

First edition: August 2022

ISBN: 978-1-958828-00-7 (Ebook edition)

ISBN: 978-1-958828-01-4 (Paperback edition)

ISBN: 978-1-958828-02-1 (Hardback edition)

This novel is dedicated to the Jefferson Ditch Gang and all my friends that I grew up gaming with. Ray, Carl, Brian, Mel, Derek, Josh, Luke, Greg, and Nick. You are the original USA Agents.

Special thanks to Danica Simone, Sally Odgers, and Nina the muse. Without you this dream wouldn't have been possible.

Last but not least, I would like to thank Silvestre. Thank you for the late night COD chats and being my first beta reader.

CHAPTER 1
A WOUND IN REALITY

The woman's eyelids trembled as they opened. Flickering lights encircled her, their source low to the ground. It wasn't enough to hold back the creeping darkness. As the ripples in her vision faded, a ceiling of dead lamp lights and dusty cobwebs welcomed her. Tingles surged through numb fingers as she explored the hard wood underneath her palms.

Attempts to move her limbs and head failed, the leather restraints keeping them in position on the table. Clouds of warm breath floated above her face with each gasp. An aroma of musty sandalwood invaded into her nostrils.

The cute blond guy... he gave me some weed... bought me a drink... the hell was in... it was spiked... had to be...

A shadow approached. Rattling accompanied each footstep as someone drew near.

"Ye be awake naa," announced a grating voice with a heavy patois accent. "That's gud. We be gettin tis undawey."

Oh my God!

Thick gnarled locks dangled just above her face as he

leaned over. She managed a glimpse of dark sunken cheeks covered in withered and cracked skin. Shifting her eyes, she could see a clay goblet clutched in his hands. The man dipped his fingers inside before running a warm and thick liquid over her skin. He hummed or grumbled. Her mind wasn't on the tune, but rather whatever he painted on her abdomen.

"Who are you? Where are my clothes? What are you doing? Let me go, please!"

"Ya hush, everyting gun be ire, pinktoe. Tis nahting personal. I jus be needin ya powah, Sara."

"How do you know my name? What power? Please, mister, I think you have the wrong person. I don't have any power. I'm just a student. My parents are the wealthy ones. They can hook you up! I can ask them to—"

"Oh, ya tink powah comes from money? Silly girl. Ya gots plenty ah' powah. See, it mostly be in da women. That's why ya ancestors had their witch trials, rootin' out da gifted. Most Europeans lost it, 'cept for a few. We embrace da otha side an' da tings dat come wiffit, Sara Duncan."

"I don't understand! How do you know my name?"

He shifted away from her view, the ceiling welcoming her once again. When his hand passed over her face, Sara managed to catch the glint of a serrated knife. The humming continued. Pain shot into her foot, climbing through the limb and coursing her entire body. She jerked in her restraints. Flesh was split by the sawing of a blade carving into her pinky toe—serrated teeth of the dull knife ground, juttering in his tightening grip. Warmth spilled over her foot as blood spewed from the wound. His filth-encrusted hand clamped down on her ankle as he pressed harder, driving through the bone.

Her shrill scream echoed into the vast area. Releasing her, he scrambled around the table, grabbing for the severed digit.

A splash came from the goblet as he plopped it inside. Tears streamed down her flushed cheeks.

"Scream all ya want, girl. Da policeman don't come callin in deez here parts."

Why?

"I told ja, I be needin ya powah. Ya bleed, so me bruddas and sistas can come tru dee udda side. See it be all about da energy. Everyting be energy, and everyting needs energy."

His leathery fingers grabbed the other ankle.

"No! Please!"

Another slice, and she was in agony again. A chain of screams followed. With a clenched grin, he continued to saw.

"Da knife made a lot of energy go tru this world, can't sharpen it, lest it lose da spirit edge."

She writhed but to no avail. The weeping continued.

"I don't understand. Please stop! I won't tell anyone, just please stop! Please—"

"Hush naa, child. The energy is everyting. I know ye be educated. Ya noe history? Ya noe bout da natives and dere sacrifices ta da serpent god? It all be bout da energy. Positive, negative, da spirits come callin when it be enough."

He watched as her bosom heaved. The tension in her body started to fade. After walking over to a nearby table, he returned. A needle penetrated Sara's arm, its contents squeezed into her. A few moments passed. Her eyes sprang open. She gasped and coughed, tears springing from her eyes.

My heart feels as if it's going to explode! This is worse than coke! Adrenaline?

"Can't 'ave ya sleepin on me. I need to bleed ya. See tis be why ya shudda mastah'd ya senses, 'stead a bein a slave to 'em."

Intense heat pressed against the wound, searing meat and

skin together. The sizzle of blood ushered the smell of cooked flesh. Sara writhed again, howling, pleading, sobbing. The leather restraint binding her head loosened. Looking through his locks, she found dark eyes glazed over, looking through her, devoid of empathy.

Necklaces of bone draped over his shoulders, long and thick. With each motion, they swayed together, rattling. He held the bloody digit that once belonged to her, measuring it with the others and nodding. A flash in her mind's eye caused her to freeze. The sobbing ceased. Her body locked into place.

The darkness closed in, draping Sara like a blanket, a chill seeping into her. A skeletal visage peered from it. Empty black sockets met her bewilderment, radiating an aura of hatred that froze her being. Sterile emptiness came with it, the images of the mortuary she visited to claim her brother's body. The cold polished silver cadaver tables filled her mind, the apathetic attendants that handled him like dirty laundry. The spout closed, ending the flood of memories. She sensed herself drowning, each breath growing more arduous as the prickling cold enveloped her.

"*Not yet, little one.*" A whisper caressed, sending her soul reeling.

It faded until only her captor stood before her, and she found herself back on the table. The pain streaked through her body. She hadn't stopped screaming. He hadn't finished removing fingers and toes. His slippery gore-stained hand lost its hold as she convulsed. He moved to a bowl of water, washing his face and hands. After taking a sip from it, he returned to his work.

"Ya see da Baron now, didn't ya? He toll me. He be muh bedda 'alf."

The blade sliced down. Her cries continued.

"Tis gun be a long night for da tree of us."

Calvin shivered when the night breeze stroked his body. The ground he lay prone on seeping his warmth away. His eyes narrowed through the shrubs their team hid amongst, focusing on the door of the small shack they overwatched from a distance.

What a shithole. I couldn't get a cushy first assignment, sniping tritons on the beaches of Miami? Of course not. Nope, I'm stuck with this asshole in the boonies, hunting God knows what.

The entrance consisted of wooden planks affixed with rusty hinges along the outer rim. His hands tightened around the resin grip of his M4 carbine, drawing it deep into his shoulder. He positioned so the chevron of his ACOG weapon optic remained center mass over the door. The cool breeze returned, causing another shiver.

"Calm yourself, Rookie," Fredrick whispered.

"Just cold, sir." *Dang it, he's on to me.*

"My ass. I know fear when I see it. Don't be fooled. We may be experienced now, but we've all been scared. Did you cover that fiber-optic tube on that ACOG?"

"Yes, sir."

"Good. These damned things will spot the red easily, even through all this shrubbery."

I don't like the sound of that. "Sir, are you going to tell me what we're hunting?"

"Nope. Semper Gumbi, kiddo. That's part of your training

tonight. Sometimes you don't know what's going to come down the pike."

Is he for real? "But this is an actual operation."

"Training is constant. Remember when you first joined the service, that OTJT you were always promised? Just bullshit to keep you awake for fragos. Shit's constantly changing, Rook. You have to always be ready for it."

"Fragos?"

"Fragmentary order." Fredrick raised a brow. "I'm sure you've heard about them during your time in the Corps."

"I was Navy."

"Griff sent me a fucking squid! I asked to work with only marines and soldiers. Were you a SEAL or SWCC?"

"No, sir. Military police. I worked with canines."

"How ironic. Damn that Griff."

Should I ask? Meh, screw it. "Sorry, sir. By the way, what's OTJT?"

"On the job training. See, this is why I wanted combat arms soldiers. I'm not running a damn acronym class here."

"Well, at least he's not another nasty girl," Callisto chirped over their communication earbuds.

"What's a nasty girl?" Calvin asked.

"National Guard." She snickered.

Don't laugh. This could be them testing the new guy's bearing. "So, I take it you were all Marines?"

"I'm Former CIA," Callisto answered.

"Nope! I was a part of the USMC." Fredrick replied.

"That's the marines, right?"

"Not quite." Callisto chimed again. "USMC means U Signed a Motherfuckin Contract."

"Yahtzee," Fredrick agreed.

"Lock it up!" Emmerich ordered. "We're almost in position. It's showtime."

"Roger, King!"

"Don't call me that! I said, lock it up, Freddy!"

"Just watch the door, Rook. Cover my brother's ass. Shit's about to get hairy. Literally."

"Everyone has their silver fulminate rounds loaded, right?" Finley inquired.

"Yeah, Egghead," Fredrick replied. "This ain't our first rodeo. Is SOAR ready with air support?"

"Yeah, Meathead," the intelligence agent responded. "This isn't my first rodeo, either."

The tall and broad-shouldered Emmerich approached the door first. The links in his combat vest held numerous twelve-gauge rounds to accommodate the pump-action Mossberg he shouldered. Behind Emmerich was Callisto, her long dark hair rolled into a perfect bun. With stern eyes, she scanned hard at their surroundings, the index finger of her right hand twitching against her M4 carbine's lower receiver.

Bringing up the rear were Badrick and Evan, the former carrying an M249 light machine gun with a plump green drum. Calvin's thoughts echoed with the first words he heard from meeting the large black man.

"I don't know what you've done to end up in our outfit. If you last beyond the first month, you can tell me your story, Rook. Until then, leave me be."

"NODs if you haven't already," Emmerich whispered.

The team reached to their Kevlar helms, snapping their night optic devices into position. They surveyed the area with newfound clarity, matching that of their daytime vision, except for the green tint. The integrated thermal imaging highlighted the bodies of their comrades with an orange coat.

Calvin spotted lights pulsing from their helmets, visible only through the device since they were on an infrared frequency. Emmerich and the strike team stacked together on the wall, leaning forward, hip to hip, ready to pounce.

"Any heat signatures in doorframe or windows?"

"I got nothing on MW thermals, Em," Fredrick responded.

Emmerich's shotgun roared into action. With a burst of force, the door erupted into splinters. A fierce kick sent it wobbling inward. After a second, he was already out of view, speeding inside. The team followed, boots stomping the ground as they streamed into the hut.

They were met with screams and whimpers. Tearful eyes peered back from dirt-covered faces with heads of disheveled hair. A mass of children caused the team to halt in their tracks. The filth covered bodies of the youngsters huddled together, shivering inside of the tattered rags they wore for clothing.

"Tac-com this is Ghost8Actual. We've sighted the children, no sign of the HVTs in the domicile," Emmerich stated over comms.

"Actual, this is Tac-com. She wants to know if they are civilians," Finley relayed.

"No idea. We haven't eyes on any bites yet. Hard to tell, they're all huddled together."

"She said it's your call, Actual."

"They're civilians, for now." *Just need to keep my eye on them.*

"This is Ghost8Golf with cordon, Em, you've got

company!" Fredrick interrupted. "Multiple heat signatures closing quickly on your position from the north!"

So much for hoping this would be easy. "Acknowledged, Golf," Emmerich replied while turning to his team. "You heard him. We've got contact." *They're too fast, too agile for us to contend with those numbers out in the open. We'll get swarmed.* "Hold here, setup a base of fire, Ghost Team."

Like the wind, they maneuvered through the forest. Hulking mounds of muscle and fur galloped with swift grace upon hind legs. Although Fredrick could see them through the medium weapon thermal sight, he heard nothing. There was no croaking of frogs, call of an owl, or even the chirping of crickets. The forest went silent as if all life became petrified by their very presence.

Fredrick felt his heart racing. Sweat from his helm rolled into his brow. *Finger straight and off the trigger until ready to fire.*

Claws pierced the walls of the hut as one climbed to the roof. Rippling back muscles spread like a cobra's hood, allowing the creature to scale with ease. Fredrick aligned his optics over it.

Gain sight alignment. Maintain sight picture.

Feral yellow eyes glistened in the moonlight as the creature scanned the area. Its thick meaty lips rolled back from its muzzle as it snapped with salivating jaws. The beast's claws flexed and curled with anticipation.

Don't want to be bitten by those. Breathe, Relax, Aim, Sight alignment, and...

The door to the hut opened, followed by two objects being tossed outside. A dozen predatory gazes followed as cylindrical metal devices landed at their paws. A flash consumed their vision. The frenzied creatures reeled away with eyes clamped shut. A deafening noise erupted. Their claws now cuffed their pointed ears. A series of high-pitched cries followed as the pack writhed. Their bodies locked, some falling over as others staggered in place.

Eyelids flickered, a dazed beast struggling to open them was greeted by the barrel of Emmerich's twelve gauge. A blast sent half the creature's skull spraying across its brethren. A cock of the fore-end chambered another round. He pulled the trigger again, and the whimpering beast's trunk caved from a silver slug burrowing into it.

"Stay with the children, Evan!" Emmerich barked.

Callisto followed with a succession of shots burrowing into the chest and head of her first target. After it hit the ground, she riddled the corpse with a few more. Her weapon barrel rose, the sight of a growling face approaching in her optics. Another torrent of gunfire sank into its chest. Muscular arms covered its heart. Callisto brought her reticle to its head, and her thumb flicked forward, snapping the fire selector into burst mode. Rounds spewed in trine at her target, ripping its forehead open, exposing brain matter to the cold night air.

"Two tangoes!" Callisto called.

More fire rang out, and the team pushed forward with Callisto taking point. Emmerich followed four feet behind to her left, with Badrick taking up a similar position on her right. Muzzle flashes lit the area as shots continued to belt out. Bodies keeled over, their gray and brown fur covered in warm stains from their gaping wounds.

...Squeeze.

Fredrick's M240B machine gun roared to life. Heavy rounds fired into the monstrosity on the rooftop. Cries came from the creature as lead punched into it. After a few staggering steps, it plummeted to the ground near the team. Emmerich inspected, chambered a round, and blasted the creature one more time.

"Em, next time, can you let me know when you're gonna go balls in?" Fredrick asked. "I mean for fuck's sake, I have no shots. The Rook and I wanted some work, too."

Dozens of howls echoed from the surrounding forest.

"Looks like you got your wish, little bro," Emmerich quipped. "All yours."

"Shit!"

"Tac-com, this is Ghost8Actual, what's the ETA on that CAS?"

"ETA for close air support is five mikes from your AO, Actual," Finley responded. "Hang tight."

"Shit!"

"Give'em hell, Freddy! Everyone else fall back inside the hut!"

The belt was sucked from the drum by the machine gun as rounds chambered and spewed. Freddy spotted the large heat signatures of enemies charging from amongst trees and bushes. Five to six shots roared from their position with each controlled burst. Howls and cries rent the air, as meat and limbs rived away.

"Barrel me, Rook! She's running hot!" *Hang in there, Ghost!*

"Gotcha, bossman!"

Calvin grabbed the handle of the sweltering barrel, pressing the release and replacing it with another. A snap signaled it had locked into the receiver. Fredrick was pulling up another drum, drawing the belt from it while opening the feed tray. He slammed it shut, cocked the charging handle, and launched back into action with sustained fire. Calvin returned to his M4, adding to the hail.

"WHOO! Get some, baby!" Fredrick bellowed. *Need to take some of the pressure off the assault team.*

Dang, Freddy really is going wild with that pig, must be fighting off a lot of tangoes. Badrick raised a brow. *Cali has that crazed look, smiling like the cat that ate the canary. That's the same grin she got when we were cornered by the Greenlee family.*

Shards of glass flew from the windows, out into the grass as the team peppered the charging beasts. Another flashbang sent the creatures reeling again. Giggles came from the entrance as it cracked opened. Callisto stood there, all smiles, pulling the pin from a grenade, and shutting the door after tossing it.

Damn, girl! Yup, I knew it! They aren't going to like that shit. That's going to rile them up.

A snarling muzzle paused, watching as the silver device fell to the ground. An eruption followed. The earth trembled, those caught in the initial explosion howled as limbs and skin were ripped clean from them. Shards of silver darted in all directions, lodging into those seized in the mayhem. Screeching cries followed. The survivors whimpered and crawled, dragging bloody strands that once formed their legs. Scratching at the ground, they tried to pull themselves away as more of their brethren stormed on the scene.

Em's nodding. Time to work.

The door opened again with Badrick's M249 spraying

rounds into the mass. He spotted the tracers from Fredrick, chewing the rear flank of their foes. The combined fire of the two machine guns halted the approach. With the last of his ammunition spent, he moved back inside the hut.

"Gotta reload, cover me!" Badrick requested.

"Gotcha, big guy!" Evan said as he left the window, taking the doorway.

"Freddy, how's it looking out there in overwatch?" Emmerich asked. "Tell me something good."

"Drones! A buttload of them, too! No sign of the big mama."

Damn it! This is going to be bad. We're steadily losing the initiative. They'll be on top of us once the rest of the pack closes behind the first wave. "Acknowledged. What's your status?"

"Em, they're still coming!" Fredrick said. "I've got dozens more signatures hounding on your position. I'm running too hot covering both sectors. I can't keep them off you!"

I hate being right. Baddy's SAW is back up, at least that'll slow them down. What would Katherine do? I know. Our father, who art in heaven—

Badrick grabbed Evan, pulling him from the doorway, reclaiming his place. "Good work, I got it from here."

A massive rumbling churned above them. From the windows, the team could see the trees and grass swaying in constant rhythm away from the hut. Leaves blew into the air, carried away by the unnatural wind.

"Ghost8Actual, this is Buzzard, we are in your AO," the pilot announced over comms.

I'll be damned, it worked. "Roger, Buzzard. Boy, are you a sight for sore eyes. Painting targets now to the north, danger close!"

"Acknowledged. We have your beacons on IR, send it when ready."

Emmerich drew his marker, switching places with Callisto at the window. Two clicks and an infrared pulse laser highlighted the position of the pack. Buzzard's minigun spun into action, spewing rounds that shredded bodies, leaving pink mist raining throughout the battered landscape. Rockets slammed into the forest, the rumble of thunder heralding their impact. Debris fell from the strike zone, followed by clouds of dust and smoke. When the minigun ceased fire, only the hum of the rotary blades lingered.

"We do not see any more signatures. It looks like you're clear, Actual," Buzzard responded. "Thanks for the work."

"Dinner on me during the next seventy-two. Thanks, Buzzard."

"Roger, we'll hold you to that. We are RTB. Buzzard out."

The helicopter departed.

"Love them flyboys," Fredrick said.

"Same here," Emmerich replied. "All right, let's get these kids evac'd and RTB so they can get vaccinated."

A scream pierced into the night. The team turned to see Evan disappear underneath a pile of claws, fur, and gnashing teeth. Their fury peeled away his uniform and armor, stripping tissue from bone. After lurching forward, one assailant's muzzle clamped down on Evan's throat. He gasped, struggling, but their vice-like grip held him in place. Callisto recoiled when a squirt of blood sprayed across her eye protection.

"The children! They've turned!" Callisto screamed, tossing her Oakleys.

"Shit!" Badrick cried, pointing his M249.

"Ghost8Actual, this is Tac-com, what's happening?"

Blood rose from Evan's mouth with a gargle as he tried to cry out. His eyes met with Badrick's, while he convulsed from the onslaught. The big man could only nod before letting out a barrage of fire into the small vicious creatures. Emmerich followed with a chain of blasts until his feed tube was empty. Once the smoke cleared from the corpses, Emmerich patted Badrick on his shoulder.

"Sorry big guy, it's always hard losing a partner." *That was my call to watch the kids. I should've had him inspect, but it just got too hot out here...*

"I was going to let him tell me his story over the weekend. We were going to introduce the old ladies and have a beer."

"Damn it!" Emmerich continued. "Tac-com, this is Actual. We have an operator KIA. Requesting dust off."

"They're dispatched and en route, Actual... Em, is it Freddy?"

"You haven't gotten rid of me yet, Egghead. What the fuck happened in there, Em?"

"Our marks were turned; we arrived here too late. They got Evan. They must've changed during the firefight." *So much for situational awareness. I dropped the ball.*

Callisto patted Emmerich on the back. "Heavy is the head that wears the crown, babe."

"Em, it's not over," Fredrick said. "I've got one more heat signature closing on your position fast. It's big."

The machinegun roared to life, releasing a salvo of lead at the giant blur zigzagging across the smoke-filled landscape.

"No impact!" Fredrick said. "Shit, it's fast and coming right for you guys! We don't have a shot anymore! It went around the building!"

"I think it's her. She's finally come out to play," Badrick said.

"I don't think she liked that we put down her pups," Emmerich added, popping slugs into his shotgun.

"Or the fact that we wiped out all her drones?" Callisto quipped, slapping in another magazine. "I think I'd be more pissed off that my pack of husbands got smoked."

A howl boomed into the night. The walls of the hut quaked from a colliding force. Specks of dust and wood rained on the team, long cracks stretching across the structure.

She's bringing it down on us! "Bug out!" Em ordered.

Badrick ran out the front door, while Callisto and Emmerich dived out windows, escaping before the hut collapsed in on itself. They scrambled to their feet, turning their weapons toward the building. Blinded by the wall of dust, they scanned as a deep reverberating roar bellowed from the wreckage.

"I can't see shit, Em!" Fredrick roared. "Get the hell out of there!"

Amongst the storm of dirt and debris, large yellow eyes glowed. A hunched mountain of hair and muscle rattled with a frenzied growl. She held her claws low, curling and flexing them, the coiled tension in her body signaling a readiness to pounce. Saliva escaped from her rolled lips as her tongue pushed against her teeth.

"The alpha," Emmerich muttered. "The queen of the pack."

Badrick sprayed into the creature. She shrugged off the rounds while bounding over the wreckage. Callisto aimed for its face, the first shot hitting the queen's forehead. The alpha barreled through the attack, continuing to pound the ground with her limbs, racing toward them. A swipe of her arm sent Callisto careening across the field.

"Bitch," Callisto grumbled, pain streaking through her ribs.

The queen leapt into the air, landing on top of Badrick and wrestling him to the dirt. The agent fell over with the creature, raising his machine gun. Her dagger-like teeth snapped on to the weapon. With her arms pinned underneath his body, her razor-sharp claws shredded through his uniform, digging into his back.

"Baddy!" Emmerich called as he put two slugs into the creature.

Badrick groaned through his clenched teeth. He could feel the warm puddle developing underneath him, having soaked through his shirt. Badrick reached on his vest, drawing a fat red tube labeled 'incendiary.'

Bright headlights flashed from amongst the trees. The rumble of a Humvee approached. The queen's eyes rose to see the broad vehicle racing over. Her face met with the steel bumper as it rammed into her.

Badrick felt the weight of the creature pulled off as the Humvee passed over him. Emmerich dived away from the oncoming havoc. The queen's body rolled until the vehicle climbed on top of her, bringing it to a halt. The armored driver's door swung open, Finley disembarked, M4 in hand, with a nod to Badrick.

"You could've killed me!" Badrick barked.

"No way, Baddy. I calculated it precisely," Finely retorted. "The hummer's undercarriage is approximately twenty inches from the ground."

"Shut up!"

The two walked around the vehicle to see the queen

writhing underneath it. Her jaws snapped, causing them to step back.

"Will incendiary EKIA this heffer?" Badrick asked.

"I think so."

"You're supposed to know these things, Intel."

"Well, let's just find out. I'd love to gather the data on something like this. Although the practicality of such applications on a specimen that isn't—"

"Yeah, yeah," Badrick said.

"Egghead, you talk too much," Fredrick added.

Standing over the queen, Badrick reached into his pouch, withdrawing the red device. He motioned close, encouraging her to bite him. With a pull of the pin, he tossed the device in place of his hand.

"Eat that!"

Smoke and yellow flames billowed from her as she clawed at the ground. Her skull melted away, devoured by the conflagration. The corpse of the creature sputtered until only a charred husk remained.

"Barbecued werewolf," Fredrick jested. "I can smell it from here."

"I'd say we have another kill method to add to our Standard Operating Procedures," Finley mentioned, climbing back into the Humvee.

"Just say SOPs like the rest of us, Egghead."

Emmerich reached over to help Callisto but she slapped his hand away.

"I'm fine—just some bruised ribs." She groaned, climbing to her feet.

"Give me a status, how's everyone looking?" Emmerich requested.

"Green to green, Actual," Calvin replied.

"We're good, Em!"

"I think my ribs are bruised, too," Badrick stated. "Other than that, I'm green to green also."

"She's calling the operation complete," Finley responded. "Queenbee says she needs us back ASAP."

"Makes sense, the wolf alpha is usually the most protected member," Callisto stated. "She would only come out if all the drones were KIA.

"Queenbee said she needs us back ASAP?" Emmerich wondered. "It must be important. All right, lets RTB. Good work, team."

"Whoo! Drinks on me after debrief, Rook!" Fredrick cheered.

"I don't drink alcohol, sir."

"The fuck you say? That wasn't an invitation. You've been voluntold to be my drinking partner!"

CHAPTER 2
SINISTER TIDINGS

Boots clomped against the gleaming floors of the headquarters' main hallway. Emmerich led with a stern gaze, his eyes peering straight ahead, oblivious to the numerous secretaries and agents watching them pass.

It all happened so fast. Evan died from my orders. I told him to stay with the children. Damn it! I forgot to keep an eye on them. I dropped my guard. I got caught up. The job has a short life expectancy, but this never gets easy.

"Em, you okay?" Fredrick asked. "Seems you have something on your mind."

The team leader nodded without acknowledging his brother. *Not now Freddy.*

"What do you think, knucklehead?" Badrick punched Freddy on the shoulder.

"Anyways, I can't get used to how dull this place looks," Fredrick continued. "I mean, let's put some paintings on the walls or pictures? Maybe one of President Obama? How about a copy of the Mona Lisa or a few statues over there—"

"Every time we're here, you say that" Finley jeered. "You

know we cannot allow such things, Meathead. They would be used as a conduit for the enemy to spy on us. We've been over this before. They inhabit idols. Why would you even propose something so ludicrous?"

"Because this place is so plain, it hurts my eyes! It's like a..."

"Like a surgeon's operating room?" Calvin suggested.

"Yeah, yeah! Like that, Rook! Just so damn sterile and plain. We could do surgery here!"

"Not with all the mud we're tracking," Finley noted. "Poor Larry."

"Meh, it's his job."

The team passed by a gray-haired man, dragging a mop bucket. His narrow eyes pinpointed on Fredrick. The operator cringed as the old man met him with a glare.

"Hey, Lar—"

"Can it, Steiner!" he snapped. "I should bash your skull in with this mop handle for ruining the polish on my floors!"

"Can you wait until after the debrief before bashing his skull?" Emmerich asked.

"Sure! We gotta date with destiny after you speak with the boss lady!"

"Calm down, Larry! You mean ole bastard! Why are you always giving me shit? I'm not the only one with dirty boots right now!"

An exchange of glares continued until the janitor was out of sight. After entering the large double doors into the war room, the team seated themselves at a polished wooden table stretching from one end to the other. Lights and humming computers surrounded them, accompanied by the clicking of keys as staff typed away at their stations.

A woman stood by a monitor encompassing the back wall, her petite and tight frame wearing her usual charcoal pantsuit and black tie. After examining a few topographical maps on display, she turned to acknowledge the team. The burning gaze of her dark brown eyes scanned over them, Emmerich smiled at her. She didn't return it, only giving the agent a nod.

Her discipline is impeccable. Many intelligence agencies around the world revere her, and so do I. The former Director of the CIA and now Assistant Director of the USA. She's a woman of uncompromising faith to the light. The forces of evil always speak her name with such contempt, Katherine Howler.

"Hey, Director—" Fredrick began.

"Shut up," she snapped. Katherine's eyes met with each of them, except for Badrick. The two shifted their gazes away, both clearing their throats.

"Good to see you, ma'am," Emmerich said. *Awkwardness... They're still doing this? I wonder if... No, they said...*

"Likewise," she replied. "Excellent work on last night's operation."

"But—"

"Emmerich Steiner, I know what you're going to say. Your concerned about Evan Smith. The team member we lost. I understand your feelings. But it's part of the job. He knew what he signed up for. This doesn't make it any easier. It's never easy."

"Yes, ma'am." *She sees right through me.*

"You took down an entire pack of lycanthropes terrorizing the region. Not only that, but you also eliminated the queen to keep them from breeding anymore purebloods. Despite our losses, I'd say that's a victory."

"We didn't save the children, though."

"Granted, we failed in that endeavor. It is a peculiar case. As you know, after a few reports of 'dogmen' in the area, I decided to lace the nearest watering holes in that region with a concentration of liquified aconitum."

"Wolf's bane," Finley said. "Lycanthropes are highly allergic to it."

"That explains why they weren't their normal ferocious selves," Callisto stated.

"Exactly," Director Howler continued. "There was a side effect though that I wasn't anticipating. It rendered the pack sterile."

"That's why they kidnapped the children?" Badrick asked.

"Correct, Agent Steiner."

"Ma'am, I wasn't paying attention. Which Agent Steiner? There's three of us," Fredrick reminded. "We're brothers after all—"

"Shut up." She continued, "The pack hadn't produced any pups in over two years. So, they decided to kidnap a few children from a nearby town and turn them. That's why your team was dispatched to eliminate the threat. While the aconitum didn't have the desired effect of killing them outright in those dosages, we believe that we can truncate the lycanthropes' numbers. In the next several months, our goal will be to lace the bodies of water in the heavily forested areas with it."

"Kind of like how they do with fluoride in the—" Fredrick started.

"Shut up. Yes, the way they implement fluoride in our water. The project has gotten a green light from the President."

"Ma'am, would that harm any civilians or animals consuming the water?" Finley asked.

"Good question, Agent Jackson. The lab techs have assured me that the dosages are harmless to other life forms, causing mild itching sensations at the most. We're only going to implement this plan for a few years. The agency is hoping to cull the lycanthrope numbers by that time."

"Do we trust the executive branch?" Emmerich asked. "Do you suspect the enemy has compromised them as it did its predecessors?"

"Not this administration. He's shown no signs of being under their thumb. Trust me, our networks have tried hard to find it. So, we'll work with them. It's better to have their cooperation on these matters. Although I will never compromise the agencies' loyalty to God, our people, and the Constitution first and foremost."

"Well said, ma'am," Callisto stated. "We share those exact sentiments."

"Ma'am, are the werewolves planning something?" Emmerich asked. "We engaged one of the largest packs I've ever seen. Granted, it was out in the deep woods and not in an area inhabited by many civilians, but it's not like them to grow this desperate. I mean, their numbers seemed fine despite being sterilized."

"I had a similar concern, Agent Steiner. Intel is working on something solid concerning that theory. I agree. Normally they don't interact with humans unless it's an older lone wolf that has better control. Occasionally, there are instances where an unfortunate hiker or hunter ends up missing, but nothing on a scale where they would attempt to kidnap several children. Of course, I'll keep all agents informed about what intel discovers. I'll be sending Trojan10Actual and his team on recon operations in Michigan and Indiana to track their movements."

"Ma'am, you don't want us to do it?" Callisto asked.

"No, I have another issue that I want your team to address. You're the most seasoned team I have currently not tasked with a major assignment. I have more important matters for you to deal with than pest control operations."

"Whatever it is, we're up for the task," Emmerich answered.

"Whatever it is, we're up for the task," Fredrick mimicked. "You're such a teacher's pet."

Freddy, don't make me sock you right here in front of Kat. The agent's eyes narrowed on his brother.

"Shut up," Director Howler said before turning back to Emmerich. "I appreciate your enthusiasm. Our Scryer Department has discovered a massive energy disturbance in Los Angeles."

"More than usual in that toilet?" Fredrick asked.

"Shut up. Yes, more than usual. A tremendous amount of negative energy was generated in a ritualistic manner, one that has caused psychic disturbances across the entire west coast. Our scryers monitoring that region have been communicating their concerns non-stop since last night."

"That's not good," Finley stated. "Something of that magnitude means—"

"Someone who possessed high levels of arcane potential was ritually sacrificed."

"Do you think the Brotherhood of Blood has anything to do with this?" Emmerich asked. "They've been quiet for a while, so maybe they've been planning something big?"

"The Brotherhood has always planned on freeing Cain from Nod," Finley added. "They would need a tremendous amount of hemoglobin, too. Well, first, they have to find his tomb."

"Why can't you just say blood, Egghead?" Fredrick moaned.

"I hope it's them," Callisto murmured. "I'd love to fill those undead leeches with some lead and add more fangs to my necklace."

"Girl, you got problems." Badrick chuckled.

Callisto nodded.

"That's who I suspected at first, too," the Director said. "But our informants inside the Brotherhood reported they are still enduring their civil war and haven't the time or resources for anything else."

"My money is on the Fera Ordini," Fredrick announced. "I hope they win because if they're the only vamps left, we'll have a much easier time finding them."

"Shut up. As I was saying, it wasn't the Brotherhood. I think this is someone working with the Nephilim."

Emmerich's eyes widened. *Things just went from bad to worse. Heard about them, but never had a mission against them before.*

"Ma'am, what are the Nephilim?" Calvin asked.

"Agent Jackson, want to get your teammate up to speed?" Howler suggested.

"The short version, Egghead," Fredrick interjected.

"Well, during the Antediluvian Period, the Nephilim were the children of fallen angels and mortal women. They were born giants, but because they didn't have the nephesh from God after their mortal bodies perished, they couldn't ascend to heaven. Their spirits remained trapped in the lower etheric layers. They became the demons that we know and love today. Oh, and they're responsible for most of the wonderful monsters we hunt now in the present. They created them in labs. It's all in the Book of Enoch, which was one of the dozens of books removed by the church after the enemy infiltrated it. They didn't want the public knowing the truth about what's going on. My guess is they tapered down the bible just enough to keep us blind, without incurring God's wrath."

"I said the short version! What the fuck is an Ante-de-wutsit?"

"It means before the flood, and that was the short version, Meathead! Not my fault you don't read. I could teach an entire semester-long course on this subject!"

"So, they're demons?" the rookie asked. "I understand the motivations of werewolves and vampires, but what do these Nephilim want?"

"In a nutshell, to terraform our planet, subjugate and destroy humanity. Oh, and bring back the good ole days when their parents openly ruled the Earth. I'm sure they have other goals. I think they plan on converting us all into animal-human or machine-human hybrids, too. That's irrelevant right now because it sounds like whomever the scryers found is trying to open a gate."

"Sorry, Fin, but I'm a little confused."

"That's okay, I know it's a lot to take in," Finley replied. "Please ask any questions you may have."

"This is why I wanted him to keep it short," Fredrick murmured, rolling his eyes.

"Okay, so these Nephilim are all dead, right?"

"Yes."

"And their spirits are trapped on the other side of the etheric layers?"

"Correct again."

"So, how are they doing this?"

"Demonic possession, my friend, the oldest trick in the book. When someone's frequency is low enough, a demon can set up shop and inhabit the body, depending on a few factors. Most of the time, it's an involuntary process, and the person possessed is a hapless victim. My gut is telling me with this kind of magic, we're seeing one of those rare cases when the person is cooperating with the demon. Like all those MK-Ultra super soldier candidates the shadow government made."

"Wait, MK-Ultra is demonic possession?"

"Yep. They torture and bring a person's frequency low enough for a demon to inhabit them. Our lesser half, the shadow government, uses them as their militant arm. A lot of these mass shootings you see happening are working for the shadow to push the agenda to undermine the Constitution, which has been a thorn in their side for the longest time. Since it's hard to convince patriotic warriors to kill and commit atrocities against their people, they resort to this."

"Unless it's the police department." Fredrick snickered.

"Technically, it's not the person doing it, but the Nephilim demon inside the person. In return, I'm sure there were promises made."

"Our government is working with these guys?"

"Not exactly," Finley said. "As with all the churches, the enemy has infiltrated and established their networks inside our beloved country."

"Okay, I'm sure I'll have more questions later, but thank you for this. I appreciate your patience. These Nephilim sound like bad news."

"They're our greatest adversaries," Director Howler answered. "That's not to downplay the threats that other unholy factions pose. The Nephilim are the main reason the USA, Unholy Slaying Agency, was established. We are still just discovering the methods of our foes. Despite how little we know, I want you to link up with Finley when you have time. Get up to speed on all the details."

"Yes, ma'am."

"Emmerich, I apologize, but there won't be much time for R&R to celebrate our latest victory. I'm going to be sending your team to locate the site of the ritual. Refit and prepare to deploy again. I want you to investigate and report back what you find. We'll go from there. I'm sending a specialist from the scryers to augment you."

"Roger, ma'am. We'll take care of it."

"Oh great, one of those creepos that meditates and talks about the spirits and energies," Fredrick scoffed, rolling his eyes again.

"Shut up. As you already have figured, I won't be able to provide you with any close air support or indirect fire support, due to the sector being heavily populated. I might be able to get local police to assist, but they'll have to be on a lesser informed basis."

"That means they'll know we're feds, but we won't inform them about which department or the nature of our operation," Emmerich explained to Calvin. *I'm not losing another rookie. He's assigned to Freddy. I'll have a word with my brother.*

"You got that look, Rook," Badrick patted Calvin. "Not much of a poker face, huh? Technically it's not lying because we have a hybrid jurisdiction that covers all junctions: Military, law enforcement, against all enemies foreign and domestic. You can thank President Kennedy's foresight for that."

"As far as any civilian authorities know, your team will be going after a serial killer," Director Howler informed them. "For the most part, you're operating light. There's a safehouse in the city, should you need anything else. Any questions?"

Emmerich looked at his team, who were all nodding with stern gazes.

"None, ma'am," he said. "We're ready."

"Good luck, Ghost Team. Dismissed."

As the members started filing out the door, Katherine's gaze fell on Emmerich. He nodded toward her, staying behind as the others left. They could hear Fredrick chattering in the hallway.

"Rook, you want to get some chow? I've been—Oh, hey Lar—OW!"

Emmerich shook his head as he turned his full attention to Director Howler. Memories from years prior resurfaced into his mind, playing back a similar scenario when he was in the room alone with AD Howler, the former Ghost8Actual. Her hair was in a perfect bun, the magazine pouches on her combat vest were riddled with dark red stains from their latest hunt.

Vampires. I remember that day. They had just finished feeding when we ambushed their nest. They popped like water balloons after rounds hit them. Cali pulled out their canines with pliers after it was over. Kat forced her to take convalescent leave and speak to a shrink after that. Good times.

"Great work as always on the operation," Howler announced. "You did well backing me in the assault. You gyrenes never fail to impress."

"Thank you, Actual," Emmerich replied.

"I know you're close to Cali, but she worries me at times. She went through a lot in the CIA."

"I'm sure she appreciates the concern in her own way, Actual. Whether she admits it or not."

"But that's not why I wanted to speak with you. As you already know, we lost Assistant Director Temples in the attack on our New York base."

"He was a good man." Emmerich sighed.

"I've been nominated for the position. The headquarters command staff will be casting a vote to see which of the candidates will be promoted to an Assistant Director as a replacement."

"I'm sure you'll get it."

"Me, too. Which is why I'm asking if you'd like to take command of Ghost after my leave?"

Emmerich paused.

"I know it's a big responsibility, but I feel you're ready."

"I'm surprised you're not asking Baddy first."

"Well, actually I did. He's a great soldier, the most selfless and charismatic out of our little family. But he expressed how he didn't want to spend any more time away from Aisha and is trying to fix his marriage. Which I understand. I should've had that sentiment about my own. Now all I have left is my career."

"Did Aisha find out?"

"No, at least I don't think so. But John did."

Emmerich nodded. "That explains Baddy's quietness during the meetings."

"We've kept it professional despite our indulgences."

"No judgment here, Actual. The heart is tricky."

"After your brother declined, he recommended I offer the job to you. An idea I wholeheartedly agree with. After declining the leadership role, I decided to keep him in command of Bravo section and elevate Dukas up to Alpha leader to act as your second. It's time to start prepping her for the future as well. We'll have to rebuild Alpha section but it's a start for now. So, think about the offer. You'd make a fine team commander. I've groomed all of you for this possibility since we reformed Ghost. With Badrick out of the running, that means you're the prime choice."

"I'd be honored, Actual. Thank you. I just hope I can be an adequate replacement for you."

"Of course, you will," Katherine grinned. "You've worked with the best."

His thoughts fluttered back into the present moment. She was in her charcoal pant suit again.

"Are you going to be okay?" she asked.

"Yes, ma'am. I—" *Yep, she knows.*

"Kat, just call me Kat. It's only us."

"I told him to watch the children."

"Those calls we make out there are tough and done with very little time to consider," Director Howler responded. "I've lost so many operators."

"Every time it hurts."

"Yes. That's what separates us from the bad guys, though. We care. Combat leadership isn't an easy thing. Even the victories can hurt. But I want you to shake it off, for now. Grieve after this operation. I need your head in the game for this one, Em. Understand? If not, I'm going to recall your team right now. Are you fit for duty?"

"Yes. I can do this. I need to do this." *My duty to our people is above all else.*

"Good. I realize I'm asking a lot of the Eighth Team to return to duty so soon after an operation. As I said, I need one of my best on this. I have a feeling there's more going on here."

"We understand the reasoning, and I'm honored. Thank you for not questioning my readiness in front of my team."

"Always, Ghost. I've got your back. I have faith in you. You're a good agent."

Emmerich nodded before taking his leave. Outside the room, Larry snickered as he continued mopping the floor. The rest of his team was already down the hall. Fredrick nursed the top of his head while Calvin patted his back.

CHAPTER 3
A CRY IN THE SHADOWS

The screaming of the C130 engine reverberated in Ghost Teams' ears. Their heads bobbed in sync with the airplane's shuddering movements. They bounced in the netting of the red fold-out seats lining the main compartment, restrained in place with thick black belts wrapped around their legs. The cold of the polyester chairs pressed through their uniforms, a constant reminder of the altitude's temperature.

"We'll be landing in March Air Force Base in a few hours," Emmerich announced. "I suggest you all try to get some rest between now and then. When we arrive, we'll be picked up by our contact who will take us to the safehouse in Los Angeles."

"What?" Fredrick asked. "Can't hear you over this old bird."

"I said we'll be landing in—"

"What?"

Emmerich jabbed his brother's nose. "Did you hear that?"

"Asshole..."

Shaking his head, Emmerich looked away to find their

newest addition. The short pale woman was sitting at the very end of the row. He unclipped his belt and walked over to take the seat next to her. She looked away, avoiding eye contact when Emmerich tried to meet her view.

That probably wasn't the best course of action to handle Freddy's shenanigans, seeing how we have a new addition that doesn't understand our team yet. "Hello there. I'm Emmerich Steiner or Ghost8Actual. I'll be your team commander for this operation. If you need anything, don't be afraid to ask. We appreciate you being here with us."

With a slow turn of her head, she revealed large glossy doe-like eyes amongst strands of raven hair. She smiled and nodded.

"It's nice to meet you, Commander. Thank you. I'm Elizabeth Turner."

"Just call me Em or Actual. None of that rank shit here in the field. I need you to think about the mission, not customs and courtesies. We'll save that for when we're doing office hours." *I respect her attitude. She has good discipline.*

"Understood, Actual."

"So, what's your specialty. Why did AD Howler choose you to be our scryer?"

The woman blinked, breaking eye contact.

That was a bit heavy handed, should probably slow it down, open up a tad for this introvert. "I apologize. This isn't an interrogation. I'm just a straight shooter. I'm asking out of necessity. I have to know what my people can do. Tell me about yourself. We only have a few hours to get to know each other before we're boots on the ground."

"Well, I—"

Her head snapped, surveying the cargo hold. The rest of the team was leaning over, listening to the conversation. Fredrick's big toothy grin was the first thing she saw, next was Callisto raising a brow, then Badrick waving with his warm smile, and Calvin's wide eyed blank stare. Finley was clutching a trash bag in his lap. The intel operator's head rolled about as he released a groan over the jet engine. His flushed face reared back as he opened the mouth of the bag, spewing the contents of his stomach.

"WHOO YEAH BOY!" Fredrick cheered. "LET THEM DAMN DEMONS OUT! FREE THOSE DEMONS! LEAVE OUR EGGHEAD BE!"

Well that's not awkward at all. Great timing, guys. "They just want to get to know you, too." Emmerich pulled her attention back.

"Nice to meet you. I'm Badrick Steiner. And her over there, that's Callisto Dukas. The gentleman next to me is Calvin Stafford. The boisterous one is our brother Fredrick and over there with motion sickness is Finley Jackson."

"Ole action Jackson is getting some over here," Fredrick continued.

"Nice to meet you, too. I'm Elizabeth. Are you three related?"

Badrick with his heart of gold. I appreciate it. Gosh, my people skills need work. "Yep, we're brothers," Emmerich answered.

"But he's..."

"I'm black, right?" Badrick interrupted.

"Sorry."

"Why? It's fine. I'm black. It's who I am. Pointing out someone's race doesn't make you racist. Not in the way you're doing it. That's a good question, though."

"We're all adopted," Emmerich said.

"And we all pretty much follow each other around through life. We've had each other's backs since day one."

The two bumped fists.

"So, what's your story, Elizabeth?" Emmerich asked.

"Wait!" Fredrick interrupted, stumbling over to them as turbulence shuddered the plane. "She needs a nickname!"

"Oh, I don't want one of those."

"You don't get a choice! Everyone gets a nickname! Badrick has two! He's Big Baddy, Baddy, oh wait and also the Badman. Correction, that's three nicknames. I'm Freddy. That's Egghead or Fin over there puking his brains out—"

"Damn you, Meathead," Finley managed before expelling into the bag again.

"—and she's Cali or just Crazy—"

Callisto raised her crooked middle finger at him.

"—Easy, easy! You know it's true. Sometimes we call Em the king. Or as I like to call him, Da Kang—"

"How are you this ghetto when we grew up in Camp Pendleton?" Badrick asked.

"—and over there is the Rook."

"Just for the record, I never agreed to be called Rook. Besides, doesn't this make her the rookie now?"

"Nope, she's a scryer! She's been with the USA for a while, just working in another department. You're still the greenest one here, Rook!"

"Will you shut the hell up!" Emmerich snapped at Fredrick. "I'm sorry about him, Elizabeth. Please go ahead."

"I'm going to call her Liz or maybe Lizzie," Fredrick murmured as he walked back to his seat.

"Well, I'm a scryer—" Elizabeth started.

Emmerich nodded and smiled.

"—my specialty is empathy and energy reading."

"That explains why the boss lady assigned you to our team," Emmerich concluded. "I'm glad to hear that."

"What does that mean, Actual?" Calvin asked. "Sorry, it's just that a lot of this occult terminology is new to me. I didn't even know it existed until about a year ago."

"No need to apologize, Calvin. I'll let Elizabeth explain."

"An empath is a psychically sensitive person that can read the energies radiated by the lifeforce of others."

"All energies are just frequency," Finley added in between gasps. "We're all designed like our radios, with receivers and transmitters—"

His mouth erupted with more half-digested contents pouring out. Finley managed to open the bag just in time.

"He's right," Elizabeth agreed. "It's all just frequencies. Everyone is attuned. Some have more potential than others. Every thought and feeling also has its own frequency being pushed out from its source. That's what I'm able to sense and with it feel the intentions of those around me. I understand that the boisterous one over there thinks I'm attractive—"

"Guilty," Fredrick acknowledged.

"—and that you are nervous."

"That I am," Calvin agreed. "This is only my second mission with the agency."

"You'll do fine, Rook," Emmerich assured. *I'll do my best to get you out of this alive.*

"You will because, despite your apprehension, I can sense bravery in your soul," Elizabeth added.

Calvin smiled. "Thank you."

"It also allows me to sense things in the etheric layers," she continued. "I can feel the energy signatures of those that dwell inside of it and their intentions as well."

"That will be useful. I'm very relieved that the director assigned you to our team," Emmerich stated.

"Thank you, Actual."

"Can you use this though?" Callisto asked while drawing her M1911 forty-five caliber sidearm.

Elizabeth paused when her eyes set on the black pistol.

"I'll take that as a big nope." Callisto grinned. "Everyone on our team needs to be able to pull the trigger when the time comes. Even you, bookworm."

"I have my weapons, but thank you," Elizabeth said, opening the black leather pack sitting in her lap.

"A singing bowl, a tuning fork, some bundles of sage, a tarot deck, several large pieces of quartz, frankincense, and myrrh," Emmerich rattled off. "Interesting, you're definitely old school."

"And well versed in the occult judging by her weaponry," Finley added.

"Blah, that shit can't stop a zom, vamp or werewolf," Callisto said. "Move, babe. I'm going to teach her how to use this. It's yours now, Elizabeth. Keep it in there with that junk. I'll find more mags for you when we hit the safehouse."

"I'm not sure—"

Cali is going to be ready for her own team soon. "Good idea," Emmerich announced. "You're going to do fine, Elizabeth. Welcome to Ghost."

Blurs started to form into fixtures around the room. When he tried to move, the leather straps bound to his wrists wouldn't allow it. That creeping feeling returned, the haze that wanted him to drift off to sleep.

What did them fools dope me with? That wasn't my meds. Where the hell am I? This ain't Moorehouse..."

Footsteps across the floor mixed with the sound of sandals clapping against soles, heralded someone's approach. Candlelight fluctuated around him, until a long rifting shadow drew near. He tried to look up, but his twitching eyelids wanted to cascade, despite his struggles. An odor invaded his nostrils, something akin to the stink of feces and rotting meat. The closer the steps came, the stronger it grew.

Is this a nightmare? No strength in my body. Feel so drained. "Who... what... are... you... do..."

"Hush, naa, son, I ain't gunna hurt ya," the thick patois accent announced. "We be needin ya services. Ya be one nuv us soon."

"Stop... ple..."

Ceramic and wood clanged as a bowl was placed beside his head, as well as a hollow plastic device next to it. The putrid fumes forced a cough, then a dry heave. Hands gripped his forehead. Calloused leather palms pressed against his sweaty skin. Dreadlocks dangled above him, a blank wizened face staring down.

"My brother... don't... do.. this..."

"Shh, the pain be temporary. I promise ya won't feel a ting aftah it's over."

The sewing needle came into view, held in the gnarled and wrinkled fingers that lowered it to his eye. A pinch, from the other hand, forced his lid shut. The needle stabbed, drove through, weaving the thread as it was repeated. The sharp pain streaked through his face. Lashes pushed inside, jamming against his cornea. Only his fingers moved, trembling, stretching, then curling into shaking fists. His eyelid twitched, fighting the threading that blinded him.

The rapping heart in his chest echoed throughout his being. Through the remaining eye, he could see the needle's glint approaching. It pierced over and under. He shuddered. The threads were tied at their ends, sinching along his skin. The menacing touch left, but the streams of pain continued, until the alarm of fear resounded in his mind, as fingers grazed his mouth. Hands pinched his lips together, with the needle following. The pointed steel continued to pierce from bottom to top. A gentle tug pulled the thread through his face from one end to the other. The sides of his mouth cinched into a seal, leaving him puckered like a fish as he groaned.

"See dat naa so bad. It be almost over, child. Ya 'ave me word, aftah dis ya feel no more pain, here on out."

Tears swelled, adding to the dampness of the wound. The plastic nozzle of a funnel penetrated the small opening of his mouth. Liquid came rushing down. Smoking noxious fluid caused him to tremble as it flowed into him. Taste buds were seared, caked over with the tang of burning liquid pain. Warmth bubbled from his stomach as its contents heaved upward. With nowhere to go, it swelled into his cheeks, before being forced back down.

He convulsed from juice going down the wrong pipe. Skin began to dry, wither and crack in his mouth, as it passed down his gullet, into his stomach and lungs. It altered, slowing in movement as it thickened. Breathing changed into wheezing.

No! What is this? Why does it taste so bad? Shit! There must be shit in this! There's blood, too. What is he doing to me?

The plastic drew away, prompting the long-calloused fingers to pinch his lips shut. Piercing from the needle returned, finishing the threading that sealed his mouth. He could feel the contents inside of him growing thicker. Breathing slowed until it became impossible.

Floating... away...

Another's gaze fell on him. He couldn't rationalize it, but someone else was there, standing with his captor. Rippling energy crept in, embracing him with a stale heat. Hollow eyes peered into his. The current in the dark pulled him. They passed each other. He screamed until it rang in his ears. Into the expanse, he continued until his cries were only faded echoes.

"Pass tru to dee udda side," his captor demanded. "Pass tru to dee udda side."

"It is done," a contemptuous whisper declared.

"Gud, tis anudda ta add to da horde. Our powah grows."

"As I promised."

"Ya always come tru, Baron. Evuh since I be a boy."

"Who else... is there?" A cry from the other side of the room. "Please, whatever you have planned... don't... do this."

"Anutha be wakin. Shh... I be tendin ta ya soon. Everyting gun be iree, I promise. Gunna drain tha elixir frum tis one an' gives it to ya, too."

"Please... I have... children."

"Shh... Papa grow angray when ya lie."

"Doubt flickers within you. What troubles you?"

"Bout tee udda day. Ya noe dat they be comin soon aftah dat powah we called. They has da gifted with dem, too."

"Let them come. It is already done. The master has passed through the veil. We no longer have to exercise caution, my friend. The kingdom grows beyond their control. When the lapdogs of El arrive, they will find only death here."

"I take it ya 'ave a plan?" he asked, rethreading the needle.

"We shall tangle them in our web. Let them struggle until they drown in the world they are trying to save."

"I sense it from ya, Baron. I can feel it rising."

"Hatred, from a lingering injustice. All of this is ours. Their weakness surrenders it. Only by his intervention was our grasp loosened. This is the reclamation. I will bleed humanity. I will stain the etheric layers with their suffering until he chokes on it. We shall bask in the wailing souls that we drain from this plane. From the ashes, we will reshape creation into our image."

Ω

CHAPTER 4
ADRIFT IN THE BEYOND

Kevlar covered heads bobbled as the van maneuvered over decaying road. Calvin peered out the window, a yellow cheeseburger wrapper flying just past it. The streets were riddled with flakes of Styrofoam, smashed cans, shards of glass, needles, and what he hoped was mud. Paint peeled from the buildings, revealing large spots of gray and white where the chips receded. He tried to read the graffitied words on them before they disappeared from view.

This is terrible. A long expression cemented over Calvin's face. *It hurts to look at the level of poverty here. These poor people. Americans. My people.*

The presence of their polished black vehicle drew the attention of the residents. Calvin examined a long face staring back at him, sagging with a heavy frown, his shoulders slumping forward. The steps the man took were slow and plodding, as if not wanting to go on but driven by something mechanical. His eyes broke away, dropping to the ground, fingers pinching an object in the rusted sewage drain between the sidewalk and the street. Pulling out a flattened soda can, he wiped it off on his tan jacket, adding to the myriad of stains. The man added it to one of the bulging trash bags heaped inside a steel shopping cart, before meandering away.

What if I had to scrape an existence like this? Just imagining it is making my heart race. I don't know how these people go on. They're strong. Stronger than me.

"We in the hood now, Rook," Fredrick said, nudging Calvin with his elbow. "Mind your P's and Q's. Don't stare at these people like you're at the fucking zoo. If they get upset with you, I won't try to stop them from busting your head open."

"You're right, sir. It's just that I can't believe we're the most powerful country in the world, and people live like this."

"The shadow government," Badrick said. "They orchestrated all of this."

"How? Why?" *There's that phrase again. This nameless and faceless foe the others keep mentioning. Why can't we just apprehend them and be done with it?*

"For power." Finely answered. "It's always been about power for them. Manipulating the world of humanity for their nefarious purposes. They give them just enough to live off, so they can siphon the negative energy. Remember what I told you in the war room, they have infiltrated many facets of our lives. All this poverty you're seeing could be ended with just some simple recalculation of our budgets, holding these so-called charitable organizations accountable and a little less military spending."

"You say that as if those institutions are—"

"Yep, corrupted. All of them. Well, I shouldn't say that. Most of them. Too many for the legit ones to have a major impact on what you're seeing transpire. Let's put it this way. Think about all those churches out there that have private jets for their leadership, dressing them in suits that cost four to five figures, or building giant ostentatious places of worship. Do you think they're doing God's work?"

"No."

"Didn't even have to think about that answer," Callisto chuckled. "Guess he's quicker than I thought."

"What the hell, Egghead!" Fredrick snapped. "What did I tell you about making up your own words! What's an ostrichtatious?"

Elizabeth's small pale hand trembled as it rose to the windshield, pointing at a warehouse ahead. "There, Actual. That's the place." *I can sense the pulses of agony, the residual energies radiate from it like a furnace.*

Flickering images in her mind's eye showed Elizabeth the dull blade, slicing into the pale little foot, shredding through the mess of red, grinding to a halt once reaching bone. The screams echoed in her psyche, growing louder along with the scryer's racing heart. Elizabeth twitched when the blonde woman rattled in her confines, her gaping mouth howling into the darkness that started to envelop her vision. *These are the death throes of Sara Duncan.*

Emmerich slowed the vehicle, turning into a large empty parking lot. He brought the van around the building, stopping in an alley. "Elizabeth, are you okay?"

"Yeah, Scryer. What's gotten to you?" Fredrick asked. "You have PTSD, too?"

"There's a gaping tear in the etheric layers, Actual. It... hurts."

"Okay." Emmerich nodded. "I understand—fuck formalities. You keep me up on what you see and feel ASAP. If it becomes too much, we'll fall back here and let you gather yourself."

"Thank you."

"The rest of you get green and give me a status. It's time to rock and roll."

Callisto slapped a magazine into her M4 carbine, pulling back the charging handle that sprang forth, chambering a round into place. She put a hand on her hip, combing over her M1911 forty-five caliber sidearm. After checking a chest pouch for her night optic device, she fingered through her magazines and pyrotechnics just below it, the pouches lining across her vest. Her hand touched the small earpiece, hearing the beep signifying active comms.

"I'm green to green, babe," she said, giving a thumbs up to the rearview mirror.

"Green to green, Actual," the others replied.

"Queenbee, this is Tac-com." Finley spoke into the vehicle's large radio. The dual receivers and transmitters of the devices hummed and whizzed at first until a beep sounded. "Queenbee, this is Tac-com, radio check."

"Tac-com, this is Queenbee, we have you, Lima Charlie. Relay to Em that you are go for launch. Be careful out there."

"Yes, ma'am," Finley responded, ending the transmission then turning to the team. "Actual, we are up on comms and encryption. That was AD Howler. She acknowledges our last and says we are a go. I'm having a little interference with the transmissions. I'm going to PM the connections on the van while you're infilling."

"Acknowledged," Emmerich announced. "You heard her, team. Let's move!"

Doors opened and slammed. The team was halfway down the alley before Finley could wave them off. They followed close to the walls, Emmerich taking point as they trailed behind, with Fredrick and Calvin bringing up the rear. Heavy breathing expelled from Elizabeth's open mouth. Her short legs pumped hard to keep up with the others. She tugged at the vest a bit. Beads of sweat rolled down her body, soaking into her uniform.

How are they moving so fast with all this gear on? My goodness they're in amazing shape.

Emmerich halted at the door on the side of the building. His neck stretched a bit as he followed the outline of the frame, bringing his nose close. He looked toward Callisto and the others with a nod.

"Breach tool up."

Badrick approached with a device that looked like a giant crowbar strapped across his back. Leaving his M4 attached to his vest by a clip and some cords, he reached over, grabbing at the breach tool, and wedging it into the door. The large man heaved and tugged, popping the entrance open within a few seconds. Badrick tossed the tool to Callisto, who caught the weapon and remounted it on his back.

Did she just catch that big thing like a soft ball? I think I would've been crushed by it!

The team stacked on the doorway, their hips touching with the muzzles of their weapons lowered and ready. Emmerich leaned back, bumping into Callisto, creating a chain reaction as she and the others followed the motion. Fredrick, at the end, returned with one going forward, reversing the process. When it reached Emmerich at the front, he was gone. The team followed his lead. Callisto noted Emmerich banking sharp right, so she turned left. Badrick followed right, and they continued, moving opposite each other.

The agents filled half the perimeter of the sprawling warehouse, their weapons pointing inboard. Emmerich raised his arm with a closed fist, causing the others to lower their muzzles. Amongst the dust and cobwebs was a table, surrounded by puddles of melted red wax blackened at their centers.

Oh my God! Is that what I think it is?

A pungent cloud filled the entire area with a metallic and salty stench. It hit them like a sucker punch. The sharp odor caused Elizabeth to recoil into a coughing fit. She covered her mouth with her tiny hands as Fredrick patted her back.

"Thanks," Elizabeth replied, her eyes reddening.

The buzzing of flies vibrated around the room as a swarm dotted the air and engulfed them. Elizabeth looked up, unable to see the ceiling. Some buzzed past her head, escaping out the door just behind her.

"We need some light," Emmerich said. "Moonbeam this place if you have them."

"Roger, Actual," Callisto responded as she and Badrick drew their flashlights.

Streaks of illumination sent roaches scampering away. A line of congealed dark stains coated the ground. Emmerich and the team approached in slow steps, their lights following contorted strips of meat, leading to a messy pile. Black dots throbbed, blended, and fumbled across it until they were close enough to notice it was only more flies. Ribs poked up from the remaining husk, the flesh of which writhed with countless maggots. Elizabeth held her stomach, coughing and spinning away, taking a few staggering steps. Her alabaster cheeks turned bright pink with the strain.

"First time seeing a dead body?" Callisto chuckled.

"Even you have to admit this is more unusual than what we're used to seeing," Badrick said.

"Give me light on the upper end of the table," Emmerich ordered.

The skull stared at them, its mouth wide open with its front teeth missing, a set of pliers next to it. Thin strips of meat were stretched over her cheeks, lashes popping up from the bottom of them.

"Poor sap died screaming," Fredrick noted.

"Are those her eyelids?" Badrick asked.

"Yeah, he wanted her to see everything," Elizabeth answered. "He needed her to see everything."

"Fingers and toes are all gone," Callisto noted. "Where the hell are they?"

Images flashed in Elizabeth's mind; gore covered, calloused and wrinkled hands placed several morsels of humanity into pockets, the warmth and wetness bleeding through the material. For a brief moment, a shimmer usurped her view, causing the scryer to pinpoint its source; the wide nail of a thumb.

"He took them," Elizabeth continued. "To keep as trophies."

"This place gives me the chills," Calvin said. "But my timepiece reads 96 degrees in here."

"You geardo!" Fredrick snapped.

"Quiet, everyone, let her focus," Emmerich ordered. He turned to Elizabeth. "You can see it? What else is going on?"

"We are not alone."

The scryer gasped. Through her mind's eye, she beheld the dark morass churning around them. It pulsated as negative energy bled into the etheric layers, stretching its corruption.

Elizabeth shivered, her eyes clamped shut. Shrill cries echoed in her ear.

A whisper carried into the air, unintelligible words lashed out with animosity. At the center, she could see it, a skeletal visage gazing back. The shadows flowed from the empty sockets, pouring into her. She couldn't feel; her body and mind went numb.

"I see you." The slow whisper strained with simmering rage, spoken through clenched teeth. *"We see you."*

Elizabeth wanted to act. Her frozen mind wouldn't let her. She tried to pull away, but paralysis took over her body. Signals sent to her limbs escaped into the darkness around her. The prickly cold stabbed at her being, tightening its grip. With every breath, freezing pain streamed into her lungs. Light from her spirit faded underneath the shroud as it smothered her.

Teeth gnashed, with claws reaching from the gloom, scratching at reality. Whispers grew into chattering. She saw them starting to pull out of the reaches. Feral eyes now stared back, growls rumbling as they drew closer. Hunched bodies trembled with furor as they surrounded Elizabeth. A tongue lashed from the darkness, slithering across her cheek with a slimy caress before snapping back into a maw of needle-like teeth.

"Let us in, Elizabeth!" hundreds of rasping voices screeched.

"*They're here, I have to—"* The cold gripped at her limbs as she fought to regain control.

Emmerich's face appeared. The darkness rushed away as she could feel her body rocking. The ceiling was just behind him in her view. Cold ground against the back of her head generated a shiver. Another gasp and Elizabeth sprang forward, sitting upright. The team had gathered around her. Badrick kneeled over to examine the back of her helmet.

"She smacked her little noggin pretty good. But it looks as if the Kevlar took most of the damage."

"You back in the land of the living?" Emmerich asked. "You just took a nasty fall."

"They're... here," Elizabeth whimpered. *I can still hear their claws dragging on the floor, I can feel the warmth of their heavy breathing.*

"Who?"

"The disembodied spirits," she answered. "The demons..."

"Demons?" Fredrick gazed around. "I mean I know roaches are disgusting, but I'd hardly call them—"

"No, stupid!" Emmerich snapped. "They're in the layers."

"—all around us." Elizabeth groaned as Badrick helped her up. "There's... a tear in the... etheric layers. It's serving... as a gate to the... negative reaches. Those eyes..."

"What eyes?" Fredrick asked, pulling back the charging handle on his M249 light machine gun. "Spit it out! We got demons to deal with and—"

"Give her a minute, you asshole!" Callisto barked. "She's going through some shit right now!"

"Something... powerful... already here." Elizabeth continued. "I think... It's responsible for all of this!"

"What else do you have for us?" Emmerich asked. "What are they doing here?"

"They want... bodies. They wanted mine. I need time to cleanse this place. So I can close the gate, Actual."

"You got it. The rest of you follow her lead."

Elizabeth drew out hundreds of incense sticks, setting them inside of wooden stands around the circle. She handed a smoldering bundle of sage to Callisto, who met the scryer with a raised brow.

"What the fuck?"

"Please walk around with this, wave it in the air," Elizabeth instructed. "It'll start clearing away the negative energies."

"Cali, just do it," Emmerich urged.

"Why can't we fight baddies that just require a bullet to the dome? Ugh, fine!"

"I'll light these," Badrick announced as he started walking over to the incense holders with a lighter.

"Since when do you smoke, big guy?" Fredrick asked.

"I don't. I just keep it handy for field ops and deployments. Never know when you need to start a fire. Ever try to make one from scratch? It's a pain in the ass when you're not in ideal circumstances."

"What you got for the Rook and me, Liz?"

"I need you both to hold hands and meditate."

"What the hell?" Fredrick sneered.

"This will help generate as much positive energy as possible."

"I don't know how to do that meditation shit."

"Okay, just repeat the Lord's Prayer."

"But—"

"Do it!" Emmerich ordered. "We don't have much time. You heard her. Demons are coming through. Damn your stupid pride. Grab the Rook's hand and start praying."

"You tell anyone outside of the team about this, and I'm going to kick you in the nuts!" Fredrick threatened.

"All right, calm down." Calvin pleaded. "It's not like I want this getting out, either."

Elizabeth handed Emmerich a bag of quartz crystals. He nodded, getting to work, placing them around the table.

"You've done this before, Actual?"

"No," Emmerich answered. "It's SOP that we all carry small

quartz in our uniforms. Some of us know a little bit about how the etheric layers and the arcane energies work."

The scryer stood before the table with her back straight and head upright. She brought her hands together, creating the outline of a diamond with them. With a deep breath, she inhaled the burning frankincense and myrrh. Badrick took his little brother's hand.

"Fuck, this is uncomfortable, Baddy," Fredrick said.

"You're the only one making it weird. Now shut up and focus like she said."

Emmerich grabbed the singing bowl. He held the rusty device in his hands, running the wooden mallet along the side of it. After a few attempts, the bowl started to resonate with its high-pitched song.

Elizabeth closed her eyes and took a deep breath. Her mind plunged back into the etheric layers. Multitudes of teeth gnashed together as the demons wheezed and growled. Claws scraped at the ground, the beings pulling themselves out of the darkness. She searched for the one at the center of it all that beckoned earlier. Her eyes only found the black void at its center, leading into nothingness.

So, you weren't actually here. You were projecting from someplace else. Where did you come from? She wondered.

The darkness withered, pulling away from the light and frequencies that gathered from their ritual. The fiends stretched their jaws, roaring in unison. Elizabeth felt a torrent push at her. She grabbed at the ether, clenching it with a singular focus and battling against the force rushing her. Their attention closed on the scryer as the full intent of their action was brought to bear.

Not this time! she rebuked.

Inside her grasp, a light sparked. It expanded until she

clutched a glowing ball. Surging rage from the demons caused her body to rock, forcing her to take a step back.

So many of them! Maintain Focus!

"Those who dwell in the abyss suffer not the light, daughter of Adam." Their thoughts bellowed into her psyche.

"We see your fear," another snarled.

Focus your mind. Do not acknowledge their voices.

The light slipped from her reach. Particles dissipated from her hands, until the warmth was replaced by the frigid cold once more.

No! I failed!

"You know the truth. You cannot win, usurper."

"We are legion. We are eternal."

"Her cord, we must sever her cord."

No!

"You will be ours forever. We will molest you. We will snuff out your spirit until all that remains is a withered husk. You will feel our teeth as we suckle the essence from your soul over the next centuries, Scryer!"

Focus!

Elizabeth gathered the light, calling its energies once more. She hurled it into the darkness, only for it to be swallowed by the mass of shadows.

"It is futile, Scryer!"

A demon leapt into the air, pouncing on Elizabeth. Its claws slashed into her spiritual presence as they toppled over. Flashes of anguish flared over the rips left in her etheric body. Another followed, its saliva drenching her hair when its mouth bit down. The sharp teeth pierced deep. Essence seeped from the deep gashes, channeling through her soul with agony.

"Sever it!"

Elizabeth felt a snap. The tension of her presence lost its

connection to her physical body. She grew light as a feather, adrift on the currents of energy flowing from the layers.

No! This can't be happening! I'm stuck!

"Drag her into the pit, so that our brethren may enjoy her as well."

"Yes, we feed the abyss!"

Claws pulled into every part of her soul, dozens of them raised Elizabeth above an ocean of demons carrying her toward the darkness.

I must focus!

The light returned, expanding from the center of the abyss. The demons howled, dropping their prey. They scampered about; the shadows that supported them now retreated. Claws slashed toward the light, hitting nothing. Turning on each other, they ripped and tore, attempting to avoid the cleansing illumination. It consumed the area, erasing their presence.

Elizabeth watched as the shadows dissipated, the room returning to normal. She saw the team carrying out their tasks for the ritual. Her body still knelt by the table. The scryer tried reaching out to it. Her etheric hand passed through.

This can't be! I'm stuck! Those cursed fiends left me trapped on the other side until my cord repairs! That could take years!

Elizabeth's empty vessel slumped over. The team halted what they were doing, rushing to her.

"Liz wake up," Fredrick said. "Shit, what's wrong with her?"

"Check her pulse," Emmerich ordered.

"She's still alive," Badrick replied, checking her vitals.

"That means she's just unconscious," Emmerich stated.

"How do you know so much about this occult bullshit, Em?"

"I read up on a little of it in my free time, just in case we ever encountered tangoes that needed more than a bullet bath."

"It doesn't feel cold in here anymore," Calvin added.

"I think she was successful," Emmerich nodded. "But at what cost?"

"Damn it, Liz, what happened to you over there?" Fredrick sighed. "I was gonna ask you out to dinner after this, but not if you're a vegetable."

"She'd still be too good for you," Callisto poked.

"Yeah, I know."

"So, what now, Actual?" Calvin asked.

"I think we can acknowledge that she closed the gate. First, we call the local authorities so they can clean this place up. Then we need to get her back to the safehouse. We'll contact Queenbee to let her know we're down one. Then Charlie Mike."

"Charlie Mike?"

"Continue Mission, jeez Rook," Fredrick said. "There's still the issue of finding the scumbag who called down all this crap."

"Oh, right."

Guys, I'm right here, Elizabeth pleaded as Fredrick cradled her body.

"Hang in there, Liz," Fredrick said.

"Ghost8Actual, this is Tac-com."

"Tac-com, this is Actual, send it."

"You've got a suit heading your way. Looks like he's PD. I spotted him approaching from the other side of the alley."

"Acknowledged."

Standing in the light of the open door was a figure dressed in a black suit and tie. He removed his sunglasses and ran his fingers through his wavy hair as he stepped into the warehouse.

"I hope you're feds, standing here with that kind of weaponry and equipment," he remarked.

"We are," Emmerich said. "I take it you're local PD."

"Yep. I'm Detective Eric Silvia."

"I'm reaching into my pocket for ID."

"Not worried. I figured you were. Just procedure."

He raised his identification card and badge to the officer.

"Emmerich Steiner with the Department of Homeland Security," the officer announced.

Elizabeth witnessed the officer's blackened aura writhing around a set of glowing red eyes. She gasped as they settled on her, and a cackle reverberated through the ether.

"Emmerich!" she screamed. *"He's one of them!"*

"I'm pretty sure you gents and ladies have this under control, so I won't get in your hair. I know better to tussle with the feds."

"We appreciate that," Emmerich said.

"Your friend going to be okay?"

"Yeah, she's just had a hard day. We have assets that will see to her needs."

"Fair enough. Curious as to why your outfit is so small, though. Usually, you feds roll with a large task force, right?"

"Not this time. We're trying to keep a low profile to avoid alerting the public and stirring any panic."

"Makes sense. Here's a helpful tidbit on your case though. Just judging by how this place looks, guessing you're dealing with some crazy cultist stuff, right?"

"Something like that."

"I'd check the Moorehouse Asylum, that's where those leather straps come from."

"How do you know that?"

"I'm familiar with the place. I've had a few cases that led me to that unsavory hellhole."

"We appreciate that."

"Just remember, you didn't get that from me. I don't want my superiors breathing down my neck about poking my head where it doesn't belong."

"Understood," Emmerich said, reaching out to shake hands.

"Want me to call in my crew to clean this place up after you're done?"

"That would be most appreciated, Detective."

"I'll get out of your hair. Good luck, Agents."

The eyes of the demon set on Elizabeth one last time.

"Watch as your friends get devoured, bitch!" Its cackle continued.

"Emmerich, it's a trap!"

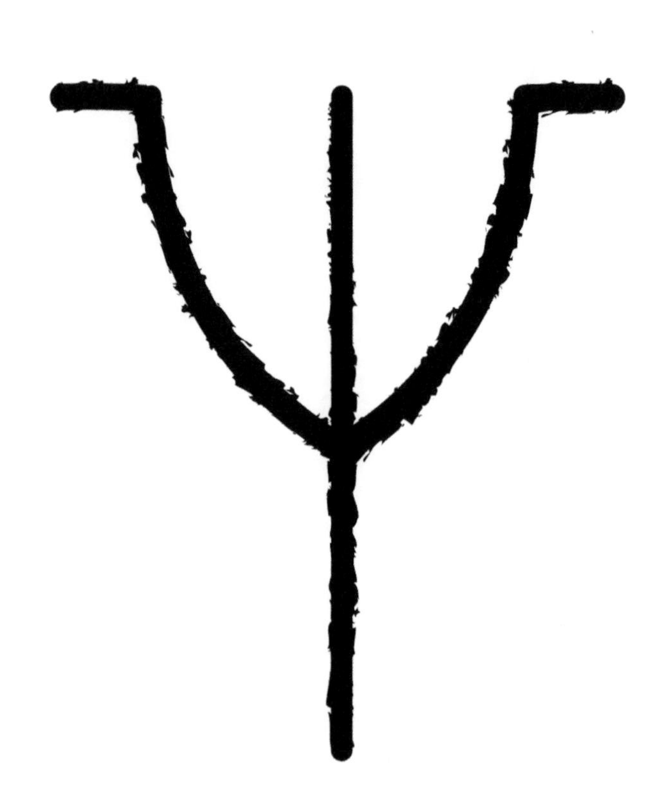

CHAPTER 5
GATES OF MADNESS

Elizabeth's motionless body was surrounded by the beeping of an EKG machine and plopping droplets of an IV, within the safehouse medical ward. Eighth Team lined the perimeter of the room with eyes fixed on their fallen comrade. Fredrick's foot tapped on the ground until Callisto turned and slapped his shoulder. He crossed his arms with a sigh of defeat.

"Go easy on the lug, Callisto," Elizabeth murmured. *"He's just worried."*

The doctor leaned over, pressing a cold metal stethoscope on her chest.

"Her vitals are normal," he announced. "As far as I can tell, she is stable and healthy despite being comatose."

"That's a relief," Emmerich replied. "I'll give my full report to AD Howler about her status. Thank you, Commander Cooper."

"Forget all that formal stuff, call me Doc," Cooper replied. "Of course, you're welcome. Least I can do to look after the welfare of my agents. You're the ones risking your hides out there."

"So, what's going on with her, Doc?" Fredrick asked.

"There are no signs of the gradual deterioration that normally occurs when someone's soul is destroyed," Cooper explained. "While my specialty is trauma surgery, in our line of work, I've learned to assess all possibilities. With what we see here, I think it's safe to say that her spirit is well. It's just trapped on the other side."

"Something must've gotten to her when she projected," Emmerich surmised. "This confirms our suspicions."

"I'll keep an eye on Agent Turner until her people arrive," Cooper said. "This area of healing is beyond my expertise. They'll know how to get her spirit back in her body."

"Thank you," Badrick replied.

"In the meantime, Ghost, if you need anything, we have a full armory, DFAC, and comms room here in the safehouse," Cooper announced. "Whatever you need is yours."

"What's a DFAC?" Calvin asked.

"What service did you come from before joining the USA?" Cooper inquired.

"The Navy, sir."

"You fucking squid!" Fredrick snapped.

"Well then, I guess you would call it a galley."

"I'm going to get on the horn with AD Howler," Emmerich said. "The rest of you gear up and grab some civies. We aren't rolling full battle rattle next hop. This mission is only an investigation."

"Damn it. I can't bring Queen Latifah," Fredrick groaned.

"Who's Queen Latifah?" Calvin asked.

"Our M240B Machine gun," Fredrick answered. "She's big,

black and beautiful, and knows how to spit that fire. My lady goes wherever I go. I'm faithful to her."

"90s hip hop was definitely the best," Badrick added.

The team started to make their way out of the room. Fredrick stayed behind, taking the blanket, and tucking in Elizabeth's body. He patted her head with a sigh.

"We'll get payback for you, Liz," Fredrick said. "Wherever you are, I hope you're okay."

"I'm right here with you. This is going to be frustrating."

Magazines locked into firearms. Callisto inspected her dual M1911s, checking the receivers, flicking the triggers, and placing them into her leather holsters. Grabbing her truncated shotgun by its pistol grip, she turned to the armorer assisting the team.

The man nodded from behind his distribution window. "What kind and how many, Agent Dukas?"

"Give me a box of slugs and buckshot," Callisto ordered.

Elizabeth reached for Callisto's hand, languishing as hers passed through.

"Please Callisto," the scryer pleaded. *"I know you're not intuitive to this sort of thing, but slow down just a second. You're all in danger, they are expecting you. The demons must have a network established. I hope you're getting this on some level. As a woman, you must have a measure of psychic ability."*

"You got it," the armory clerk acknowledged, shuffling around the boxes of ammunition.

What's going on? Callisto wondered. *Why am I feeling this? Imminent danger? Worry? Am I losing my nerve? Get it together, Cali! There are only a few female combat agents. I can't lose my edge.*

"Ghost Team is walking into an ambush," Elizabeth continued.

And again, the dread. It's coming in waves. I can't shake it. Screw it, I'm going heavy. Stupid Freddy will probably squawk about this, but I don't care. "Wait." Callisto's eyes narrowed. "On second thought, nix the slugs. Let me get the M17.50BMG rounds. A lot of them."

"Cali, what the fuck?" Fredrick said. "It's just an investigation and C&E. Not even a recon mission. Don't you think you're going a bit heavy for a few interviews?"

Right on cue. "Shut up, Freddy," she said, switching back to the armorer. "And also, can I have more mags for my sidearms, please. Thank you."

"Please? Thank you?" Fredrick scoffed. "Are you feeling all right today? Who are you, and what have you done with my future sister-in-law?"

"Here you go, Agent Dukas."

Callisto snatched up the boxes of ammunition. Emmerich entered the room, patting their shoulders as he passed.

What was that flood of thoughts?

"Just got done talking with AD Howler," he informed them. "We're Charlie Mike even though we are down one. She's sending someone from the scryers to assist us and help with Elizabeth's situation. It's going to take twelve hours for them to arrive in sector. In regard to Moorehouse Asylum, she was able to scratch up some intel. Turns out the place isn't sponsored federally, or even by the state. We don't know where they are getting their funding to run such a large facility."

"No private donors?" Badrick asked.

"AD Howler didn't find any paper trails."

"Em, will you talk to your queen?" Fredrick interrupted.

"What's wrong with her, Freddy?"

Callisto rolled her eyes. *Great, now this idgit, is bringing attention to me.*

"This is just an investigation and C&E mission, right?"

"Yes." Emmerich's brow rose. "As I stated before."

"Well, she's packing enough heat to take down the Jaysh Al Mahdi!"

"I just have a feeling, damn it," Callisto retorted. "And don't speak about me as if I'm not here or I'll pistol whip you, Freddy."

"Now you're sounding normal again. Anyways, you turning into a scryer now?"

"Permission granted to slap the teeth out of his mouth, Cali," Badrick interrupted.

If only he was in reach. Freddy knows to keep his distance when he's showing his ass.

"You have a feeling?" Emmerich asked. "What kind?"

"I can't explain it, something is telling me we're in for more than just checking the local looney bin," she explained. "If I'm wrong, then I'll be the one heaving around the extra weight. No biggie. I'll just stand in the back while you do the interviews."

"But you're our interrogation expert, former CIA!" Fredrick exclaimed.

"I've trained Em on it thoroughly. He'll be able to take my place."

"The rest of you double tap on ammo, too," Emmerich ordered. "I'm also going to bring a little something extra as an insurance policy."

"Yes, sir," Calvin acknowledged.

"Already on it, Em," Badrick agreed. "I'm taking a small med-pack, too. Nothing to obvious, just something I can slip into my coat."

"Em—"

"Just do it, Freddy! Have your shit ready. We leave for Moorehouse Asylum in fifteen mikes."

Thanks for always having my back, babe. I think I know where those thoughts were coming from. Maybe...But how?

"Good." Elizabeth exhaled with relief.

The blue of the afternoon sky faded, replaced by an orange that signaled the beginning of sunset. Stale heat from the afternoon started to die down, giving way to a dry cold, augmented by the occasional caress from the evening breeze. Calvin's eyes traced the outline of buildings they passed while driving deeper into the city.

Rows of tents were pitched on the sidewalks of alleys, with some trickling into the street. Clothes hung along the fences, trash cans crackled with flame, as shivering individuals huddled around them.

"This place is a dump!" Fredrick stated. "And I thought the spot we were at earlier sucked."

"It just keeps getting worse," Calvin agreed. "This hurts to look at."

Weak vibrations of dimming light radiated from the inhabitants. Elizabeth shivered, her face growing long with a frown, as she examined each of them. The wide-eyed onlookers froze, spotting the team's vehicle. Some shook off their apprehension, others fled into random directions. Elizabeth felt a heart racing. It wasn't hers. The scryer's hands quaked as goosebumps rose along her shoulders and arms. The generated fear subsided as they passed, and the link between her mind and the inhabitants' faded.

"They're terrified," Elizabeth said. *"I can feel it exuding from them. From this entire place."*

Rumbling from the van's engine cut off as Emmerich put the vehicle into park and killed the ignition. The lot was empty except for a few cars. The sprawling compound was surrounded by thick iron gates encompassed in a murky film. Tall bushes made it challenging to peek in from the outside. Emmerich gazed up at the top floor, noticing none of the windows displayed a source of light.

"Actual," Calvin called out. "There aren't any homeless around these parts."

"Yep," Emmerich agreed. "I caught that, too. Stay tight when we go in."

"Did you want me to accompany the team inside?" Finley asked.

"Scared to be in the hood by yourself, Egghead?" Fredrick jeered.

"Just want to stretch my legs, that's all."

"Uh-huh."

"That's a negative, Finley," Emmerich replied. "I'll need you here on comms with Queenbee, just in case this operation goes live."

"I see. Understood, Actual."

"You're talking as if we're expecting some serious heat," Badrick said.

Emmerich glanced at Callisto before exiting the vehicle. She returned with a stifled smile. The team walked to the gate. A dust-covered speaker flared to life with the static of a transmission upon their approach.

"Welcome to Moorehouse Asylum," a feminine voice greeted. "We appreciate your patronage but must sadly inform you that visiting hours are over. You're more than welcome to return between the hours of 12 and 4 PM. Thank you."

"We're not here for visitation," Emmerich answered. "We are a team with the Department of Homeland Security. We are here to speak with your leadership and staff about some disturbances."

"Oh, I see. Well, may I ask what this is regarding?"

"We believe there may be a connection between supplies pilfered from your establishment and a culprit that we are searching for."

"I understand, Officer—"

"Agent. My name is Agent Emmerich Steiner."

"I don't want to gain a reputation as someone difficult to work with, especially since we operate thanks to federal funding. Please come inside and take as much time as you need for your investigation. There are several staff members currently on shift if you need to interview anyone."

"The aura of this place..." Elizabeth's spirit felt the grip of cold radiating from negative energy saturating the area. A mountain of shadows writhed in the background, its slithering reach escalating, disappearing just before reaching the murky clouds below the starless night.

The gates shuddered and whined as they receded from the entrance. Ghost Team started their way up the paved lane, flanked by large bushes and trees. Badrick tapped his brother on the shoulder.

"Yeah, big guy?" Emmerich asked.

"Em, you caught what she said, right?"

"Yep. There's definitely smoke here."

As the team took the steps leading to the double door entrance, metal on metal clanged and rattled underneath Callisto's coat. As Emmerich reached for the knocker, the door unlocked from the other side and opened. A long pale face met them with drooping eyes. Graying brown hair draped over his ears as if it were escaping the rest of his scarred and balding dome.

"Hello, and thank you," Emmerich greeted him. "We appreciate your institution's cooperation in this investigation."

With bloodshot eyes, the orderly peered down at them. When his gaze lowered, Emmerich noticed small holes lined across his lips. The man turned away, heading down the main hall. They started to follow.

"What the fuck, they have Lurch from the Adam's family working here?" Fredrick whispered to Calvin, who responded with snickers.

Emmerich shot off a stern glare. The duo's laughter faded. A few of the ceiling lights began to flicker as they continued. Towering orderlies passed by them. Badrick examined one. Their expressions didn't change, paying no attention to the team as they continued about their way.

The etheric layers flowed like smoke. Elizabeth's vision blurred, the shapes around her distorting and flexing, as if wanting to twist and braid. The place was immersed in shadows, rippling with negative energy. The muffled light of Ghost Team's souls managed to shine, but whatever they followed, Elizabeth could not make out from the surroundings.

"Something just isn't right," Elizabeth said. *"I've never encountered this before. What's going on here?"*

"So, are there size requirements around here for your orderlies?" Badrick asked. "I'm guessing for dealing with the unruly folk?"

Stone-faced, the guide continued.

"Not much for conversation, I guess."

"Tac-com this is Ghost8Actual," Emmerich announced

over comms. "We've made contact and are en route to speak with the doctor of the facility. How copy, over?"

The tall man came to a halt in front of a door, pointing at it while turning to them. His unblinking eyes fixed on the team.

"I take it this is the doctor's office," Emmerich said. "Thank you."

Once they entered the room, a woman dressed in a doctor's robe rose from behind her desk. She smiled, her wrinkled, pale face scrunching together underneath the thin frame of her glasses. The doctor walked over to greet each of the team members, shaking hands.

"Greetings Agents, I hope that you've found my staff cooperative thus far in your investigation," she said. "If not, they're all going to get a serious talking to. I've made them aware of your presence, and they should not get in your way."

"We greatly appreciate that, ma'am," Emmerich replied. "So, can we ask you a few questions?"

"Of course, I'm at your disposal."

"Her aura..." Elizabeth struggled, feeling resistance when trying to read the etheric layers around the woman. *"It's impossible to see through the ether near her. Like staring into muddy water."*

As Elizabeth took a few steps closer, she felt pressure pushing back against her. The doctor's gaze broke away from Emmerich's to meet hers. The weak semblance of a smirk started but faded once her attention shifted back to the team.

"Can she see me?"

Elizabeth waved, a hand in front of the doctor's face. Her eyes remained fixed on Emmerich. The scryer expelled a sigh of relief.

"At the scene of a homicide, local PD notified us some of the equipment used came from your asylum."

"Agent Steiner, we prefer the term 'hospital.' We know our official name is Moorehouse Asylum, but that terminology is so outdated, which is something I mean to remedy. We aren't just a place where the undesirables are locked away. We give people what they need here. We allow them to have a new life that they otherwise wouldn't be able to enjoy."

"You're right. My words were callous. My apologies, Doctor."

"Apology accepted, Agent Steiner. I understand you're a soldier, after all, with a job to do. I can appreciate your straightforward attitude toward your work. My subordinates have a comparable mentality."

"I've noticed. They don't seem very chatty," Badrick said.

"And you are?"

"Agent Steiner as well, ma'am. We're brothers."

"Hmm... so one of you was adopted?"

"All three of us are adopted, ma'am," Fredrick said.

"I see. Your parents must have a big heart. I hope that you find us the same way here at Moorehouse. My suggestion would be to start in the eastern wing by the sixth block."

"Why there?"

"One of my orderlies complained about missing supplies in that area. Mostly just pens, syringes, medicinal containers, and the like. Perhaps there's a correlation with your investigation?"

"Perhaps. Thank you, ma'am. We'll get out of your hair and try to keep our interference to a minimum."

"That will be greatly appreciated, Agents. I'm very curious to see what comes of this investigation. Just give us a holler if you find something. We are here to serve."

CHAPTER 6
SWALLOWED BY DARKNESS

Only one of the four lights in the eastern wing's dining hall functioned. The team weaved between vacant tables covering the sprawling floor draped in shadow. A ceiling lamp flickered behind the serving counter, illuminating the back area near the kitchen.

"We've wandered so deep into this cesspool of decay," Elizabeth murmured. *"Every step I take is like walking in the backyard of a dog owner who never cleans up after it."*

"That cougar gave me the creeps," Fredrick said.

"I hope you're joking, you pig," Elizabeth scoffed. *"Ugh! I can't even tell with you sometimes."*

"Cougar?" Badrick recoiled. "No, Betty White is a cougar. That back there is just nasty to consider, Freddy."

"I mean, yeah, I'd still give her the D," Fredrick responded. "Don't judge, Baddy. You know I'd smash a ten or a two. I don't discriminate."

Badrick shook his head.

"I didn't like her either," Callisto chimed in.

"You don't like anyone who isn't part of the team," Badrick chuckled. "Em, you're quiet. What's on your mind?"

"Just not enjoying this place either. Let's just get this over with. Tac-com, this is Ghost8Actual. We are in route to the eastern wing housing region. How copy, over?"

Emmerich waited a minute then halted. "Tac-Com, this is Ghost8Actual. Radio check, over."

A few seconds passed.

"I'm thinking we lost comms with Finley and thus Queenbee."

"This place is doing something to the equipment," Elizabeth muttered. *"The aura is making more than just—"*

"After we complete the investigation of this wing, Freddy and Calvin, I want you both to go check on Finley. And no rebuttals, Freddy. So help me God, I'll nut tap you."

"I remember the last time he got you good, Freddy." Badrick reminisced with a grimace. "I can still picture you in the fetal position on the weight room floor, groaning for ten solid minutes, and turning purple."

Callisto cackled as Calvin's eyes widened.

Fredrick's hands cupped over his crotch as he frowned, "Ok, I'll do it. I'll check on Egghead. No need for violence."

Static fizzed over the dusty face of the intercom, drawing their attention upward. The sound from the device skipped, followed by a high-pitched squeal as the machine came to life.

"Hello Moorehouse, this is Doctor Metzger speaking—"

"There's your cougar, Freddy." Badrick nudged his little brother.

"—Our lovely home has some visitors from the Unholy Slaying Agency—"

The team exchanged wide-eyed glances.

"How did she—" Emmerich stopped as she continued.

"—Please give them the welcome they deserve. That means all of you, my children. Orderlies, I command you to release the horde. Have your fun, but save the last agent left standing. Leave them alive so that we may plant a seed. Whoever captures that final one, gets a special gift from our master, Baron Samedi. You'll find them currently meandering in our eastern wing. Now fill these halls with their screams. Show these interlopers that we are legion!"

The compound awakened as gears ground, and rusty locks unfastened. The clicking echoed throughout, giving way for those that dwelled within. Dozens of footsteps pounded the floor just outside an entrance to the dining room. Callisto grabbed her pump-action shotgun by its pistol grip, pulling it from her coat and chambering a round into the receiver.

"I told you assholes, I had a bad feeling," she said, her narrow eyes and weapon beaming on the door.

"From that commotion, I'd say we're surrounded," Emmerich stated. "There's two doors, split sectors of fire between them. No incendiary until we can identify exactly what we're dealing with."

"Roger, Actual!" Calvin acknowledged as he drew a sleek brown M17 nine millimeter pistol.

"If we survive this, Cali, I owe you an apology," Fredrick uttered.

She gave him the middle finger.

"Lock it up!" Emmerich ordered. "Get your head in the fight. We've got contact."

The doors of the cafeteria pushed open, swinging inward, and slamming against the adjacent walls. Writhing masses of humanity piled forward through the narrow opening. When their glazed eyes settled on the team, dozens of loud and shrill screams belted from their stretched maws. Arms grabbed, pulled, pushed, and shoved amongst their number as each of them struggled with the next to get closer. Unfortunate souls were trampled underneath the feet of their brethren, only to rise unfazed.

Elizabeth examined their warped snarling faces. Darkness gripped the bodies of those before them, leaving their etheric presence appearing as an extension of the negativity drowning the area. The spirits that dwelled in these poor vessels weren't the original hosts. In their eyes, the light was missing, devoid of a soul.

"They're all possessed!" Elizabeth screamed. *"Lesser demons are inhabiting these bodies!"*

A blast from the shotgun sent the first one's chest caving inward. Its rag-dolled body flew back into teeming masses of its brethren. Callisto cocked the weapon, placing a round into the next one in view. Fire rang out as the team continued to unload their volley.

"Ghouls!" Badrick roared. "I think we're dealing with ghouls! Aim for the head!"

The ghoul Callisto shot raced back to his feet. With bared teeth, he hissed, charging with outstretched arms. A dumpy round from Emmerich's M1911 collapsed the face of the creature, sending it back to the floor. It twitched as the lifeforce seeped from it.

"Baddy is right!" Emmerich said. "Aim for the head! Do not use pyro or chem!"

"Kill them!" Doctor Metzger screamed over the intercom. "Feed! Feast! Murder them! Tear them apart! Rip them limb from limb!"

Shots continued to ring out. Foes stormed the room. The wailing grew louder.

"Bitch shut the fuck up!" Fredrick yelled. "I can't hear my own damn thoughts in here! Fuck, there's a lot of them!"

"Fall back to the rear door!" Emmerich hollered.

Calvin, Fredrick, and Badrick ran to the other entrance as Emmerich and Callisto walked back, providing cover fire. Once the other three were set, they turned to fire from the entrance. Emmerich and Callisto broke from their engagement, catching up with the rest of the team. Feet pounded across the floor as ghouls sprinted at them. The team withdrew, shutting the exit behind them. Fists thumped against the wobbling doors, a loud slam buckled them, shaking the hinges. Calvin wedged two chairs underneath the handles as the rest of the team held it shut.

"Double time it down the hall!" Emmerich ordered. "That shit isn't going to hold for long!"

As they ran down the corridor, groans materialized from the shadows. Emmerich stopped, raising his weapon as he was just able to make out silhouettes. Wheezing strained from worn vocal cords as figures staggered amidst the dark. Shaky outstretched arms greeted the team with crooked and trembling fingers. They walked toward Ghost in slow trembling steps, fighting to remain upright. Their dismal unblinking eyes fixed on Emmerich. The first approached, with threads dangling from its quivering lip, over rust-brown teeth.

"They're possessed, too!" Elizabeth said. *"What happened to these people?"*

Emmerich aimed. Two rapid trigger pulls sent rounds slamming into the creature's dome, ripping open its forehead. Black liquid jettisoned from the gaping hole, oozing from the corpse.

"That's not blood," Calvin murmured.

"No time to explain, Rook!" Fredrick barked. "Let them have it!"

Muzzle flashes lit the corridor. Bullets found their marks into flesh, and bodies riddled the floor. Emmerich saw his receiver lock back after the last round fired, smoke billowing from the barrel. Training and instinct had him reaching for another magazine. Metal clanged against the floor as the empty one was discarded. He slapped in a full load of ammo, giving a flick of his thumb to launch the receiver forward, sliding a round in place.

"Actual, Run! Keep moving! They're through the door!"

Emmerich peered back into the blackness that filled the hallways. Screams from the other group grew louder.

"Push through!" Emmerich roared. "Avoid their hands! Stay out of their reach!"

The team moved forward, skirting along the outside of the hall. They continued to fire upon those shambling from the shadows. Hands reached out, as one stepped toward Calvin. The rookie placed a shot that snapped its head back, sending it reeling into the dark. A tight sensation grasped his arm. Grime-covered fingers wrapped around his wrist with a pincer-like grip. The wheezing in his ear paused as he saw a mouth of flat yellow teeth opening. He tried to pull away, but its strength rendered him like a toddler in the grasp of a parent.

The dry opening of its mouth snapped shut around his hand. Bones crunched as pain channeled through Calvin's arm. He screamed, weeping to the ceiling as he felt two of his fingers disappear down the creature's gullet.

"Rook!" Fredrick hollered.

Two rounds from Fredrick's weapon ripped into its temple. The attacker's corpse fell over, dragging Calvin to the floor. The rookie agent pulled, his face turning red from strain.

"Stand clear, damn it!" Callisto barked.

She placed the barrel of her shotgun at the elbow of the fiend. One trigger pull severed the arm from the corpse. Fredrick grabbed Calvin, heaving him up to his feet. The rookie groaned, clenching his quivering blood-soaked hand.

Callisto turned to see arms reaching out for her. She fired and cocked her shotgun until they receded back into the shadows. After she pumped the gun's fore-end, nothing chambered.

"I'm dry," she yelled as her fingers popped more rounds into the weapon. "Have to reload!"

Ahead, Emmerich saw glimpses of a door within the muzzle flashes. They continued to press on until reaching it, where he ushered the team inside. The agent slammed the door, turning the lock on the knob. He leaned back against it, feeling the jarring thumps coming from the other side. The screams grew louder, closing in on the door.

"Let me see it," Badrick said. "Give me some light."

The big man grabbed Calvin's hand while reaching into his coat to draw out a small olive-green box. Fredrick pulled out his cellphone, turning on its flashlight. The rookie's entire arm trembled, his face locked in a deep wince. Badrick drew out a small brown bottle, uncapping it with his mouth and pouring the contents on it. Calvin gasped as the wound sizzled with sparks of pain. Shreds of tissue foamed up when the liquid touched, creaming the area with a pink mixture.

"Damn, this hurts!" The rookie cried out.

"Hang in there, Calvin!" Elizabeth pleaded.

"Hold still, young blood," Badrick demanded. "You're not in danger of bleeding out, but I still want to stabilize it."

"Please!"

Badrick wrapped the wound with cotton balls and gauze.

"Now this hand is out of commission. Try to stay off it. Just fire with your left."

"I lost my weapon in the firefight," Calvin said.

"Here, take one of mine," Callisto volunteered.

"Thanks. Reloading is going to be hell with only one and a half hands."

"I'm glad you're keeping a sense of humor about this," Emmerich patted the junior agent. "You'll be fine, Calvin."

"What the hell were those things, Actual?"

"The first wave was ghouls. The second were zombies."

"Wait, what? Actual, am I going to become one of those damned things?"

"No, they're not the plague variant. We encountered those during a project gone awry with Tamco Pharma and the biological weapon they unleashed on a town outside of Baton Rouge. These are products of sorcery, not science. So, they're not contagious. We ran into this type of classification before."

"During our deployment to Louisiana," Callisto added. "The Bayou Wars we fought alongside Tenth Team against the Leroux Clan."

"Oh yeah, Cali, I remember, those crazy ritual sorcerers," Badrick agreed. "Primitive but effective magick."

"Right, these are products of voodoo," Emmerich continued. "I find this strange because most voodoo practitioners are benevolent helpers of the community. They aided us when facing the Leroux Clan."

"I thought voodoo was just silly superstition used in movies," Calvin groaned as a layer of tape was affixed to his wound.

"Those silly superstitions nearly killed you," Badrick said. "And would've torn your body to ribbons if Cali and Freddy hadn't gotten there first."

"Voodoo is one of the oldest and most powerful systems of magick in the world," Emmerich said. "We're not dealing with some Lewellyn paperback pest."

"Those goofy edge-lords that watch the Craft and dress in all black?" Fredrick chuckled. "Yeah, I think it's safe to say whomever we're up against is well versed."

"Magick originated in Africa, with its direct traditions carried to the Caribbean. A voodoo practitioner with great spiritual potential could cause a lot of mayhem. Even destroy an entire town."

"You're referring to Roanoke," Badrick asked. "Yeah, chilling stuff. Magick doesn't always have to work instantly. It can slowly chip away at you, until there's nothing left."

"The old colony that disappeared, I remember reading about that in history class," Calvin inquired. "I thought it was an abandoned settlement that failed. Voodoo did that?"

"One of the slaves they brought over was the daughter of a powerful practitioner," Badrick continued.

"Serves them evil honkies right," Fredrick snapped.

Badrick rose a brow at his brother. "I don't even know how to respond to that level of ignorance."

"I do." Callisto's hand went upside Fredrick's head.

"I don't completely understand the system," Emmerich continued. "But, I know they manage to remove the soul from the body, keeping it alive so a demon can take over. Usually, it's a low-level mindless one. These become ghouls. Over time, the body starts to decay. The wear and tear on it, combined with the inability to heal itself since technically it's dead, leads to a breakdown of the muscle tissues, turning ghouls into the slower moving zombies."

"Well said, Actual," Elizabeth agreed. *"You're correct. I guess you are more than just a typical gunslinger."*

"So, the good news is you're not turning. We won't have to put a round in the back of your head," Badrick quipped. "The bad news is that this is the best I can do until we get you to a medical facility."

"Thank you, sir."

"Now, to orient ourselves and find a way out of this hellhole," Emmerich said. "Have to let Queenbee know about this infestation ASAP."

"Then what?" Calvin asked.

"Want some payback, huh?" Badrick wondered.

"She'll probably drum up Badger, Monarch, or Pitbull teams to wipe them out," Emmerich answered.

"Of course, I want some payback. Why not us, Actual?"

"They're huge assault teams designed for large scale confrontations. That's not our role. We're designed for variable threat recon, investigations, search and destroy missions."

"Knowing the Assistant Director, if she doesn't hear from us in a few hours, she'll probably launch a QRF to augment us."

"A quick reaction force?"

"Yes."

"That's a relief, Actual."

"I'm sorry, Rook," Fredrick said. "This is my fault. I shouldn't have taken such a lax stance. I didn't think anything would happen going to this facility. Thought it was just another meet and greet with some civies."

"Hate to say I told you so, asshole," Callisto quipped. "I'm lying. Actually, I love it. I told you so, asshole."

"It's not your fault," Calvin said. "No need to apologize."

"Give me that moonbeam over here," Emmerich ordered.

The light revealed televisions mounted on walls and rows of couches. Several ping pong and foosball tables were stationed at the end of the large room. The stale air reeked of long burnt cigarette smoke, the remainders of which sat in ashtrays throughout the area.

"I feel something," Elizabeth said. *"I see nothing. Damn this fog of negative energy."*

"A game room," Badrick stated.

"Does anyone else hear a tapping," Callisto asked.

"I think I hear it," Emmerich replied.

"Guess even crazies need a hobby," Fredrick said. "You know, besides munching off people's hands."

Calvin shook his head.

"Shut up, asshole!" Callisto snapped.

She stormed off ahead with Emmerich, the others in tow. The cellphone's flashlight caught a shadow fluctuating low to the ground, behind a table. Callisto raised her shotgun.

"I got movement over here, Em!"

Fredrick illuminated the area. "I got nothing."

Emmerich sidestepped in a wide arc, his pistol trained where Callisto pointed her shotgun. He cleared the corner, seeing nothing.

"It's gone."

"If there was even anything there," Fredrick said.

"When are you going to stop doubting me, asshole?" Callisto grumbled. "I saw something!"

"Hey, calm down, I'm just saying the dark has a way of playing tricks on people."

"Shut the fuck up!"

"You're going to make such an awesome in-law."

"At-ease, you two," Emmerich ordered. "I think I saw something also. Whatever it was, it's gone now. Eyes open and call out all contact."

A loud slam across the way urged Fredrick to bring his light over to the other exit. The wide-open doors still rattled and swayed. Standing in the entrance was a dour-faced individual, towering just below the height of the door's frame.

"It's an orderly!" Fredrick shouted.

The man stretched open his mouth, resonating a deep bellow as he stomped forward. A flip of his arms and couches flew out of his way, against the wall. The orderly dipped his face during the rampage, showing his forehead. He stormed over to the ping pong table, bringing his meaty fist down and shattering it in half with one blow. The pieces were hurled at the team, and they dived out of the way.

Callisto pressed the release latch just below her shotgun's receiver, pumping the fore-end to jettison the remaining rounds. Her hand scrambled over her jacket pockets, fingers gripping each of the shells in them, searching for the long ones.

"Get them damn BMG rounds out," Fredrick screeched, firing at the orderly.

"Shut the fuck up! I know what I'm doing, you asshole!"

"Keep the light on the tango!" Emmerich yelled.

Emmerich's fingers pulled the trigger in rapid succession, and the orderly's head snapped back. Flesh peeled from its dome. Amongst the mangled tissue, a metallic layer reflected in the cellphone's light. Badrick circled the brute's right flank, firing several shots at the side of its head. The orderly turned its wailing visage on him as he reloaded.

"Someone gave this moefoe a steel plate in its dome!" Fredrick screamed. "How the fuck are we going to drop it?"

"Give me a light, dumbass!" Callisto demanded.

She continued to fumble through the many twelve-gauge rounds in her pockets. Fredrick brought the light over to her.

"Hurry, damn it! Load those BMG rounds!"

Furniture crashed against the wall, followed by a loud

cracking that seized everyone's attention. Badrick began to holler in agony. Emmerich paused as he stared at the shifting shadows. His trigger finger trembled as he aimed his weapon.

"Badrick!" he screamed.

The orderly continued its howl. Badrick wailed to the ceiling in anguish.

CHAPTER 7
THE CONDEMNED

"Badrick!" Emmerich cried out for his brother. "I can't see shit! I don't have a shot!"

The grating tear of cloth followed a thud. Metal pounded with flesh and bone, from Badrick pistol-whipping the orderly. He panted and groaned, his heavy boots stomping as he staggered off. A roar came from the agent, and steel collided with the floor as a magazine discarded. Shots rang out, the barrel of his gun spewing rounds. Flashes from the weapon illuminated quick glimpses of Badrick stumbling from the hulking assailant backhanding a chair out of his way.

"You want some?" Badrick roared. "Come and get it, you big ugly son of a—"

Fredrick brought his light over. The orderly reached out, grabbing Badrick's pistol and ripping it from his grasp. One jerk from his large hands and the weapon snapped in half, tossing the grip in one direction while the receiver flew in another. Badrick's rear hit the corner of the room. Heaving deep with each breath, he nursed his side with a chicken winged arm, raising a knife in the other.

"I still got some fight in me!" he roared at the orderly. "You're going to have to earn this one!"

Badrick twisted his hips while stepping forward, launching a punch. His fist crashed into the orderly's jaw with a loud pop. He cocked his hand back into position. The orderly's dislocated mandible hung open, his eyes still fixed on the agent, leaning forward, and reaching out to grab him. Badrick lunged, bringing the knife up, ramming the six inches of steel through his skull. The blade pinned the assailant's mouth shut again, causing his head to snap back.

The orderly reached out, his large hands closing on Badrick's forearm. The operator punched with his other arm, groaning as he felt surges of pain coursing through his torso. Badrick twisted his body, delivering a fierce hook, sending the orderly's head turning, dislodging the knife from its jaw. The orderly grabbed his arm again, holding Badrick in place. The agent placed a boot against his opponent's hip. Veins stretched in his forehead as he tried to pull away with everything he could muster.

"Duck!" Callisto screamed.

Badrick dropped to his knees. The shotgun roared. Globs of brain matter rained on him, followed by a substantial piece of metal falling on his back. The orderly swayed leaning forward, its decapitated corpse falling on top of him.

"Get this thing off me!" Badrick hollered. "It's heavy!"

The team ran over. Fredrick and Emmerich struggled to break their brother free. Badrick staggered to his feet, his elbow tucked into the left side of his buckled body. Emmerich reached out to help.

"I thought you were a goner there," he said.

"Me, too," Badrick replied. "Just some fractured ribs. I've had them before. I'll live."

"Just?" Emmerich asked, shaking his head. "We got to get you the hell out of here."

Fredrick shone the light on to the corpse. "Look at that!"

A rip across the orderly's turtleneck exposed the skin below. Moldy stitching stretched across the bottom of his neck, joining his pale epidermis to a darker russet skin tone. Emmerich unbuttoned the jacket, opening it and tearing the rest of the sweater. They spotted another line of stitching with hairy tanned skin.

"This guy has three different types of skin?" Fredrick asked.

"Yes, he was pieced together," Emmerich answered. "He was created from the parts of others."

"A fucking Frankenstein's monster. Let's just add that to the list of weird shit we hunt."

"That's not good," Calvin said. "Is that why they want one of us alive?"

"Let's hope not," Badrick answered, lowering his head as his eyelids clenched together before delivering a little groan.

"We're getting weaker by the moment," Callisto added. "We need to fall back and rendezvous with Fin, then counter once QRF gets drummed up."

"She feels it. This place, it's doing more than just clouding the ether. The energies here are ruinous."

"My thoughts exactly," Emmerich agreed. "Baddy, are you going to be able to keep up?"

"Not as though I have much choice. Just give me a gun, that thing broke my last one like a child's play toy."

Callisto handed him one of hers, patting the big guy on the shoulder.

"Always can count on you," he struggled to say, giving her a weak smile. "Thanks, sis."

"M-medicine," a faint voice managed.

"What the—" Fredrick said, spinning around and shining his light.

An emaciated figure scampered behind a nearby table. The team followed the patter of small bare feet across the floor. Their light pursued, flashing over a set of gleaming eyes that ducked behind a table.

"Who's there?" Fredrick demanded.

"Get that bass out of your voice, Freddy," Badrick groaned as he walked over.

"Didn't you see her?" Emmerich scolded. "You're going to scare her off."

"Her?" Fredrick scoffed.

"I can barely see her aura in the ether. It melds into the darkness with only a faint signature of her existence. I could've easily missed it if I weren't focusing."

The team moved closer, walking around the table. The skinny girl scurried across the floor, unkempt strands of lengthy blonde hair trailing her. She halted at a counter, opening one of the cupboard doors and crawling inside.

"Wait!" Callisto exclaimed.

"We mean you no harm," Emmerich pleaded.

Faint beating carried through the counter along the wall. Calvin opened a door on the opposite end. She shifted away with occasional glances, her blinking eyes gleaming in the flashlight.

"Please, we aren't here to hurt you," Calvin said. "We're the good guys, I promise."

"We're human like you," Emmerich added.

Calvin reached out, her thin grungy fingers accepting his hand, assisting her from the crawlspace. The team gasped, seeing the girl's gaunt frame, draped in rags soiled with patches of black and gray.

"You poor thing," Callisto said.

"I'm Emmerich, and these are my teammates, Callisto, Badrick, Fredrick, and Calvin. What's your name?"

"I'm M-Madelyn."

"What are you doing here?"

"M-mommy and Daddy took me here a long time ago. I—I escaped."

There's so much pain coming from her aura. Gosh, this girl is so hard to read. She keeps slipping through my reach like water between my fingers. I hear voices around her. They're crying out. Curses, I keep losing the connection. Can't hear what they're saying.

"Kid, hate to break it to you, but you're still here," Fredrick said.

Emmerich slapped his shoulder.

"How long have you been here?" Callisto asked.

"Th-three years. They turnt people into m-monsters. Th-they said I was too s-soft and small t-t-to use."

"Whoever is doing this wants adult subjects only?" Calvin wondered.

"Kids aren't as effective in combat," Emmerich deduced. "This is the breeding ground for an army."

"Poor girl," Badrick groaned the words. "I can't stand when people mistreat children. Nothing gets my blood boiling faster."

"Yeah," Emmerich patted his brother's back. "I know. I remember, the hunt in Santa Fe." *We tracked one of the Cucuy species of fae during that operation. I can still hear the scrapping of its sharp nails dragging across the floorboards of the home it invaded, a combination of the long arms and fingers it used to walk on, on account of short legs. Although tall, its height wasn't abnormal to onlookers who would usually be fooled if it tucked its arms behind its body, usually adorned in a long black coat. The rim of its hat managed to hide its shining eyes with pupils that opened and closed like a camera's aperture.*

I didn't understand the reports I had read before hunting it, I just remembered that they hid behind the power of illusions. The one we battled that day didn't. We got lucky I suppose, only having to deal with a juvenile one. The ambush was quick and brutal. Badrick didn't even wait for Kat to give the order. I could see it in his eyes when he hacked it apart with that carbon steel machete, hatred. Iron weapons can damage them since they naturally disrupt the flow of magick.

We all hurt knowing that we didn't arrive in time to save some of the children of that city. Badrick took it more personal than the rest. Perhaps because he lost his little brother to domestic violence. Before our father adopted us, when we were at the orphanage together, he didn't say a word to anyone for the first few months. Then he broke down and told us the story during sharing time. His little brother, savagely pummeled by their mother's drunk boyfriend, over a piece of cheesecake. They hadn't eaten in days before finding it in the fridge. Badrick let his two-year-old brother eat it, thinking it was the right thing to do until they were discovered...

Emmerich witnessed the fervor rising in his brother's eyes as the seconds of silence passed. Badrick nodded to him.

"You're such a big softy," Callisto chuckled.

"M-medicine?"

The girl pointed at Badrick.

"Yeah, sweetie, I sure could use some strong stuff right now."

"C-come."

Madelyn leapt on the counter, pointing at the vast gray air vents. She removed the faceplate and started to pull herself into it. Her blinking eyes looked down at the team.

"Sweetie, we aren't going to fit in that, and even if we could, two of us are in no shape to climb up there."

The girl hopped back down and dashed to the door, cracking it open and poking her head out. She looked back at the team, waving for them. Madelyn started down the corridor with slow steps, close to the wall but never touching. Ghost Team followed.

"Find them! Feeding time isn't over until I have their heads on my desk!" The doctor screamed over the intercom.

"E-Evil lady," Madelyn murmured. "Evil lady. Evil lady."

"It's okay, we won't let her harm you," Badrick whispered as he took the girl's hand. "We're going to get you out of here. I promise."

"O-okay," Madelyn smiled.

Arriving at a door, Madelyn pressed her ear against it for a few seconds. She nodded to the team, cracking it open and peering into the room, the lithe girl slipped in. Chairs lined one side of the room, facing an open counter door.

"A pharmacy, thank you, sweetie," Badrick whispered. "Looks as if this is where they store the meds. Right on. Now to score some morphine for us, Rook."

"That sounds amazing, sir."

"If only she can find us some chow," Fredrick jested.

Madelyn reached into her torn shirt, walking over to him with a thin brown chip. The operator raised a brow and took it in his hand, feeling its hard-outer shell and rigid appendages. Fredrick yelped, dropping it.

"What the hell is the matter with you!" Callisto scolded in sharp whispers. "You're going to let that swarm know our location if they hear your stupid ass!"

"It's a roach!"

Callisto rolled her eyes.

"Jackpot." Badrick grinned. "The Rook and I are good for now. I snagged some other stuff, too. Just in case."

"It's going to be such a relief once it kicks in. Thank you, sir."

"Don't thank me. Thank the little lady here for saving our behinds."

Madelyn smiled.

"Do you know a way out of here?" Emmerich asked.

Madelyn nodded. "Y-yes, b-but lots of b-big guys."

"Just what I wanted to hear," Fredrick groaned.

"Makes sense, though. Remember, on our way in here, all the orderlies we passed. They're just sentries guarding the entrances."

Madelyn nodded. "Follow!"

She exited the room, with the team tailing her down the corridor. They passed by doors lining the wall, some of them with little windows. Calvin peered into one, seeing a man sitting by himself at the corner of a bed. He looked up, spotting the rookie, and ran over.

"Help! Help us!" Muffled pleas came through.

"Keep moving, Rook," Callisto said.

"But—"

"We can't do anything for him or any of the others now. We don't even know how to unlock these doors. The best thing we can do for them is to return with a larger force."

Calvin sighed. "Understood, ma'am."

"There," Madelyn said.

They traversed the hallway until reaching another door. Emmerich nodded, racing ahead to crack it open. He peered over to see a room with a double door. Through the windows, he spotted the lamps illuminating the tall hedges and benches of the garden. Heavy footsteps trudged on the other side of the door. Without a sound, Emmerich eased the door closed.

"Madelyn," Emmerich whispered. "Does that lead to the backyard?"

"I-I think s-so." She shrugged.

"Okay, I didn't see anyone near the entrance, but I heard them in the room. We double time for the door. Cali, you take up the rear and keep them off us."

"With pleasure."

Badrick took Madelyn by the hand. "Stay with us, sweetie."

Her eyes widened.

"Here we go," Emmerich announced.

The team burst through the door, bolting into the room. The handles to the exit would not budge. Callisto spun around with her weapon aiming for the orderlies rising from their seats. Their glares fell on the team. Mouths dropped open to usher out ear-piercing screams. Plodding forward, the beasts closed on Ghost Team.

She aligned the sights of her weapon with the forehead of the first, pulling the trigger. The shotgun bellowed its payload, caving in the frontal lobe of her target, sending him collapsing on the floor. A puddle of blackness gushed below the back of the head, mixing with the chunks that sprayed out.

Teeth bared, she cocked her twelve gauge, aiming it again at the next foe. The large round struck the monstrosity's throat, burrowing clear through its massive Adam's apple. A torrent of its inner fluids spilled out of the stump where its head had once been.

"I got it, Em! Back away!" Badrick roared.

The large agent raised his boot, stomping on the front of the door. It shuddered, flexing under pressure. He stepped forward again, delivering another mighty kick. The busted lock gave way.

"I should've thought of that," Emmerich said. "Thanks."

A shrieking reverberated over the intercom. "The interlopers are escaping out of the southeastern entrance!" The doctor's roar echoed. "After them! Devour the children of El! They must not escape!"

"N-no! Monsters out-outside!" Badrick felt the tiny hand slip from his grasp. He turned to see Madelyn, eyes wide, mouth agape, and whimpering as she fled back into the asylum.

"No, sweetie, where are you going? We're trying to save you!"

Elizabeth witnessed the girl's vibratory rate rise in the ether. The grip of the darkness loosened on the layers, the closer they came to the exit. Madelyn's aura dimmed, plummeting once more and blending into the haze of shadows, just before disappearing from the scryer's reach.

"Come back, Madelyn!" Elizabeth pleaded.

"Let her go, Baddy!" Fredrick said. "We don't have time for this shit! All the damn crazies are going to come down on our asses!"

With another shot, Callisto felled the next orderly in her sights. She maneuvered through the door, popping rounds into the feed tube as she caught up with the others. Tall hedges, bushes, and trees provided cover in the gloom of the night, save for the few areas illuminated by the moon. Screams followed them as they slipped away, disappearing amongst the foliage.

"Tac-com, this is Ghost8Actual. Radio check. Over."

"Anything, Em?" Fredrick asked.

"Nothing still."

"Damn, I hope Egghead is alright."

"Fuck it. Break protocol, everyone try using your cells."

"I have no signal, Actual," Calvin replied.

"Yeah, same here, babe. It's safe to say this place is a dead zone. Literally and figuratively."

As they continued, Emmerich felt slender arms wrapping around his torso. Callisto's rosy scent was a welcome relief from the unwashed masses that were bearing down on them. He placed his head against hers.

"Thanks for covering our six back there," Emmerich said.

"Anytime, babe."

"Can we please get the hell out of here?" Fredrick asked.

"Let them have a moment. We almost ended up KIA in there!" Badrick slapped his brother upside the head. "I need to hug my lady when I get home, too."

"He's right," Callisto agreed. "As much as it pains me to agree with Freddy."

The next path between hedges began to widen. A tall figure stood amongst the shadows of the moonlight. Weapons rose with sights and barrels aligning on it. The team moved closer, seeing a stand below its feet. The tension dropped from their shoulders as they lowered their firearms.

"Stand down, Ghost Team. It's just a statue." Emmerich read the inscription along the bottom, "Let those who were washed away by cruelty and lost to this world, find their home here, -Dr. Alfred Moorehouse."

"How ironic to put something like that here," Callisto said.

"We've come too far to turn back now. Let's keep moving, team."

"But where, Em?" Freddy pointed at the three breaks in the hedges.

"We're on the southeast side, so let's go left, keep pushing east, and working our way north to link up with Finley at the van."

Emmerich's head snapped in the direction of the asylum, his attention seized by barking and screams echoing in unison throughout the night sky. Rumbling growls carried like the wind, augmented with heavy breathing and the snap of slavering jaws.

CHAPTER 8
LAMENTATION OF SERVICE

Paws sped across the ground, their nails tapping against the cement of the garden walkway. The union of growling and screams carried through the night sky, growing louder with the drum of each approaching step. The first abomination sprinted through the break in the hedges. Sharp fangs bared from its bobbing head, its mangy body churning its legs hard to close the distance. On its back, held by frayed sutures, the face of a man stared up at the moon. Its trembling mouth gaped, screaming with every fiber of its being.

"I can't believe they've done this to innocent animals!" Elizabeth gasped in horror.

A shiver crawled down Emmerich's spine when the beast's feral eyes homed in on him. "Line abreast formation!"

Shots rang out. Muzzle flashes followed. Rounds disappeared into the bushes, some of them peppering the galloping beast. Its momentum continued, leaping into the air and pouncing on top of Emmerich.

"Actual, watch out!"

The large blond man toppled over. As his back hit the ground, his breath seized out of his lungs. With a snap of the beast's jaws, it locked on his forearm. Teeth pushed into the sleeve of his coat, rubbing against his skin. The ear-ringing screams continued, resonating just over him. With a violent shake of the creature's head, Emmerich thumped on the pavement as he was thrashed about.

"Get the hell off him!" Callisto yelled.

A blast from her twelve gauge sent the beast flying off Emmerich. It snarled, rearing its head around as it rose once more. Another bellowing shot from Callisto ripped its canine head clean off. Blood and fur sprinkled across the hedges, yet its body scampered away, the head on its back still screaming into the night.

"Are you oka—" Badrick tried asking.

The big man's attention was usurped by more paws rapping across the ground. His pistol rose, aligning the sight with the opening in the hedges. More of the beasts came storming through. His finger pumped the trigger, releasing consecutive shots at the fanged pair before them. The rest of the team continued firing.

A beast's head snapped back as lead punctured its skull. The hail sent its body collapsing to the floor. Another creature leapt out from behind it, tackling Badrick to the ground. The big man groaned and winced as he brought his pistol over and bashed its skull.

Callisto aimed, firing a round into its stomach. The blast toppled the creature, tumbling it across the ground. The second shot that followed struck the human head across its back, caving its skull. The screams ceased as its lusterless corpse slumped over.

"Not getting away this time," Callisto announced. "Babe, are you still with us?"

"Sir, are you okay?" the rookie asked Badrick.

"I'm good, check on my brother."

"Rise to your feet, Actual. More are coming. I can feel them. The shadows of their dark essence are pushing through the remaining light."

Emmerich rose, cradling his forearm. "Good, just got the wind knocked out of me and a sprain."

"Walk it off, babe."

"Yeah, let's keep moving before more show up."

Monitors surrounded Dr. Metzger, flashing through various locales of the asylum grounds. She leaned over the microphone on her desk, clearing her throat, then shaking her head.

"I have nothing." She mouthed the words as her trembling hand reached into her coat pocket. "I have no other option."

The bright screen of the doctor's cellphone reflected against her glasses. A slow press of her fingers punched in a sequence of numbers, her hand pausing before pressing the last one. Metzger shivered, though it was warm in the room. She sighed, hitting it, and sending the device into a call sequence.

"We be listenin."

"I need to speak with the master." Her lip quivered. "I-is he there?"

"We are here. Utter your report."

"Master, you were absolutely correct about them being USA agents—"

"Tell me what I need to know." The voice seethed between clenched teeth.

"We lost the rest of them in the gardens."

"So, they have escaped."

"No, Master they're still—"

"Sounds like dey escaped, mon."

"Master, they were heavily armed, well trained and managed to fight off the horde—"

"Are you trying to entertain me with your babbling excuses, Dlo? You think that's what I want to hear?"

"No, Master."

"When I arose from the abyss, I reached back and grabbed you to be among the first to join me. I gave you a chance at a new existence because I foresaw potential in you. Now I am starting to comprehend the error of my ways. Optimism in my minions seems to be a foolish trait these days."

"Master, please—"

"I've given you the bulk of my army. Your task was simple; kill the agents and capture one. Your failure has exposed our designs. I have no doubt they will return with more of their ilk. This will happen after they manage to contact their superiors and report everything they have witnessed."

"I have managed to capture one of the agents, my master."

"Then, your endeavors were not a complete waste of my time."

"What do you wish of me?"

"Slay them before they can escape. If they return with reinforcements, set loose the full strength of the horde. Show no mercy. Do not relent."

"A full-scale attack? Won't that compromise our entire operation?"

"Only in Moorehouse. If that's the price we must pay, so be it."

"As you wish, Master."

"I will have Alcanor assist you should they reach outside of the asylum grounds. They believe him to be an ally. He will catch them off guard."

"Yes, Master."

"Do I need to iterate what will become of you should this fail?"

"No, Master."

"Good. You have work to do. Now begone."

"Don't fail'im, girl. I be far more kinder ta my victims den da Baron be to his."

Through the sting of wounds and clouds of warm breath heaving from their lungs, Ghost Team jogged through the twists and turns of the gardens. Hedges, bushes, trees, and benches disappeared from view in their rapid trek. Emmerich stopped, raising his fist. The team halted in their tracks.

Damn it this looks the exact same. "We've passed by this area a few times."

"How do you know, Actual?" Calvin asked.

"The flower arrangement on that hedge over there. I made a note of the pattern these have died in. Many of them in the center are missing."

"Damn it. Stupid ass maze is just wasting our time!" Fredrick snapped.

"There's more coming, Actual! Keep moving!" Elizabeth pleaded. *"I can see their auras now that we're no longer in that cursed place!"*

"We have to keep moving though," Callisto urged. "I'm sensing it's not over."

"Em, how about we hoist someone up on that gazebo over there and try to get a vantage point?" Badrick suggested.

Good thinking, Baddy. So much weighing on my mind. Glad you're here. Emmerich nodded. "Freddy, you're going up."

"I knew it. All right."

"I'll go, babe."

"No, I need you on the ground with our firepower," Emmerich answered. *I can't have you doing everything, my love.* "Badrick and I will hoist him up on the gazebo. You and the rook keep watch for any tangoes."

"You got it, babe."

"Acknowledged, sir."

"Don't get too comfortable being the big gun, Cali," Fredrick quipped.

She replied with her middle finger and a smirk. "I'm always the big gun."

"Come on, let's get your ass up there before she mistakes you for a tango," Badrick suggested.

The two hoisted their brother upward. Fredrick grabbed at the corner of the roof, pulling himself up. The gazebo creaked, swaying a bit from the agent's steps. He poised himself, looking over, past the gardens, to the gates that surrounded the vast empty parking lot.

"What you got for us, Freddy?" Emmerich asked.

"Yeah, we aren't too far from the front. I'd say about a hundred meters. I see the parking lot, but the main building is blocking my view of Egghead and the van."

"Tac-com, this is Ghost8Actual. Radio check. Over." *We're definitely in range. Yet no response.*

"All right, I'm climbing down. This shit feels like

something's going to give. Help me, so I don't bust my ass and end up a broke-dick like Baddy and Rook."

"You know you're getting popped for that when you get down here, right?" Badrick said.

"Hurry! I feel their approach!"

The hair is standing up on the back of my neck. It's about to get heavy. Damn it, I was hoping to avoid any more engagements. Baddy is slowing despite trying to keep his bearing and Rook is wincing every couple of seconds. The morphine must be wearing off. I have to get them the hell out of here.

Fredrick dropped down from the gazebo, his brothers catching the fall. Screaming came from an adjacent passage within the hedges. With arms flailing and legs pumping, the swarm poured into the area. Callisto's shotgun spewed its payload into the oncoming menace. Calvin's pistol barked, the receiver churning with each round it spewed.

"Tangoes incoming!" Callisto roared.

We need to fire and maneuver to give our wounded time to escape, or else they're going to be on top of us! I'm not losing anyone else!

With weapons drawn, the Steiners joined the fray, adding a salvo of lead to the mix. Bodies collapsed as holes punched into their skulls. Black liquid flowed from their piling corpses, streaming like a small river over the walkway.

"To the rear!" Emmerich instructed. "Bounding withdrawal!"

"Roger, Actual!" Calvin acknowledged.

"Bravo section move with me," Badrick commanded.

Calvin, Fredrick, and Badrick disengaged, running to a break in the hedges behind them. When set, their weapons rose, firing into the screaming hordes. Callisto and Emmerich turned and ran backward, their hands in a swift motion, reloading their weapons. They raced through the opening, appearing before a long stretch of foliage aligned with benches. They continued down the corridor of shrubbery. Covering fire from the other three rang out until positioning themselves on each side.

"Set!" Callisto shouted.

"Hurry! Go, go, go, run!" Elizabeth pleaded with everything she could muster.

The three came rushing through, wailing foes in pursuit gunned down by Callisto and Emmerich's cover fire. They continued to the far end of the corridor. Crooked hands raked the air just in front of Emmerich's face. Their shrieking rang in his ears. Through his core, the echo of his racing heart pulsed into the palms of his hands.

"Set!" Badrick hollered. "Em, get the fuck out of there!"

"Almost dry!" Fredrick yelled.

"Here!" Callisto tossed him a magazine as they passed. "I have more when you need them!"

Loading his pistol, Fredrick rejoined the torrent of fire. Their foes continued the onslaught, sprinting over the bodies that littered the ground. Large arms swung, knocking aside smaller comrades. Bones snapped, skulls shattered, dark blood flowed. A dour expression of a wailing orderly locked on them as it bulldozed through the lesser minions. Squirts of liquid added to the nurse's uniform, already covered in a myriad of stains with the juices of those it pummeled.

"Orderly!" Calvin yelled.

"Cali!" Fredrick cried out. "Drop this big Frankenstein sombitch!"

The hulking figure grabbed at an ally, hefting the writhing ghoul into the air, and tossing it at Calvin. The rookie dropped to his knees as the body flew over his head, crashing into a bench with a loud snap. The broken ghoul's body folded over on impact. Agony zipped through Calvin's hand, churning up his trembling arm. He groaned, the three remaining fingers trying to balance his frame as he pushed back to his feet. The bushes near the bench shuffled as the broken ghoul crawled from underneath it. Calvin turned, watching the shrieking foe crawl toward him with its legs dragging on the ground. Two shots in its head halted the crippled body.

"Set!" Emmerich shouted. "Move!" *There's too many. Everyone is almost dry. They're gaining on us. I have to do something.*

The rest of Ghost Team sprinted past Emmerich and Callisto. The orderly plodded its way in close pursuit. Callisto raised her weapon barrel, aligning it with the abomination's face. With a pull of the trigger, the large round burrowed into its forehead. Dark chunks sprayed out the back end of its skull, it swayed and collapsed on top of those to its rear.

"Set!" Badrick shouted.

"There's too many, Actual. I know you're all exhausted and hurting but keep going! You're almost there!" Elizabeth pleaded.

"Here!" Emmerich shouted, pointing at the steel gates leading to the parking lot. "We're hopping them! Rook, you're first!"

"Roger, Actual!"

Fredrick and Emmerich hoisted Calvin up. The rookie grasped the top of the gates, groaning through his teeth as he pulled himself up and over. Once his feet touched down, he began firing between the steel bars. His pistol's receiver snapped back, holding into the rear position. Its smokey chamber was devoid of any more bullets.

"I'm out!" Calvin said.

Fredrick slipped his weapon between the bars, handing it to Calvin.

"Cali, you're up!" Emmerich barked.

She broke contact, shouldering her firearm, and catapulting into the air as the two launched her up. Callisto was over the gate in seconds, adding to the hail of cover fire with Calvin. The horde continued, their numbers swelling, their screams echoing throughout the gardens. They smashed through the smaller bushes, leaping over the benches, and trampling their fallen. Badrick fired, dropping a few just out of reach.

"Baddy!"

"No, send little Freddy first."

"Little?" Fredrick raised a brow.

The pop of a foam dart shot from a plastic gun, usurped Emmerich's thoughts. He heard the laughter of his brothers echoing into his mind, as they ran through the halls of their childhood home, aiming their toys at each other. Fragrant cinnamon scented the air from the French toast their mother cooked every Sunday morning. His vision shifted, immersed with the images of a long-faced Fredrick walking with his head hung low, his arms swinging with a rattling and broken toy gun. Another flash, and there was Badrick handing his to their little brother, whose face light up with the renewed vigor of a toothy smile. Snarls and gunfire brought Emmerich back to the present, but the memories lingered. *That's what he used to call Freddy when we were children...*

"Get your ass up there now!" Badrick snapped.

"All right, damn it!"

Fredrick bounced up, holding on to the railing and lying prone along the top of the gate. He reached down.

They're closing. I have to get my team over the—

"Em, you're next!"

"No, my team goes firs—"

"Get your ass up there!" Badrick snapped. "We don't have time for this shit!"

Emmerich paused. His brother downed more foes. The horde continued to surround him.

He knows he can't make the jump and his mighty pride won't allow him to admit it. The rib fractures are taking its toll. I'm surprised he kept up this long—

"God damn it, Em! Go already!"

"Thank you," his voice cracked, before leaping up and catching Fredrick's hand. "I love you, brother."

"And I love you, both."

"Badrick, don't!" Elizabeth cried out.

The two climbed over the gate, landing and joining the salvo. Snarling ghouls fell, but the swarm continued. A hand flew out, grabbing Badrick's weapon arm. He swung his huge balled fist, knocking the wailing foe's head sideways. Teeth sprinkled the cement. It reared back, biting down into his sleeve.

"No, God damn it!" Fredrick snatched his weapon back, emptying his magazine into the horde. "Badrick! Em, do something!"

More arms reached out, locking Badrick in place. The wailing rang in his throbbing ears, drowning out his thoughts. His finger pulled the trigger, spewing lead into the nearest body. He struggled, but they continued until he crumpled from the sheer weight. Badrick disappeared underneath a pile of tearing hands and gnawing mouths. His screams washed away in their wailing.

"Badrick! We have to go back for him!" Fredrick hollered. "Em!"

"We're moving," Emmerich order. "We can't—"

"No! Em! Baddy—"

"He's gone!" The words stung Emmerich, the chill of sorrow flowed through with alarming resonance. "We need to move, or his sacrifice will be for nothing!" *I failed my own brother...*

Fredrick turned, the ravenous pile continued to claw at the strewn remains.

"I said move, Freddy! Double time it!" Emmerich barked.

The team continued through the parking lot, jogging over glass shards shimmering on the pavement. Scattered around the van were dozens of corpses. All four tires sagged. The air had escaped from gaping tears across them. Inside more debris from the smashed windows littered the seats.

"They must've gotten Egghead!" Fredrick exclaimed.

"Yeah, and they took all the radio gear, too," Emmerich said. "That means our crypto graphics are compromised. We have to get the hell out of dodge."

"Babe, we have incoming!"

"Keep going, Actual! Clear the reach of darkness!"

Feet touched down from the shuttering gates. A body plopped to the cement, only to rise back up and begin racing over toward the team. The horde scratched, pulled, and strained to scale the gate. A few more of their members trickled over.

"On me," Emmerich said. *I must gather myself for the sake of the others. Fall back now, vengeance later.*

As the team ran for the front entrance, a loud shudder caused them to look back. The door to the main building had flung open. A tall, wailing orderly pointed as his lifeless eyes spotted them. The horde streamed around him and into the parking lot.

CHAPTER 9
CASUALTIES

We must keep moving. It's what he would've wanted.

"On me," Emmerich boomed. *I will avenge you, Badrick. No matter the cost.*

Ghost Team sprinted across the parking lot. The horde spilled into the area, rushing to close the gap. The cries of one grew closer as it broke away from the rest of its numbers, catching up to the team's rear. Calvin turned, putting two shots into its skull. As its carcass plopped to the ground, countless eyes bore down on him, their savage gazes emanating rage.

"Keep moving! You're almost there!"

"Another gate to scale!"

"Rook beat feet!" Fredrick yelled.

Calvin shook his head, turning to catch the others. The damp sweat stains made their garments cling to them. Their lungs burned from the cold and exertion, mouths heaving, expelling white clouds into the night air. Despite the muscles in their legs swelling with agony, adrenaline coursed through them, propelling them through the parking lot. Their arrival at the main gate forced a halt.

"Rook, first!" Emmerich said. "Cover us when you touch down!"

"Roger, Actual!"

With combined grasps, they spring boarded Calvin up the tall gate. A groan escaped his mouth as he pulled himself over. Calvin glanced up after landing, firing at the snarling horde looming behind the rest of Ghost Team.

"Freddy, let's go!" Emmerich yelled.

Cali fired a chain of blasts, dropping the first arrivals. "Babe, get your ass over!"

"Cali!"

"Do it! We don't have time to argue!"

"Go, Actual!" Elizabeth pleaded.

Emmerich leapt up. Fredrick grabbed onto his arm from his perch at the top of the gate, pulling him up. Once situated, Emmerich turned to reach down for Callisto.

"Jump!"

Shouldering the weapon, she leapt, grabbing Emmerich's hand. He pulled with everything he could muster but couldn't lift her. Callisto howled in defiance, kicking one of her legs downward, her boot crashing into the face of the zombie grasping her. Its head snapped back, but the screaming didn't stop, the zombie's gaze returned to Callisto. Another reached out, grasping her other ankle. Emmerich hollered in despair, as her hands began slipping from his.

"Hang on, Cali! Don't you give up!"

No, I can't lose her, too! I can't live without her...

Shots through the gates dropped the creatures. Fredrick jumped from his perch. Emmerich continued to pull, gasping as his face turned cherry red. He heaved, the extra weight still clinging to Callisto. She started her ascension, and Emmerich dropped back using this momentum to propel Callisto upward. Fredrick grabbed at Emmerich when he came into reach, pulling them both over. With a crash to the ground, Callisto reached for her shotgun to blast off the ghouls clinging to her.

The team rose to their feet. Rattling from the gates drew their attention, a mass of sneering faces peered through the bars, halting in their tracks. Their mouths closed, stopping the macabre choir of screams. Unblinking eyes trembled with rage as they watched Ghost Team disappear into the city. Their numbers dispersed, creeping back into the asylum.

Five vans drove along the road, tires kicking up grime and trash as they sped through. Magazines popped into carbines, rifles, and pistols. Belts of ammunition locked into machine gun chambers, and batteries fed into night optic devices.

"Give me a status, Monarch," Curtis ordered in his deep voice. *Divide the elements during the assault, keep them focused on the main attack group while the secondary approaches from the rear. There's thirteen members in each squad, that should be enough for one to infiltrate the rear of the grounds and secure any avenues of escape for the enemy.*

"We're green to green, Actual," a team member announced.

"Second squad is green to green, Actual," another reported over comms.

"Third squad is green to green, Actual."

"Queenbee, this is Monarch2Actual, we have arrived in the

AO and will be conducting rescue and sweep. Any status on Ghost Team?"

"Acknowledged, I haven't had radio contact with them in several hours," Howler answered. "As you already know from the briefing, their last known location was en route to investigate Moorehouse Asylum."

"Understood, ma'am. We'll be arriving there in thirty mikes."

"Good. Something major is happening here, Curt. We're down one scryer, and I haven't an update on Ghost Team's status. They were initially tasked to investigate a wound in the etheric layers. That led them to Moorehouse."

"Acknowledged, ma'am."

"How's Madam Dupree?"

Curt looked into the rearview mirror for the grayed woman. A blanket draped over her head as she leaned back in her seat.

"The BOW is napping." He chuckled.

"I can't believe she chose that callsign."

"Me neither. The jet lag took its toll on her. I promised I'd only wake her when we needed. I'll relay everything to my team, ma'am. We'll find Ghost and link up with them."

"That sounds like her. Be careful out there, Curt. I'll be on the horn waiting for the status, Queenbee out."

"All right, Monarch, listen up," Curtis relayed over comms. "One of our teams has gone missing in the sector, a scryer is down, and the boss lady herself just told me she feels something big is happening here. So, all squads be ready for stiff resistance when we are boots on the ground." *I have a feeling we're about to enter a war.*

"Acknowledged, Actual," his squad leaders replied.

"Who rules the battlefield?"

"MONARCH RULES THE BATTLEFIELD!" the team roared in unison.

Em, hang in there. I hope we get to you all before it's too late...

Sharp, heavy breathing filled the air as Ghost Team ran down the street. They zipped past buildings, the paint on them either gone or flaking away, replaced by illegible graffiti. Windows were cracked or boarded, doors barred over, or not even present. Emmerich rose his fist, halting the team.

"You're in the clear, Actual. The lesser ones can't travel that far from the negative energies that fuel them. I feel your weariness. I know you're tough soldiers but rest a bit before the fatigue gets the better of you."

"How far did we run?" Fredrick asked, leaning against a building. "Are we clear?"

"About four klicks," Emmerich answered. "They didn't pursue after the gate, though. I was expecting otherwise."

"I found it odd, too. They could've just opened the gate and gone for it, but stopped instead. Why?"

"We'll figure out the reason later. Let's focus on getting back to the safehouse and contacting Queenbee. We need a QRF, and we have to hit that place with full battle rattle. What's everyone's status?"

"I'm good, just trying to figure out where the hell we are," Callisto stated, popping some shells into her shotgun. "These are my last ones, babe. After that, I'm down to my sidearm and two mags."

"Running low here too, Actual," Calvin answered. "Other

than that, my hand is killing me, but I'm ready to Charlie Mike."

"I'm never going to be alright after this," Fredrick answered. "But, I'm Charlie Mike, too."

Emmerich looked at his brother and nodded. His big hand covered Fredrick's shoulder as he sighed. "Me, too."

"I'm going to miss them, too." Callisto sighed, cocking her shotgun. "I say we make a pact, no matter what happens, we find the asshole who started all of this and finish him."

Fredrick nodded, eyes pink and glistening. He turned his head away from the others.

"We're in agreement, Ghost?" Emmerich asked.

"Yes, sir," Calvin responded. "I know I just joined, but Badrick saved my life twice in there. This could be infected right now and a lot worse. I'm going back after refit and avenging them."

"Cellphone battery is dead," Fredrick announced. "I was going to try phoning the safehouse for pick up."

"Mine, too," Calvin replied.

"Damn it, that place did something to our electronics."

Sneakers scuffed along the ground, proceeding the arrival of a short man, wearing a gray coat with jeans frayed at the knees.

"You came from that ole asylum, didn't ya?" a creaky voice asked from an alley.

The man's smudged face reeled back as Callisto's shotgun barrel greeted him. Emmerich raised his hand, getting between the two as the stranger dashed behind a dumpster.

"Callisto, no! He's a civilian!"

"I'm sorry! I'm sorry!"

"Cali, stand down!" Emmerich ordered.

"Sorry, babe. He startled me."

"Hey, bud. We apologize about my fellow agent pointing her weapon at you. My name is Emmerich Steiner."

From the shadows of the alley, trembling eyes peered at them, then ducked behind the dumpster.

"Damn it, Cali. We need the locals to give us some kind of orientation."

She shrugged, tucking the weapon inside her coat.

"Sir, we mean you no harm. We're the good guys."

"As hard as that may be for you to believe at this point," Fredrick jeered.

Emmerich and Fredrick took a wide approach around the dumpster. The man was crouched, his arms wrapped around his knees. Unkempt strands of hair draped over his shoulders, his beard dragging over his forearms as his head rose to acknowledge them.

"The horrors he has seen. That place is on his mind. It haunts him and the other unfortunates. Every day is a battle for survival."

"Don't hurt me," he pleaded.

"Be calm, they are here to help."

"I swear we aren't going to hurt you."

"Callisto is always on edge, buddy. That's all."

"We did just fight our way out of Moorehouse Asylum. I have a feeling you locals know a bit about it," Emmerich said.

"I-I heard the gunshots. There's rumors about that place..."

"What do you know?"

"The police bring us there whenever they managed to make their way over to these parts, which luckily isn't that often anymore. They grab a few of us to take there."

"Hey, I'm sorry for flagging you down," Callisto said. "I'm just riled up after this evening."

"It's fine, lady. Not my first time, won't be the last even though ya scared the daylights outta me. I understand why you're so jumpy. I been on these streets for twenty years. It's been goin on since I can 'member. First, I thought it was a good thing they were doing. You know, gettin folks the help they needed."

"But then you never heard from then again?" Emmerich asked.

"Yeah. Exactly. I had a few buddies of mine. I know for a fact that they wouldn't have just up and quit talkin with me. Police took 'em. I ran. Don't know why. Something just told me to get away from 'em. They stank. Not like, you know, I do. It was different. So, I slipped away, acted like I had other things to do during the round-up. Luckily, that time wasn't like the others."

"You mean like when they forcibly rounded up unfortunates?" Emmerich prodded.

The man frowned as he lowered his gaze. "Yeah, I know to leave when they come 'round. I see the lights and their squad cars. I know to run before they get out of their vehicles. I tried to warn others. Most folk 'round here didn't start catching on until later about them. And if we try to leave to other parts, when the snobs with money call the cops, they take us to Moorehouse after picking us up."

"It's all making sense now. This massive population of homeless that's been created..."

"Whatcha gonna do? Does the government even care?"

"You bet your ass we do!" Fredrick stated.

"It's a bit more complicated than that," Emmerich added.

"Whatcha mean? You don't have to butter it up for me. I know you have better things to do than worry about us folk."

"What I meant was, we do care. But we are fighting against internal corruption."

"Yeah, sure..."

"We need to charge our cell phones so we can call for help," Emmerich said. "You happen to know a place around here we can get that done?"

"Yeah, I know a place—a warehouse a few blocks from here. For some reason, the power is still on in there. None of the lights work, but the outlets do."

"That's perfect!" Fredrick exclaimed. "I have a charger. We'll just plug it in, sit tight until we can call the safehouse for extraction."

"The agency will compensate you for your time," Emmerich announced.

The man ushered them to follow as he led them down through the alley. "Aight. Follow me. Name's Jerry, by the way."

"Thanks for your help," Emmerich said. "It's been quite an unpleasant experience so far in L.A."

"Yeah," Jerry chuckled. "But this place has a way of growin on ya. I know that might sound weird coming from someone like me."

"Nah, bud." Fredrick's voice cracked. "Shit, home is where the heart is. Right now, my home is in the strip clubs of Jacksonville, North Carolina."

The agent's aura dimmed in Elizabeth's view. The mask of his social skills was not there, only the coldness inside of him aching through his soul. His mind wandered, trying to read the graffiti they passed, seeking to hear what Jerry had to say, wanting to be close to Emmerich. Anything that could take his mind off the torrent of sorrow trying to push through.

"Fredrick, I feel you. Actual isn't doing much better himself, but he's holding it together."

"Freddy, you don't have to..." Emmerich declared.

"I do. It's the only thing that'll keep my mind off it."

"You alright there?"

"Yeah, Jerry. Thanks."

"Jerry, please tell us more about these feelings you had when you met the officers," Callisto said.

"Well, like I said, it was weird."

"Try us."

"Like it was hard to breathe near them and so damn cold whenever they were around. Gave me the chills. My instincts was tellin' me to get away from 'em. I was tryin' to warn the others, but they blew me off. I know that don't make any sense, but that's the best way I can 'splain it."

"It makes sense to us."

"He's like me."

"Oh yeah, we work with your kind all the time."

"I'm sorry, Ms..."

"Just Callisto."

"That's a pretty name. You don't hear that often around here."

"Thanks, my folks are Greek."

"I'm sorry, Ms. Callisto, ma'am. But what do you mean?"

"Just Callisto, I said. I work for a living. What I mean is that you have psychic potential. Not sure what category you fall under; there's so many. We have a classification of trained agents that specialize in assisting us with their gifts."

"What agency do you work for again? You guys FBI or something?"

"That you'll find out in time," Emmerich said. "It's confidential until you've passed the qualification course."

"You're thinking it too, babe?"

"Yep. He'd be a good candidate. We'll clean him up and fly him over to Queenbee after we make it to the safehouse."

"You're offering me a job?"

"I'm offering you a tryout," Emmerich said. "As a team commander, I can scout and recommend talent for selection and eval."

"You're a team commander? So, you're like a big dog?"

"Not quite. But I like to think I have some clout."

"Katherine loves you like a son," Fredrick said. "She's grooming you for the next step. Anyone can see that, King Emmerich."

"Anyways, you might be a bit older than our usual recruits, but I'm sure I can get a waiver for you. You're helping us here. It's the least I can do."

"I don't know what to say." Jerry's voice started to crack. "Even for the chance, thank you."

"It's settled. Let's gather your things, and we'll take you to the safehouse with us. You'll be shipping off in a few days once I get HQ to process the paperwork."

"Paperwork is always a pain," Calvin said, shaking his head. "I just finished the Operator's Q-course. It'll be easier than what you're doing."

"What happens after that?"

"Well, then you'll be trained up as a scryer," Emmerich said, patting the man on his back. "Have to ask, but you're not on drugs or anything, right?"

"No, sir."

"Good. It would be awkward if you failed that test."

Scraps of newspaper blew past them as they turned into an alley. The path led to a rusted door of a grime covered warehouse.

"My stuff's inside. I got some friends watching it while I was huntin for grub." Jerry knocked five times on the door. "No one ever knocks five times. Always three but never five."

Emmerich nodded.

"Who's it?" a voice asked through the cracked door.

"It's me, Jer. Come on, open up. Quit playin around, Karen."

When the door opened, a woman popped her head out. Locks of thick curly hair flopped about the sides of her wizened face. Through narrow eyes, she scrutinized them from top to bottom, while sniffing hard at the air to recall the contents of her running nose.

"Jerry, ya brought cops here?" Karen's gravelly voice rumbled like a growl.

"Nah, they're cool. They're feds. They're the ones that we heard fightin' at Moorehouse. They need our help."

"So, your bright idea was to bring them here?" she snapped. "We don't want to get involved with any of that crap!"

"They're here to help us! They fought—"

"Look, bitch, we don't have time for your bullshit!" Callisto roared. "There are two downed agents back in that hellhole! They gave their lives fighting against what's been plaguing this area. So, let us charge our cells so we can be on our way." Her nails rolled against the charging handle of the shotgun.

"Whoa, be cool!" Karen said. "It's fine, use the outlet, but go away after you're done."

"That's the plan."

Massive headlights beamed down the alley. Large tires scraped against the ground from pebbles and debris caught underneath them. A full SUV rolled along, stopping short of several yards. When the vehicle doors opened, men in suits came out.

Elizabeth gasped. Three of them lacked the light, their souls containing the ruinous energies of the shadows. From the darkness glared eyes overflowed with rage. The negativity they radiated made the scryer recoil in disgust. Their writhing auras stretched around the vessels they wore. Their wheezing filled the etheric layers, the only thing she could hear until their breathy laughter.

"Three of them are possessed. I recognize the one in the driver's seat. It's that Detective Silvia."

"So, what are you citizens doing with those open-carry firearms?" the officer from the passenger seat asked.

"They're operatives of the USA," Detective Silvia answered. "And this bum is aiding them."

He grinned, withdrawing his Glock from the holster in his jacket. His arms lurched forward, putting them into the sights of his weapon before firing two shots.

Jerry cried out. His body rocked with violent force as rounds bored into him.

CHAPTER 10
SLAYING CORRUPTION

"What the hell are you doing, Eric?" his partner pleaded. "You said we were just going to question some suspects!"

Detective Silvia aimed at the officer and fired. A round pierced through his skull before he could finish raising his arms in a futile defense. He toppled over, blood streaming from the kill shot and spilling across the pavement.

Just like they teach at the farm. Callisto's instincts flared into action again. *No hesitation, no mercy. Swift and deadly.*

Callisto returned fire, her shotgun's roar echoing in the alley. The first blast bored into the driver's side door. Silvia keeled over, falling to the ground. A cackle left his mouth as he rolled to a nearby dumpster.

"Their bitch is using some heavy stuff, that ain't buckshot she's packing!" Silvia yelled. "Kill them all!"

"With pleasure," his remaining partners murmured together.

Bring it! I don't scare easily, demonic scum!

The other officers drew their weapons. Emmerich grabbed Callisto as Fredrick bulldozed his way into the door. A hail of pistol rounds dotted the thick walls as the team disappeared into the warehouse.

"You brought this on us!" Karen sobbed.

"Ma'am, we are trying to fight the men that are—" Emmerich tried to explain.

"Jerry is dead because of you!"

"We didn't kill him, you stupid bitch!" Callisto snapped. "He was murdered by these assholes working for the Shadow Government!"

"And you will be too if you don't help us," Emmerich continued. "Now, is there a back door?"

"Yeah, it's on the other side of the warehouse."

They gazed around the building illuminated by a small crackling fire contained in a trash can. The moon's light shone through the glass ceiling panes thirty feet above them. Metal debris riddled the floor, none of it recognizable due to the thick, flaky coat of rust everywhere.

"I suggest you all escape out the backside now," Emmerich suggested. "If I know the police, they're going to call for backup and surround the place."

"The hell is goin on out there, Karen?" a man in a beanie asked, warming his hands.

"Jer brought'em here! He was tryin ta help them, and them cops killed him!"

"What? There's cops outside? What they want?"

"They want them!"

Elizabeth's attention drew to the corrupt stains of Silvia and his fellow officers. She watched as their tainted auras began to maneuver, disappearing from the alley and out of sight. Their intentions echoed through the etheric layers, streaking through Elizabeth's mind with imagery of Ghost Team's bloody corpses and Callisto's screams. A blot of darkness returned, rounding the rear of the building, signaling an arrival.

"We don't have time for this shit!" Callisto barked. "Get your asses out the backside before they get to it first! Make a run for it before you get caught!" *Em, is wrong. They're not calling for backup. Silvia and his scumbags are surrounding the building. How do I know this?*

The swinging door on the other end of the warehouse echoed as it collided with the wall. Shots chimed as pistol fire illuminated the area. Bullets pierced into the whimpering homeless, shuddering as each shot hit their mark. Their cries were drowned out by the growing maniacal laughter of their foe, echoing in the vastness of the building.

The team dived behind a large worktable. The brief flickering of light stopped along with the gunfire. The detective reloaded an extended magazine into the weapon as his eyes scoured the area. Homeless scattered in all directions, sobbing, gasping unintelligible pleas for mercy. One dropped to her knees in front of the officer. Her hands clamped together in prayer with eyes shut and tears streaming down her face. She didn't see the handgun raised to her head. Their cries continued until halted by the gunshots that snuffed the life from them.

"Come out and play, USA Agents." The detective chortled like a hyena. "Don't be scared."

That son of a bitch killed all those civilians. Callisto's index finger twitched with eager anticipation on the trigger. *Running low, have to make these shots count.*

The soles of his oiled leather shoes squeaked as he stepped across the ground, except for the moments when he bounded over the dead. Echoes from his wailing amusement filled the area, growing louder as he drew closer. His laughter's pitch shifted, going higher, losing its sharpness and bass, becoming softer until they only heard the soft giggle of a little girl.

"Why don't you want to play with me?" The voice matched the laughter. "I promise I'll make it quick. Don't you want to pla—"

The team rose from behind their cover, aimed their weapons, and unleashed a volley of lead. Bullets ripped holes into the detective's quavering body. A round hit his shoulder, knocking his arm away, sending his retaliatory shot careening into the depths of the building. He staggered with each hit punching into him, tripping over a corpse and plunking to the floor.

"I'm always up for playtime, asshole." Callisto smirked. Fredrick gave her a high five.

"Good ambush, Ghost," Emmerich said. "Our first time encountering something like this, and I'd say it went well."

"Thanks, sir," Calvin replied.

"That's what I'm talking about!" Fredrick cheered. "Finally, some damn luck this operation."

"It's not over. There's something more inside of them. Something different than what we are used to seeing. Something... greater."

Giggling filled the room again. The detective's leg twitched. He rolled over, patting the ground for his pistol, pushing himself up to his knees and starting the climb back to his feet. A murderous gaze covered his flushed sneering face as he fired shots at Ghost Team. They ducked behind their cover once more.

"Freddy, I think you spoke too soon," Emmerich quipped.

Gunfire whizzed overhead. Lead splinters ricocheted through the area. "Ya think?"

Emmerich peeked over the rust and metal. The pistol's blare forced him back into hiding. He rummaged through his jacket pockets.

"Em, we need you to do some of that leader shit right now," Fredrick said as he blind fired two shots over the workbench.

"Working on it. I brought something for an emergency."

He sighed with relief as his fingers ran over a spherical metal device. When Emmerich withdrew his hand, he was holding a bulbous M67 grenade. The brothers grinned at each other.

"You always have a plan. I appreciate you."

"Don't get weird on me." Emmerich drew the pin from the device.

The detective watched as the plump green ball of metal flew through the air and landed at his feet. A flash consumed his vision. His eyes clamped shut. A deafening eruption launched him off the ground, the force propelling him from where he stood.

That's why I love that man.

The detective's body plopped to the floor. He flailed about as smoke and dust blanketed him. When the warm air cleared, his senses returned. The ringing in his ears faded. Blood oozed, and he felt the dampness surrounding the rips across his body. When the detective tried to get up, the dust-covered stumps that were once his legs beat on the ground.

"My body!" he bellowed at Ghost Team. "You destroyed my body!" he wailed, his jaw-dropping open as he thrashed about like an unruly toddler.

A blare from Callisto's shotgun ripped the top of his skull clean off. As bone splinters and brain matter showered the area, the remainder of his mouth and chin slumped to the ground.

"Shut the fuck up!" Callisto snapped.

"The dark signatures are back. I can feel them closing on us."

Glass shattered above them, and shards from the ceiling windows rained down as gunshots broke through. Before covering his face, Emmerich could see Silvia and another, shooting down at them. Rounds from the top backside of the building went into the large workbench.

"We need to move!" Emmerich ordered. "Freddy, you and I are going to cover Cali and Rook as they make a break."

"Gotcha, Em!"

"Now!"

Emmerich and his brother rose, returning fire at the officers. The remains of the downed detective began to rattle with a boisterous cackle. Meat sloughed around, spilling out of the gaping head wound.

"We will find you!" the other detective howled. "I'll get another monkey suit, and we will find you! You've already lost! This is all futile!"

"Damn it! They're getting away!" Silvia roared.

Calvin and Callisto waited as Emmerich and Fredrick joined them outside. A hail of bullets chased until the barrier of the door protected them. The team rushed through the alley, stopping at the SUV parked there. The driver's side window gave after Emmerich pistol-whipped it. He reached in unlocking the vehicle and hopping into the driver's seat. The doors slammed shut as the rest of Ghost joined him.

"What about keys?" Callisto asked.

"Trying to hotwire it," Emmerich replied.

"Get the hell away from my car!" Silvia yelled from the rooftop.

Cracks streaked through the front windshield, extending from holes punched by Silvia's indiscriminate fire. He and the other detective continued until the receivers of their pistols locked back, unable to chamber any more bullets from the empty magazines. They disappeared from view as they moved to the backside.

"Anyone hit?" Emmerich asked as he continued to fight with the starter.

"Good, babe."

"Still alive, Actual."

"Em, get this damn thing started!" Freddy pleaded.

"Hurry, Actual! They're coming!"

The warehouse door flung open. Silvia and his partner rushed out, firing more shots at the vehicle. The team ducked in their seats, as bullets sank into the car. Emmerich peered just over the steering wheel. One moment he saw the bursts of their pistols, and then Silvia's body thrashed about. Light blared in the alley as loud shots came from behind the car. Rounds shredded Silvia and his partner; blood poured from the two as they keeled over.

Ghost Team looked to the rear. Dozens of smoky M4 barrels lowered to the ready. The familiar black uniforms and body armor brought sighs of relief. Monarch had arrived. Emmerich left the driver's seat, greeting Curtis with a firm handshake.

"We owe you," Emmerich announced.

"Just a cold one when we get back in the rear, will do," Curtis said.

"How'd you find us?" Fredrick asked.

"Queenbee was sending us to Moorehouse as QRF for you.

But, as we were infilling into the sector, we heard the contact and mayhem. Figured you were over here."

"Good figuring," Callisto said, shaking his hand.

"I love you, grunts," Fredrick added.

"Monarch, sweep the area, get our scryers checking all civilians you encounter." Curtis turned his attention to Ghost again. "We'll get you guys back to the safehouse for recovery."

"No," Emmerich said. "You have any more weapons and rattle in those vans?" he asked, pointing at the other vehicles parked on the street.

"Yeah."

"We'll do an infield refit."

"Em, you can't be serious. You all look like shit. Your team is pretty banged up—"

"Which vehicle has the refit supplies, sir?" Calvin asked.

"Damn, you are serious. Okay, it's over there. Speak with my intel agent. She'll get you all armor, uniforms, pyro, and weapons. There's MREs, too."

"Thank you, sir."

"You smug apes think you've achieved some kind of victory?" Silvia hollered. "Ha! Our master has already won!"

The agents watched as the gunshot riddled body of Silvia pointed its blood-drenched fingers at them. A whirring motor sound emerged from the vans.

"Silence, you fiend." A stern woman's raspy voice rebuked as she arrived with the assistance of an automated wheelchair. She reached up from the controls to brush away a few strands of gray hair from her glaring hazel eyes. Despite her withered disposition, she met the demon's gaze with an arched brow of overwhelming tenacity.

Silvia's lips closed. His teeth clenched together during the stare down.

"It's Madam Simone Dupree. The Grand Scryer, leader of the order." Elizabeth smiled. *"Never did I think I would be happy to see that crotchety old shrew again."*

The old scryer rummaged through a backpack sitting in her lap. Her burning eyes never broke from Silvia's. Her wrinkled and veiny hands drew a massive quartz spike from it. A sparkle appeared from the item's fine sharp point, gleaming down the blade's shaft, into a hilt that possessed a small crossguard and rounded pommel. She handed the weapon to Emmerich.

"This demonic scum has been giving you grief the entire time correct, Agent Steiner?"

"That's correct, ma'am."

"Well then, I'll let you do the honors. Make it count please, those quartz daggers are expensive and a pain to fashion. I have a few left in this baggy for his friends, too."

"Thank you, ma'am."

"Fuck you, Scryer!" Silvia screamed.

"Oh no, it's you that's getting penetrated, boy." She smirked.

Emmerich's fingers gripped tightly around the weapon, its point aiming downward. Silvia's eyes widened as he watched the dagger rise, then plummet into his chest cavity. The transparent crystalline quartz dulled into an opaque and frosty white. The writhing darkness that formed around Silvia's spirit faded as it was slurped into the weapon. A whimper left his mouth as it jutted open. The heaving from his struggled breathing stopped. His arms dropped back, hitting the ground. The baleful frenzied look faded from his eyes.

"What just happened?" Emmerich asked. "Is it done, ma'am?"

"Yes. It's done. You've erased that demon's soul, Agent

Steiner. I know you can't see what's happening on the etheric layers as I do. But you did just fine dispatching that scum."

"Thank you, ma'am."

"You're going to need quartz from here on out since we're dealing with a lot of demonic possession this operation. The stone is a natural remedy for breaking down and cleansing negative energies that the Nephilim use to sustain their existence."

"I see. Thank you, ma'am."

"Meh, don't thank me yet. We're not done here. I brought some quartz ammunition that is compatible with weapons that use 5.56. There's not much, mind you! The damn things are hard to make. I can't even promise they'll be accurate since they don't work in rifling like a normal round. Use them sparingly, Agents."

"We will, ma'am," Callisto responded.

"Keep in mind they might cause a jam or two. The weight of the rounds is different from your standard ball ammunition. So, try to ensure those weapons stay clean, although I understand and anticipate that we're going to be quite busy soon. Take some more daggers."

"Acknowledged, ma'am. Thank you for the quartz." Emmerich and Ghost slipped the weapons into their pockets.

"So, I'm a crotchety old shrew, huh?"

"Ma'am, um no one called you that." Emmerich raised a brow.

Elizabeth's eyes widened. *"Ma'am... I... uh..."*

"Save it, Turner. I actually expect that kind of banter from my rival's apprentice. I'm just glad you're okay."

"Wait," Fredrick raised a brow. "My Elizabeth is here?"

"Ugh! Did he say his Elizabeth?"

"I think he's taken a shining to you, Turner." Madam

Dupree smirked. "Yeah, she's here. Elizabeth has been following you through the etheric layers the entire time."

"This is going to sound weird," Callisto said. "But I felt she was with us."

"Nothing is weird, Agent Dukas. You should learn to trust your feelings more. I can sense you have the spark."

"I guess that's something to think about, ma'am."

"Elizabeth, let's get you back to your body."

"I can't, ma'am. I know it's dangerous, that I can be lost to the ether. But I feel I can help the team better from here."

"You're diving deep, girl. Are you sure? This bunch is kind of brain dead except for Dukas."

"Hey!" Fredrick frowned.

"Yes, ma'am. I'm willing to risk it. I think I was able to reach them during a few crucial moments."

"Okay, I guess you'll continue to be their eyes and ears in the etheric layers. If things get too ugly, you report back to me."

A few members of Monarch passed by holding quartz daggers. Screams came from the other demon-possessed detectives a few minutes later.

"That concludes this Frago," Curtis announced over comms. "One more sweep of the area and then all squads mount back up. We are Charlie Mike to Moorehouse Asylum."

"Let's gear up, Ghost," Emmerich ordered. "We have a score to settle."

"Acknowledged, Actual," Calvin replied.

As they headed for the vans, Emmerich felt Madam Dupree's hand touch his.

"My condolences, boys," she said.

The two lowered their gazes.

"I know it hurts. Get on the horn with Kat when we get back to the vehicles. I think it'll do her some good to hear your voice. She worries about you. After all, she was your former team leader."

"Will do, ma'am."

"All right, enough of this sentimental BS! Get your butts in gear! You all have evil to slay!"

♄

CHAPTER 11
DECLARATION OF WAR

Engines switched off as the vehicles halted before the gates of Moorehouse Asylum. M4 charging handles were drawn back, feeding a round into place, making the weapons ready for combat. Doors slid open and boots hit the ground as agents stormed out. Barrels pointed at the gates, Curtis and the first squad made their way to the entrance.

The large steel gates began to rattle, coming to life in an ominous welcome. Curtis' eyes followed the empty road that led to the main building. He raised a fist and his team halted their approach with their weapon sights remaining forward. The Monarch team leader shook his afro covered head and smirked.

"They're expecting us," Curtis said over comms.

"Well, let's not keep them waiting," Emmerich replied.

"Indeed. They're looking for a fight. We'll give them a fight."

"Curt, we ran into some civilians in the asylum, particularly a little girl named Madelyn that was very helpful," Emmerich stated. "We need to rescue them."

"I'll pass the word about their presence to my elements. All squad leaders listen up. There are civilians trapped on the premises. We will run standard rules of engagement for this operation. To prevent any innocent casualties, ensure that you only use force if you feel threatened. How copy?"

"That's a solid copy, Actual," the first squad leader acknowledged before the others. "We will make sure all fireteam leaders are aware of civilian presences."

"Monarch2Actual and Ghost8Actual, this is Tac-com. Queenbee says you are go for launch, be safe out there."

"Yes, do indeed be wary," Madam Dupree chimed in over comms from her post in the vehicle. "I feel hundreds of negative entities congregating in the layers."

"We will, ma'am," Curtis replied.

"We're scaling the rear gates with third squad, now. I'll have them securing the back area while I take Ghost in through the rear entrance," Emmerich said.

"Understood. I have second squad guarding the vehicles, and fourth squad doing cordon perimeter sweeps."

"Acknowledged, Monarch. Happy hunting."

"You too, bud. Mancini, are we up?" Curtis asked.

"Just checked, Actual," Christopher Mancini replied. "My squad is green to green and ready."

"All right first squad, advance on me."

The double doors to the main building flung open, slamming with a loud thud. Harsh screams packed the area as the denizens of the asylum charged out of the building. Countless feral eyes fixed on first squad as ghouls sprinted toward them.

"Line abreast, maintain sectors of fire!" Curtis yelled.

"Weapons free!" Christopher added.

Carbines spewed their wrath into the coming masses. The

squad's M249 light machine began to consume its ammunition belt as it slung copious amounts of hate. The first line in the swarm fell like dominoes, the succeeding shots following their marks deeper into the enemy ranks. Fiend after fiend was cut down by the firing line until the focus became those rushing through the doorway. Ghouls trickling out were met with a furious salvo of well-placed shots, felling them before they could pass the archway.

"That's how we do, give them the business, first!" Mancini said.

A large shadow appeared, pushing past the others over which it towered. The pile of accumulated dead was flung out of the way in one mighty effort. Weapons trained on the orderly across from the team. The nurse's uniform splattered with black goo as wounds opened along its massive frame. The tall menace plodded forward, his wide arms outstretched, fingers flexed and ready to crush whatever he grasped. The creature bellowed as it waded through the hail of gunfire.

Boots touched down as Ghost and third squad finished climbing the rear gates. The tall hedges were before them, lining the back area in an array of paths. The popping of small arms fire echoed into the night. Emmerich nodded.

"That's our cue, maneuver on me. Limit of advance for third squad will be the rear entrance. Keep your eyes open for the canine sentries that will be roaming this section."

"Roger, Actual," Calvin responded.

"Roger, Ghost8Actual," third squad leader, Hendricks, acknowledged.

"This place is clogging my perception of the layers again. But I can feel a majority of the darkness shifting to the front entrance. The diversion of force must be working."

"We're not seeing shit so far!" Fredrick exclaimed as they continued.

"Yeah, but keep your eyes open, Freddy. Complacency kills," Emmerich warned.

"They're open. I'm going to find them."

"I know. We aren't leaving without either of them."

"I'll ring that little stuck up bitch's neck until she tells us where they are," Callisto grumbled.

"Fine, but I get to shoot her in the head after you're done," Fredrick agreed.

"We take the doc alive, Ghost Team," Emmerich ordered. "No vendetta shit in there. We need to interrogate her for intel. There's not only the matter of finding our fallen brothers but getting answers about the gate that was opened."

"All right, babe."

Emmerich sighed. "If she is possessed, it's not going to be an easy task trying to pump information from a demon."

"A greater demon at that," Callisto added.

"Yeah. You're right. I'm not looking forward to this."

"I can make her talk, Actual. Don't worry about that."

"Actual, how do we know the difference?" Calvin asked.

"Well it's simple. The minor demons are more bestial, with limited thoughts except to follow the commands of higher-ranking ones. I'm not sure if this is due to the toll taken for spending so long trapped in the void or the abyss. I forgot the terminology Finley taught me for it."

"The abyss are the lower reaches of the etheric layers. The void is the area beyond that which no one has traversed."

"A minor demon wouldn't have entertained us like the doc did. It would've just torn us to shreds instead."

"I'm tracking. Roger, Actual."

"So, when we were escorted by that orderly, it most likely was given instructions from the doc to stand down," Callisto said.

"Affirmative. As you've guessed, Calvin, this job entails some detective work. You'll figure it out. How's that hand doing?"

"It's good for now, Actual. The medic gave me fresh bandages, cleaned the wound again and hit me with another shot of morphine."

"Good."

"The darkness is trickling from its confines. Be wary. They are coming!"

"Contact!" a member of Monarch screamed.

The rapping of paws against the cement prompted the teams to raise their firearms. It scampered before them, the four legged and two headed menace. The lips of its canine snout curled upward, exposing sharp glistening teeth. The cries carried from its back, its face stared up into the stars, wailing into the night.

"What the hell is that?" Hendricks asked.

"That's one of their sentries!" Emmerich answered. "Weapons free! Try to hit the humanoid head on its back!"

Fingers pulled triggers, spewing lead and tracers into the creature's body. It reeled about, struggling to keep its footing, each hit knocking it around. The monstrosity collapsed, its face reduced to a husk of shredded meat sagging from its neck, hitting the ground. The dark gore spewed from the mess, streaking through the protruding remnants of bone and staining the cement.

"Well, they know we're here now," Fredrick said. "The fire fight and the screaming are a good indicator that another force is coming from the rear."

Callisto raised a brow at him.

"I know. I'm shocked I said something intelligent, too."

Canine fiends sped through openings within the hedge, closing around their position. An M249 light machine gunner held his finger down, unleashing a vicious barrage of force at the new arrivals. The creature's canine head and front legs were ripped off. The humanoid head screeched into the air, the mangled front side of its body piled on the ground. Its rear legs still pushing forward, dragging its remains against the cement of the walkway.

"Lesser demons are encased in these animals. Their minds are feral, devolved beyond that of a predatory beast. They know only to seek and devour."

A galloping beast zipped around the fallen. Lead flew, showering the hedges as more snarling monstrosities darted forward. One leapt at a Monarch agent. Large teeth locked around his forearm. The beast dropped back with all its weight, tugging in snarling ferocity. A cry escaped the agent's mouth as he was lunged forward, tripping over his own footing.

The creature shook its head, flapping his arm about in its steadfast grip. Grinding of his shoulder preceded the loud pop before his arm pulled from its socket, followed by a loss of sensation through his entire arm. Pain flooded his mind, overwhelming his senses. The warmth rushed in along with the dizziness; he could only think about grabbing his caved shoulder. The growling rumbled in his ear, as the shattered remnant of his arm beat the side of his head when the creature shook.

"I don't have a shot, it's too damn close!" Hendricks said.

Cries stretched through the etheric layers, the high pitch and sorrow causing Elizabeth to wince. Misery carried with it, causing the scryer to shiver down to her core. Images of long yellow teeth and claws fluttered her mind's eye. They sank down on the diminishing light within, thrashing around the hapless soul in its grasp. She covered her mouth with her trembling hand, her big brown eyes widened each time her body collided with the suffering energies.

"I see it now. The souls are still there, trapped within the darkness. A plaything to the demons inhabiting their temple. The torture within gives further fuel for their presence. I can sense the spirit of the animal in the deepest recesses. It's weeping for release!"

"Just shoot the damn thing!" the downed agent cried out.

Weapon sights zeroed on the creatures. The first volley of shots rattled one of the abominations, each bullet causing a convulsion as the monstrosity tried to keep its balance. The reticle of Emmerich's Close Quarter Optic hovered over the last beast. He struggled to keep it in his aim as it flailed about so close to his fellow agent.

"I'll take it," Emmerich said.

One quick trigger pull and lead struck the creature's forehead. It reeled back, its jaws slipping away from its grasp on the man's forearm. Emmerich put two more shots into it, stepping to the side for a clear shot on the humanoid head. He scanned with his glowing red sight until finding the blank eyes and trembling mouth that never stopped wailing. Relaxing his body, he breathed and fired. The creature's frame capsized, the last of the screams cut off.

"Get that man evac'd now!"

"Roger, Ghost Actual," Hendricks acknowledged.

A member of Monarch jogged up to his fallen comrade. A bulging pack bounced around on his shoulders as he made his approach. Dropping to a knee beside his moaning squad-mate he flung the backpack to the ground. He rummaged through it, withdrawing splints and needles.

"This is going to hurt, bud," the medic warned.

Emmerich turned his gaze away, trying to ignore the man's screams as his arm was reset and stabilized. He sighed, his gaze falling on the towering manor.

"Tac-com, Monarch2Actual, this is Ghost8Actual," Emmerich called over comms.

"This is Monarch Actual, send it." Gunshots rang out in the transmission's background.

"The comms are actually working? The darkness that grips this place peels away with each demon we dispatch. Their magick is withering."

"We've got one agent down and having him Medevac'd before Charlie Mike."

"Acknowledged, Ghost Actual. Take care of my people."

"Will do."

"This is Tac-com we are sending a response vehicle to the AO's backside. ETA four mikes."

"Acknowledged, Tac-com. We'll have him there. Ghost8Actual, out."

"Alright," Hendricks said. "Now that we have him splinted and stabilized, I'm sending two members to carry him back. Doc thinks he's still susceptible to shock."

"Good call, Hendricks," Callisto agreed. "Best not to have him move with an injury like that."

"Those damn things are vicious," Fredrick added.

"You don't have to tell me," Calvin said, looking to the remainder of his hand.

"We push into the manor," Emmerich announced. "Time to finish this."

The fluid poured out of a plastic nozzle, splashing on the floor of the cage. Each ounce that touched down washed away the filth that lined the enclosure. Waves flowed against the bare feet of an individual. Shaky green eyes peered out from strands of disheveled brown hair, meeting the fierce gaze of her captor. Her blackened soles became drenched in the liquid, some of it washing away the months of grime.

"W-what are you d-doing?" she asked.

"Shh..."

"Stop, please!"

"I sed ya hush naa, child. Lest I be addin ya to da pile."

Her eyes followed his grim finger, pointing to one of the candlelit tables. Next to a dusty white skull, she found a pile of slimy meat, most of it pink in color while some had purple hues. From underneath the pile, streams of blood stretched out to the corner of the table, dripping to the ground.

"My God, th-that's why they were screaming. The pain I sensed—you took th-their tongues!"

"Girl, I be warnin ya..."

She covered her mouth with her trembling hands.

"Good, girl."

"Excellent my friend," Baron announced through harsh whispers. *"Continue with the preparations."*

“Ya don’t ave much faith in Metzger, eh?”

“Dlo has proven incompetent throughout the remainder of our operation. The only reason I have not snuffed the life from her is because we have already concluded the most important objectives of our quest. Luckily you and I have brought over many of my legions.”

“All we ‘ave is each otha, Baron.”

“Indeed. Greater honors await you, my friend. Your service to the throne will not be forgotten. We have long memories. You seek power. You will have it and more.”

“Ya been so generous.”

“Finish your work here. Ensure the captives line the outer perimeter. This one before us is the strongest. Leave her here at the center.”

“Not ta be doubtin ya methods, but dis ‘ere ritual is different from tee uddas ya be showin me. Won’t this be quicker den normal?”

“No. We aren’t conjuring anyone through the abyss. We don’t need to expunge the layers. We only have to momentarily terraform the immediate area.”

“Okay. Then wut?”

“Then, you hide until I’m done with the agents...

CHAPTER 12
QUEEN TAKES KNIGHT

Weapons roared, spewing rounds at the horde. Bullet riddled corpses littered the large parking lot of the asylum. The teeming number of foes continued to push through the entrance, breaking out in a dead sprint just to be gunned down. Heads snapped back as steady shots neutralized each menace speeding through the doorway.

"Damn, how many of these things are there?" Curtis murmured to himself.

"Many, Actual," Madam Dupree answered over comms.

"Ma'am, you know I hate when you do that."

"Yes. Yes, I do."

"Ghost Actual, this is Monarch Actual. How are you looking with the rear breach?" Curtis asked over comms.

"Monarch Actual, this is Ghost Actual. Your squad has set outside for outer cordon and has locked the area down. Ghost Team has infiltrated the rear entrance. We are en route to the doc's office."

"How's it looking in there?"

"We've encountered minimal resistance so far. I think you've gotten the attention of the enemy's main body."

"Acknowledged. Time to bring out the big gun."

"That's not a very ladylike nickname for me," Madam Dupree said.

"We're ready for you, ma'am," Curtis continued. "Monarch2Delta this is Actual."

"Monarch2Delta acknowledges, Actual. Send it."

"Bring up 'the Bitch on Wheels'."

"Excuse me, Actual? I don't follow."

"He means me, sweetie." Madam Dupree interrupted.

"That's the callsign the Madam chose. Now give her two escorts from the vehicle guard."

"Roger, Actual."

After a minute, the faint whirring of Madam Dupree's motor approached in between the sustained volley of gunfire. She arrived behind the line of agents. Her stony gaze fell on the snarling foes. In her left hand she clutched half a bottle of orange juice, bringing it to her lips for a chug, before handing it to one of the escorts that flanked her.

"Good to see you, ma'am," Curtis greeted her. "Are you ready?"

"This is quite the choke point you've set up, Curt. I am ready. Are you sure this is the majority? We only have one shot at this and I'm going to be out of commission for at least a week."

"Yes, ma'am. Ghost is inside and they reported that the bulk of enemy forces are here, trying to repel our frontal assault."

"Okay then. Just let me get a little closer."

"Will do, ma'am." Curtis said. "All right, squad. We're firing and maneuvering to the limit of advance."

"Acknowledged, Actual," Mancini announced. "Squad is set and ready."

"On me!"

Curtis pressed forward, acquiring one target after another. The glowing crimson reticle of his optic hovered over an enemy, his finger pulling the trigger in rapid succession. With each step he took the team followed on his flanks, maintaining a perfect line of fire. The whirring sound of Madam Dupree's chair followed as she rolled behind. They approached closer to the door, and hundreds of ravenous eyes peered from dark silhouettes in the unlit main hall.

Be with us, father in heaven, Madam Dupree prayed.

"Ma'am, this is as close as we can get without losing our vantage point," Curtis announced.

"It will suffice, Curt. Thank you."

She closed her eyes, bringing her hands together, lowering her head. The Madam witnessed the darkness around them, its writhing mass reaching out with a cold embrace, wanting to consume her presence. A pulse emanated from it, chilling her being with a dull inner pain. Her steadfast mind focused, blocking out the misery she felt.

This isn't my pain, it's theirs, she chanted. *I must cut off the connection.*

Her mind settled as she quieted all thoughts, guiding her attention to her own inner light. The pain faded, drifting away as the darkness recoiled from her. Light rose through her, illuminating the area around her chair. The shadows watched the old woman, halting their steps, ignoring the gunfire still ripping away at their physical bodies. Hissing escaped from their mouths as they pointed at Dupree. Raising her head, she met their glares with one of her own.

I am the daughter of the most high! Gifted with the sight!

Created in His image! His breath, light and love reside in me! And by the authority of His everlasting will, I banish you back into the void! In His glorious name!

The light sparked outward, sending the darkness withering back into the recesses of the manor. It enveloped the teeming masses in the main hall. They scrambled, clawing at one another, wailing, sobbing, shoving, but to no avail. It covered them, erasing the darkness from the bodies they inhabited. Their screams reverberated in the etheric layers as the light took them, the negative frequencies fading, their presence losing all grip on reality.

Curtis looked back at Madam Dupree. She twitched in her chair, her eyes fluttering, and a groan escaped as her mouth dropped open.

"Ma'am? Are you okay? Please say something."

The demons' cries faded with the darkness swallowed by the etheric layers. The shadows that formed their presence evaporated. Dupree pressed on, pushing the light outward with everything she could muster.

Curtis watched as swathes of foes collapsed where they stood. The team ceased fire, their eyes widened at the carnage that laid before them. Hundreds of bodies now littered every inch of the large corridor.

In the ether, Dupree witnessed tiny balls of light rising from where the darkness had been. Their faces gazed at her, smiling. She felt their love, thankful for their freedom.

It's okay, Madam Dupree told them. *You're free now. Cross over. Trust me. Feel His love.*

We trust you. We feel it. Thank you.

She opened her droopy eyes and greeted Curtis with a weak smile. "Something."

A sigh of relief escaped the agent's mouth. "I was worried there for a second."

"I'm too tired to make a joke. I know one's supposed to be there."

"Get her back to the rear and make sure she has more orange juice," Curtis ordered her escorts.

"Roger, Actual."

"No," Madam Dupree declined. "She's still here. I can sense it. It'll take more than charging the etheric layers with positive energy to remove the doctor. I must interrogate her."

"Understood, ma'am."

"But that orange juice would be nice right about now." She grinned. "After all, it'll help me replenish my psychic energy faster."

"Will do, ma'am." Curtis smiled with a nod.

"Now, let's go find that evil bitch and exorcise her, too."

The armor piercing tips of the 5.56 ammunition fired from M4s, striking into the cranium of an orderly. The hulking figure's head flung back as it reeled away. Its large feet stomped at the ground, struggling to regain its balance. When it turned to face Ghost Team again, rounds dented the metal plate in its forehead. A final burst of fire roared from Fredrick's weapon. Black blood poured from the wound, splashing to the ground as the orderly toppled over.

"Monarch Actual this is Ghost Actual," Emmerich called over comms.

"Send it."

"We're cutting through the enemy's rear guard as we speak. Still minimal resistance. Almost at the doc's office."

"That's good to hear, Agent Steiner," Madam Dupree transmitted. "Monarch Actual and I are heading over to join you. Be sure to take her alive. The doctor and I are going to have a little chat. I have a feeling she isn't the one responsible for all of this. Rather, I believe she is merely a servant to something far more nefarious."

"Yes, ma'am. I acknowledge your last. We will apprehend her alive."

"Tell Elizabeth that I'm going to need her help. I've been substantially drained of my energy dealing with the horde."

"I am here, ma'am."

"Yes, ma'am."

"Em, I'm sure Elizabeth is with us," Callisto said. "I can still feel her."

"Good. Well, you heard the Madam."

"Yeah, taking a demon alive," Fredrick said. "Piece of cake. Sure. Not going to hurt one bit."

"We have our orders."

"If I remember correctly, the doc's office is right down this hall," Calvin mentioned.

"Good memory, Rook." Fredrick patted the junior member on the shoulder. "I can't seem to remember anything about this place. Maybe all those bumps to my noggin are adding up."

"Lock it up," Emmerich ordered. "We do this by the numbers."

"Roger, Actual," Calvin acknowledged.

"I'm ready, babe."

"I'm with you, Actual."

Barrels pointed low at the ready as Emmerich led Ghost

Team down the corridor. There wasn't a sound throughout the manor except for the echoes of their steps. Elizabeth felt the darkness grow stronger, the etheric layers were impossible to distinguish at this point. Her vision was consumed by a churning morass of shadows starting to blanket her.

Emmerich positioned himself in front of the door, looking to the others until each of them gave him a nod. He took a deep breath before booting the entrance open with a mighty kick. The door shook and swung inward, canting off the hinges tearing from the frame. He lowered his weapon, rushing shoulder and helm first, raising his M4 as he turned sharp left. Callisto followed, banking the corner to the right. The rest of the team poured into the room, until all weapons were pointing inboard.

Doctor Metzger's lips curled in disgust as her narrow eyes examined them. Her thin hands balling into a fist trembling with fury. She sighed, letting her fingers unfurl and shaking her head.

"You can't kill me, Agents. Not with those weapons."

"We each have a magazine of quartz rounds and a quartz dagger, Metzger. You knew that already because you could sense their presence in the room, Nephilim scum. Now start talking, before I give the order to fill you with shiny rocks," Emmerich barked.

"You make any sudden movements or smart mouth us anymore and I'm going to light you up, bitch," Callisto threatened. "Please, make my day."

"My brother and Finley. Where are their bodies?"

"Not sure. I get you apes confused so often, Steiner. Is your brother the overgrown nigger or the geek we brutalized in the parking lot?"

Emmerich reached underneath her desk, lifting it up and

toppling it to the side. With a smirk Metzger crossed her arms, not budging from her chair. The agent raised his weapon, firing a round into her foot. Doctor Metzger's eyes widened as she belted a scream to the ceiling. Before she could bounce out of her seat, the crashing force of Callisto's M4 buttstock kept her down. The doctor's head flung back, numerous teeth pelted the wall.

"Damned apes!" Metzger howled.

"Keep talking that big ole shit!" Callisto snapped. "I got more for you."

"I've got something up my sleeve too, demon."

"Demonic scum like you doesn't fall under the Geneva Convention guidelines. We're not the CIA, FBI, or regular army. We will get what we want, one way or another," Emmerich declared.

A whining motor accompanied by marching boots echoed in the hall. Madam Dupree and Curtis passed through the doorway a few moments later. Curtis nodded at Ghost Team before glaring at Metzger with disgust.

"He's right, you know," Madam Dupree added. "We don't fall under typical jurisdiction. That means your booty is going to get tortured, little miss. There's two scryers here. We'll take turns peeling away at that evil little soul of yours. You're going to suffer a lot, unless you give me the goods. So, while you're trying to act tough and give us the run around, keep this in mind. When I'm done, whomever infernal Lord, Duke or Prince you serve will get to have their fun. Right after I banish your sorry hide back to the abyss."

Metzger's unblinking gaze dropped to the ground, her breathing gaining pace. She shook her head, sighing. When her eyes met with Madam Dupree's again, they had turned reddish, swelling with wetness in her tear ducts.

"If I answer everything truthfully, then what?"

"If you tell me everything I want to know, with none of your demon bullshit, we can make a deal."

"I'm a demon, Scryer. We make the parameters of the deal."

"Not today, little missy. So, what's it going to be?"

"You can't banish me."

"I'll think about it."

"No, Scryer. That's one of the parameters I want in the deal. You're not going to send me back to get tortured as a traitor in the pit. That's the whole driving force behind these negotiations. Without that promise you have no cooperation from me, and you might as well get on with it."

"All right, but you can't keep this poor woman's body."

"Fine. What body do I get?"

"You're going to be contained in a nice quartz skull, held inside of a consecrated box where you can't escape or harm others. No one will get to see you warping the skull either, since you'll be locked away in my vault. Don't worry, there will be other low lives to converse with there. Think about it as a prison sentence. If you behave well, I might even let you out once in a while."

"You mean to trap me in an idol?"

"If you don't like that, there's always an all-expense paid trip back to the abyss to answer for your failures."

"Fine!" Metzger shook her head. "Put me in the idol."

"That's a good pet. Now we're going to probe your mind to make sure you answer everything truthfully. If I sense a hint of betrayal, the deal is off, and you'll be exorcised. Understand?"

"Let's just get this over with. Ask your questions, you insolent mortal."

"Are you ready, Elizabeth?"

"Yes, ma'am."

Madam Dupree and Elizabeth extended their will into the etheric layer. Maneuvering their intent felt like swimming through muddy water. They only just managed a glimpse of the demon's vibratory rate, its negative state being almost identical with the rest of the dark, save for the faint outline that surrounded it. A thought flickered, and the rippling energies of its frequency faded into the rest of the darkness. Elizabeth lost sight of it. She felt the hand of her elder, seeing her presence like a lone star in the night sky.

"This way, my young Scryer," Madam Dupree instructed.

"Thank you, ma'am."

"She's just ahead of us."

They found Doctor Metzger. The seven-foot lithe figure before them possessed wide hips and hind legs with protruding claws. She used her talons to remove strands of thick black hair from her face, setting her serpentine yellow eyes on the two scryers.

Madam Dupree reached out with her will, locking onto the shadowy presence of Metzger. The dire essence of the demon chilled her soul, generating shivers beyond the layers, racking her body into the cushions of her chair. Elizabeth followed her example. She couldn't hold onto the entity. A huff escaped her mouth when the nauseating essence of the creature pressed against her.

"You're an amateur, girl. What would you do if your master wasn't here to coddle you? Your silver cord has been torn from your measly little soul. I would drag you back to the void and pass you around like currency to the other knights."

"Silence, fiend!" Madam Dupree scolded.

"You will only speak when spoken to, beast," Elizabeth rebuked.

"Good, Elizabeth. They are subject to our will. Understand that you are made in the image of the creator. Their power is only an illusion of the mind. This is why we human beings are able to conjure them, because demons are low on the cosmic scale. No matter how great one may appear, their power is miniscule to that which a self-realized child of the creator commands."

Elizabeth's willpower clamped down on the demon like a pincer. Metzger howled in pain, the crushing force of light locking her in place.

"Yes, let her taste your power. These damned abominations are difficult to deal with. Show her you're not to be trifled with. We might have to get our hands dirty with her if she continues this level of belligerence. I won't be surprised to be honest. It's in their nature."

"Go ahead and give us a hard time, this will only get worse. Give me a reason to let loose," Elizabeth snapped.

"Ask your damned questions! Let this be over with!"

"What is your name?" Dupree asked.

"I am Doctor Heidi Metzger—"

The light closed on the demon, clamping hard on her stomach. She reeled over in pain, reaching out for anything but only swiping at the air as she tucked her arms, clenching her body.

"I warned you. Now, no more smartass answers. You know what I meant. What is your real name, demon?"

"Dlo. I am known as Dlo amongst the people of this world. But I am also known as Paimon amongst my kin."

"Dlo. Like the voodoo loa that lures men to their doom by drowning them?" Dupree inquired.

"Yes. One and the same. Although the drowning legends are metaphorical. I submerge men in negative energy until they are susceptible for my brethren to commandeer."

"I'm not familiar with your other name, Paimon."

"To know one is to know both, Scryer. I'm being transparent for once in my existence."

"Now we're getting somewhere. Elizabeth, what do you think?"

"She's telling the truth. Her aura didn't fluctuate any further into the lower frequencies."

"Good, I was just testing you, girl. You are correct. This little skid mark is telling the truth. Okay, Dlo. You're only a lowly knight. Just barely above the level of these mindless drones. Who are you working for? A Lord? A Duke? A Prince? The Queen bitch herself?"

"He's a duke."

"And his name?"

Dlo looked away. Her eyes shifted to the darkness, lowering her head. *"I get to stay in the skull, right? Under USA protection?"*

"That's our deal. If you stop being difficult," Madam Dupree assured.

"What happened to transparency, demon?" Elizabeth snapped. *"Get on with it, answer the question."*

"His name is Baron Samedi. Well at least that's what he convinced the mortal he's been working with."

"What's his demonic name? The one imprinted on his signature in the layers?"

"Andras, a grand duke, commander of thirty legions, slayer of men and herald of the Princes."

"I know that name," Madam Dupree announced. *"He is a merciless killer and commander of many forces for one of his rank. He detests humanity and his forces are purely devoted to killing people. Why would he work with a human?"*

"That mortal is like you, Dupree. He's very gifted with tremendous levels of psychic potential. Something we have found prevalent amongst the people of the Caribbean and Western Africa."

"Did you just compliment me, Paimon? You trying to butter me up?"

"Perhaps."

"I won't drop my guard, demon. This ole bird has many scars from lessons of my youth. Now get on with it."

"For the record, Dupree, you're still a youngling to me. Anyway, Andras' vessel, Edjewale, harnesses his gifts through the ancient ritual sorceries of voodoo. My master needed a host with lots of power to carry out his mission. Voodoo has a very efficient zombification process that provided a means for us to give bodies to the legion."

"The staging point of an invasion."

The demoness nodded.

"Andras has been bringing his forces over through this operation. Finding mortals your society discarded and turning them into vessels for our forces. You know the sad part? If you actually listened to your master's son, we wouldn't have had so many...recruits."

"You're taking advantage of capitalism and democracy? Or should I say, the shadow government has done that."

"Correct, Scryer. You're not as dumb as you look."

"I'm sorry, did you just say you wanted me to strangle you again with the light? Because that can be arranged, my dear."

"Calm yourself, young Dupree. No need to be hasty."

"You were saying?"

"As you just mentioned, we have a foothold in your government. I will admit it took us longer than with others. Communist regimes, monarchies and despots were a lot easier to manipulate into submission. But the pesky United States and their constitution has been difficult to override. Not to mention having to erase capitalism, which has created an annoying sense of self efficacy amongst your people."

"This is why politicians have sabotaged industry in some areas of the country?"

"You're learning, Dupree. Look at you. So, it can be taught."

Paimon felt the gripping energy from the light closing around her body. Her neck strained as the area around it started to tighten.

"Don't!" the demoness pleaded.

"You done sassing me, skid mark?"

"I'm a demon. A being of negative energy. It's in my nature."

Brightness erupted around Paimon. The demon sizzled as light peeled away at the negative energy of her body. She raised her head into the air with a howl, collapsing to her knees. Claws stabbed the ground, scratching and pulling. The etheric body of the demon crumbled with bits of her essence floating into the void.

"No! We had a deal, Scryer! Dupree! Don't do this!"

"It's not me, demon." The Madam turned her head to see Elizabeth's glowing eyes amongst the darkness. *"Calm yourself, girl. We still need her."*

The light receded. Elizabeth's irises returned to their usual chocolate brown. Her brow arched over the deep frown on her face. The young scryer's fists balled white knuckle tight, shaking with the urge to strike.

"One more smartass remark and I'm tossing that filth back into the pit for her buddies to deal with her. Then I'll put an echo out into the etheric layers letting every denizen know that she squealed."

"Mercy!"

"Elizabeth!" Dupree ordered. *"You will stand down!"*

"I'm a USA agent, it's in my nature. You can court martial me when we get back, ma'am. I don't care."

"Might I suggest you do as she says, Paimon. She's quite gifted,

and after exorcising your buddies, I don't have the energy to stop her."

Paimon wheezed, her fingers still digging into the layers, maintaining a death grip.

"I should've never brought you, Elizabeth." Madam Dupree winked. *"You are too young and hot headed. Now, where were we? So, these poor souls you converted into vessels are...?"*

"Let's just say the homeless situation we've constructed, and the open borders policy have created a massive population of undocumented cattle to draw from. Our mortal foot soldiers do the rest."

"Gangbangers, organized crime, human traffickers?"

"Yes. Not to mention the large number of police officer vessels we have. We try to control both sides of the coin, leaving nothing to chance. Once they get us the bodies we need, Edjewale converts them for the legions to inhabit. The process is faster and requires less effort than trying to break someone for traditional possession, although the body becomes effectively dead. Everything was running smoothly until he requested that girl be sacrificed. That brought the attention of your agency."

"Why would he sacrifice an innocent woman with that much psychic potential and open such a large wound in the etheric layers? He had to know we would discover it. Kind of sloppy for someone of his rank."

"I don't know." Paimon's head snapped toward Elizabeth. The young scryer's eyes illuminated again. *"I seriously don't know! He never told me the reasoning behind it. That ritual was done far from here! None of us knew why he did it!"*

Elizabeth, she's lying, keep it up. Madam Dupree informed. *Silly undisciplined demons. Fear is causing her mind's defenses to slip. I can see her thoughts now, escaping from the recesses of her psyche. Paimon knows why the ritual was done. There's images of Edjewale and Baron*

Samedi, stuffing greasy reddened toes into their pockets. The girl's screams are horrendous. The gate was opened to bring—I lost it, the walls are going back up. We have to keep her mind off her defenses.

"Does Andras plan on bringing his entire military force over?" Madam Dupree asked.

"No, we have too many on the other side for that. Usually after he prepares a body, he'll randomly choose a lesser demon to carry over. Then we house them here until it's time to unleash them. After your pappy flooded the planet and left our souls trapped in the abyss, the bulk of us were driven mad by the unjust punishment. Most of our kind devolved to the bestial state you've encountered here."

"You almost wiped out humanity during the antediluvian period. You get no sympathy from me." Madam Dupree turned to Elizabeth. *"This should be no surprise to you. Think back to your training."*

"It was somewhere in the synoptic gospels," Elizabeth recalled. *"The last days will look like the days of Noah. He meant that the Nephilim would walk the Earth again. He never mentioned that they wouldn't be giants this time."*

"Exactly. They have returned, just as he prophesied. But not as we expected. This is why the scum removed the book of Enoch from the bible."

"We removed just enough from your bible to avoid your pappy's wrath, while keeping you blind to our plans. Hey, human institutions are easy to manipulate. If you think about it, we're not really at fault here."

"I didn't ask to hear your twisted demon logical fallacies. Now, where is Andras?"

"His base of operations is right below us."

"The basement?"

"No, literally below ground."

"The undercity, the tunnels of old L.A?

"Correct. We compartmentalize things. So, don't relish too much in your victory here. The real games are about to begin."

"So, I gathered."

"Let me ask you scryers a question. Why do you serve a people who would soon as shun you due to their dogma? Over the gifts their own master has bestowed upon you? Not long ago they would've burnt you at the stake as a witch. It's pathetic how you serve such an undeserving lot. We would greatly appreciate and award such talents."

"A wise man once said, forgive them for they know not what they do. Plus, we all know it's you demons that have infiltrated the faith, manipulating it into the wrong direction and the level of corruption we face today," Dupree answered.

"Where are the bodies of the fallen agents?" Elizabeth asked.

"The nigger is being used as a chew toy in one of the zombie pens—"

A shock of light slammed into the demon, sending it crashing to the ground. She screeched, curling into a ball and shivering.

"No! Mercy! What did I do?"

Good, her defenses are down again. I see the rest now. Their intentions... They wanted to bring over... NO!

"Don't use that word around me, skid mark," Elizabeth said.

"Hey, you stole my name for the new pet," Dupree remarked. *"She's right though, skid mark. We don't tolerate racism here."*

"Really? You all seem so susceptible to following it when we program you through the media."

"Not all."

"Where's the other agent?"

"Maybe still alive. He was being interrogated for information by the master."

"I see."

"Does that about wrap it up, Scryers?"

"Yes, for now. There will be more questions in the future, skid mark."

"So be it. I take it you want me out of the body?"

"Yep."

When Dupree's eyes opened, she saw the faces of Curtis, Emmerich and Callisto hovering over her.

"It always freaks me out when you scryers go under." Curtis smiled, patting her shoulder. "Glad to have you back, ma'am."

"Good to be back. I need a shower after all of that. Ugh."

She rifled through her pack until drawing out a small wooden chest. When she opened the lid, the aroma of frankincense and myrrh entered the room. A gleaming skull shaped from quartz sat inside the small container which she presented to the doctor. The body of Metzger slumped over, falling out of the chair and smacking her head on to the floor. The agents felt a cool gust of air caressing their bodies, leaving goosebumps as it passed. Dupree grinned at the skull, rolling her index finger over the forehead.

"Comfy?" Dupree asked.

"I hate you!" Paimon snapped.

"Better than getting tortured by your superiors for centuries."

"Leave me be, Scryer. Now I rest."

"Steiners, I know where your brother is located. Let's retrieve his body and give him the burial that a man of his caliber deserves."

"Thank you, ma'am," Emmerich replied.

Fredrick sighed with relief.

Callisto lowered her fierce gaze, nodding.

"There's much to discuss. Lots of intel to pass along. I have to meet with Kat and talk about some dire situations brought to our attention. From what I know, Finley is still alive, and I have the location of the scum that started all of this."

"Understood, ma'am," Emmerich said.

"This is as far as I can go with you. I don't have much left in me anyway. I'm going to recommend to Kat that she dispatch a member of Fifteenth Team to accompany you."

"A tunnel rat?" Emmerich asked.

Callisto and Fredrick raised a brow.

"Yes. You're going to need them where you're going."

CHAPTER 13
THE SHATTERED REMNANT

Knocking jolted Howler's eyes open to her dim office. Her head turned to the door. She leaned forward, her creaking chair realigning to become flush with the floor. After blinking a bit, she rubbed away the crusty mucus lining her baggy eyes. Another knock on the door and she shook herself out of the sleepy stupor.

"Come in!"

Max, one of her assistants, rushed into the room, centering himself in front of her desk. "Good afternoon, ma'am. Sorry to disturb your nap—"

"Nix the traditional pleasantries. Give me the details."

"Madam Dupree will be arriving back to HQ within an hour with an enemy prisoner of war in tow. Ghost and Monarch have locked down the asylum and are mopping up the last of the enemy combatants. They are trying to recover Agent Badrick Steiner's remains. It has been reported Agent Finley is still alive. Ghost Team will be going underground into the old tunnels of L.A. to pursue the perp. Curtis will be augmenting them. We have dispatched Agent Nhi from

Muskrat to reinforce them. The AO is currently considered yellow."

"Finally, some good news." She took a sip from the stale lukewarm coffee in her mug and gagged.

"Ma'am, I can get you a fresh cup after this."

"That would be lovely, Max. So, what else do you have for me?"

"They will be calling in civilian medical assets to help with the asylum's captives that weren't turned into zombies."

"Good. Protecting the innocent is our priority. Is Psy-Ops on top of the media coverage?"

"Yes, ma'am. Psychological Operations are spinning a story right now about a massive abuse scandal, involving corrupt medical staff, human trafficking and illegal medical practices."

"Excellent. No need for the public to go crazy about this."

"Ma'am, permission to speak freely?"

"Granted."

"Why are we always hiding the truth from the public?"

"Because most humans are irrational. Also, we are sinful creatures by nature. Think about the abuse of power we already have to deal with. Now imagine if the majority of humanity knew that magick, demons and the like existed? The panic alone would be impossible for the government to control. During the Covid-19 epidemic, the anti-eastern xenophobia ran high, and many innocent Asian Americans were given unfair treatment because of it or worse."

"I see where you're going with this," Max nodded. "I didn't quite grasp the severity of the situation, but you're absolutely right, ma'am. Things could become uncontrollably worse around the nation."

"Indeed. Imagine people running around accusing others of

being a werewolf, vampire, or sorcerer. We already endured those days and many innocents died from the irrational fear, with little actual evil being slain. Not to mention the number of recruits the dark would receive from the corruptible and power hungry. You see what a few dictators are capable of in these foreign countries. Now imagine if every angsty psychically gifted teen in the world knew how to harness their arcane power. We'd have a huge mess on our hands. We can't fight the world, Max."

"In that regard I'll have to disagree. Yes, fear would cause them to take some irrational measures, but for the most part, wouldn't their decisions be rooted in a desire to do what's right? I don't think we give people enough faith."

"My faith is in God, the constitution, my agents and myself. Not people. People will let you down most of the time. Well, that's been my experience. I'm not going to risk the lives that could be lost if the truth is revealed. It could be catastrophic."

"I didn't think about it that way, ma'am. Those are all good points. You're right. The risk outweighs the reward. It's not worth risking anyone's life from the panic or the power mad individuals that could arise from it."

"You're new here. I like these questions and conversations we have, though. Can you guess why?"

"Because it shows that I'm thinking outside the box?"

"Yes, but more-so it tells me that you have a good heart. You care about the people we are trying to protect. It's the dedication we need in the agency. But sometimes we have to protect humanity from themselves."

Max nodded. "Oh yes, I almost forgot, ma'am. You still have the morning brief with Teams Butcher and Diver about launching the New Mexico operation. Also, the other assistant directors wanted to know if you were ready to add your Jane Hancock to the paperwork."

"What paperwork?"

"The acknowledgement to move forward with the Chemically Augmented Physical Enhancement program."

"That's right, CAPE. I see. I thought they were going to give me more time."

"AD Grimes is pushing hard. He made the request. Fourth Team is going to be the first implemented in the program. He said to remind you the prophecy says they will be returning in full capacity. Even if we try to resist with conventional resources, it's only a matter of time. We need to meet them on the field of battle with an even ground. Whatever that means."

"Ugh, Grimes. All he cares about is combat applications. I need time. Tell them that I haven't made my decision yet and that I won't any time before the deadline. I understand that Fourth Team is willing to volunteer for this. But I have to think over the proposal. I have questions that need answering before subjecting some of our best to something that could radically alter their humanity. Remember, sometimes we have to protect people from themselves."

"Understood, ma'am."

"If Ghost is going underground to dig up the perp, I want you to get SOAR ready so we can authorize use of the DBM."

"DBMs, ma'am?"

"Deep Burrowing Missiles. Precision guided missiles that will provide a small amount of support for the team down there. They penetrate the ground with small craters we can claim in the media are sink holes. The AO seems sparsely inhabited so we should be clear. Anything else to report?"

"Permission to continue speaking freely?"

"That's a little redundant. Shoot."

"I think you need another hour of rest, ma'am. You look..."

"Ate up? Like a soup sandwich? Go on, be honest."

"I guess that's the right term. I was trying to choose something a bit more tactful. You've been up for nearly two days straight."

"So have my field agents."

"Understood, ma'am."

"Just keep my mug full and I'll be fine. Tell the rest of the staff, I'll be in the war room in ten mikes. You're dismissed, Max."

"Yes, ma'am."

The door to the cell flung open. Carbine barrels pointed into the room, their aim following the sound of gnashing teeth and rumbling growls. Emmerich switched on the mini light clipped to the side of his Kevlar helm. The inhabitants of the room roared, the brief flash of illumination revealing their rise from a crouching position. With heavy plodding they sprinted for the doorway.

Emmerich stepped backward, shouldering his weapon, and firing into the entrance. Bodies wobbled with each shot, some toppling down. The first of their brethren leapt over the fallen. The ghoul was greeted by the M26 twelve gauge attached to the underside of Callisto's M4. Her left hand grabbed the magazine, using it like a handle as she pulled the shotgun's trigger and split the tango's skull with buckshot spray.

The splatter covered the doorway, pelting the next arrival. Calvin and Fredrick released shots from their M4s, sending the enemy reeling back into the darkness of the room. Emmerich peeked in again, seeing a corpse lying at the center.

When his light surrounded it, his weapon lowered as he let out a sharp exhale and closed his eyes. The combat boots and torn jacket looked familiar.

"We found him..." Emmerich announced to the team. "It's Badrick."

"Babe, you don't have to go in there. I'll take care of this with Rook. Why don't you and Freddy stay out here?"

"No, I have to see him one last time."

The blood-soaked padded floor squished with each step, sliming the soles of their boots. Emmerich shouldered his weapon, kneeling to touch his brother's hand. There were no fingers, only shambles of meat drenched in saliva. There was pressure underneath Emmerich's boot, given rise from stepping on numerous small, rock hard objects. Only after picking them up, did he recognize the greasy bone fragments slipping from his grasp, as the remains of his brother's hand. A sigh of anguish fled from him when his touch ran over the indentions of numerous teeth marks across the ridges.

Fredrick's eyes glanced over to his brother's face, the gore covered skull had been gnawed at until all that remained were grisly tufts. "I can't... I can't..."

In a split second, Fredrick's psyche catapulted him back to his childhood home. He was slumped over at the dinner table with a thick book sprawled across it. Badrick sat next to him, pointing at an array of numbers, and nodding as he explained the process for each math problem.

"I know your teacher explained this in class, but you were probably daydreaming," Badrick chuckled.

"Yeah," Emmerich ruffled Freddy's hair as he sauntered by the table with a plate full of peanut butter cookies. Fredrick reached for one, feeling the warmth of pastries near his fingertips, until the stinging slap of Emmerich's hand ushered him away. "We're taking time away from football practice so you're going to learn this stuff. Luckily for you, we already took this class during our freshman year."

Badrick snickered as Emmerich offered him a cookie. "Just focus, Freddy."

"This stuff is too hard, Baddy. I don't even know where to begin. I'm grounded until I can bring my algebra grade to at least a B."

"PEMDAS, Freddy," his brother explained. "It helps you understand the order for solving math problems. Or there's a little ditty, that goes Please Excuse My Dear Aunt Sally. Parenthesis, Exponents, Multiplication, Addition..."

The white walls of the house faded, peeled away, replaced with the gore slimed padded room. Stench invaded his nostrils, replacing the scent of his mother's kitchen, the sweet aroma of pastries gave way to the harsh reek of feces and dried blood. Badrick's eyes still glistened through the remains of his face, Fredrick peered at them, before the torrent of memories caused his being to shatter.

"I can't," Fredrick whimpered, turning away. "I can't..." His voice started to crack.

"It's okay, Freddy," Callisto said. "I'll take care of him." She unfurled the plastic body bag.

"He... didn't deserve this. He had such a good heart. He wasn't a shit bag like me. It should be me getting put in that bag."

"Don't say that!" Emmerich snapped. "Baddy gave his life for us."

"Em, I—"

"No, damn it. Get your shit together. I know it hurts. But he was taking care of his little brothers. That's why we're seeing this to the end. You will live, damn it. You will go on fighting. Because that's what he wanted."

"We'll honor his memory by sending as many of these demons back to the pit as possible," Calvin added.

"That's right, Calvin," Emmerich agreed. "Let's finish wrapping him up and get his body back to the rear."

He turned his head as Callisto pulled the zipper over the body. Calvin grunted as she piled Badrick onto his shoulder. Fredrick remained looking away, keeping his back to everyone. Emmerich patted his brother on the shoulder. Fredrick sniffled and walked out of the room.

"Don't worry about a thing," Bob Marley's soulful voice blared through the radio. She hummed with the rhythm. "Don't worry about a thing."

The child clutched his face. Tears streamed through his fingers and down the sides of his obsidian cheeks. The sting from her slaps still rang in his head, causing his face and ear to throb with his escalating heartbeats. The scent of cocoa butter from her body clung to his nostrils. The aroma always stuck with him for a few hours after each ordeal. When it ended, the event faded from his mind, leaving only the quaking residual images in his memory, like a dream after waking up. If only the fear and ignominy did the same.

"I told ya, doncha be fightin' back. Ya tawkin' dog aint gun save ya tis time," his mother didn't look at him as she put her pants back on. "Ya scared me, last time wiv that talk, but ya not gun fool me again."

The boy stared at the ceiling, hoping the warm clamminess would hurry up and fade. His chest heaved with ribs protruding, rising with each gasping breath, and every tear that cascaded to the sheets.

"I wuz gud, wasn't I? Gatha yaself, get da chicken for the ritual tonight afta ya dun. An' stop ya cryin. Yuh cyaa duh nutt'n bout it."

"Ya, mooma," the boy responded.

"Listen to da music, Eddy. Like I always say, everyting gun be irie."

Her looming presence pulled away from his peripheral vision as she made her exit. His hand smeared the wetness from his face. The sting of the assault faded, along with the humming of pain in his ear. The boy didn't want to shower anymore. He recalled the first time, being struck, and forced. Washing never fixed the problem anyway, so his instincts shifted to urge him into going through the motions of the day.

Evuh since me pa left, the boy wondered as he shook his head. *Why she always do tis to meh?*

"Power."

The boy's head snapped over to the corner of the room where a large pointed eared Dobermann Pinscher laid with its front legs crossed. When he stared at the dog's eyes, his own twisted reflection gazed back from the sheen of its pupils.

"Power," it continued. *"Life is about power, my dear Edjewale. Those who have it, imposin' it upon those who do not."*

I wouldn't be doin teez tings to mah own blood if I 'ad powah. Why ya not come save meh, Baron?

"I know ya be hurtin' each time. But tink a dis as a learning

experience. Exercising power makes ya stronger. She understands this. You must learn it."

Ya dun speak patois, do ya?

"No. It's a rather new language that I haven't quite picked up yet."

Jus be real wiff meh.

"You're quite the brilliant child. So be it. Right and wrong is merely a matter of perspective. It doesn't truly exist. This is why the natural order of the world is chaos, fabricated by the opinions of those observing the pandemonium of existence. I can grant you the power, my dear Eddy. May I call you that?"

Ya, but wut bout tis powah?

"Your mother and father tutored you early in the basics of Voodoo and the way of the saints. But ascension requires more dedication. Only when you've tapped into the left-handed path, can you master it. I've scoured the world for the perfect amalgamation of talent and character. You're gifted, but that will not suffice for what you seek. Innate ability can only go so far without my refinement."

How I go bout tis?

"First, let me in, Eddy. I can be your family. We are the same, both discarded by a cruel world that allowed us to suffer. We've spoken about this before. I'm tired of watching her victimize you. I can only help if you let me in."

Edjwale lowered his head. *Ok, but what's next?*

Freedom is our next step. We go into the kitchen and grab a knife. Then I'll show you true power.

The wooden hilt of the knife was warmed by his clammy grip. Wetness from his tears moistened the palm of Edjewale's hand. Smoke from her cigarette scented the hallway leading to the living room. He followed it, along with the rumbling sound of her loud snoring. But it only guided him back to reality, his mind pulling into the present.

Edjewale was seated on his throne, the cold and moldy flesh that formed it brushing against his own. He rubbed his hand over the arm rest, caressing the hair follicles within it, before gazing around the room with his watery pink eyes.

"The power of the mind, the ultimate time machine. I can sense your aura plummeting further into the recesses. You went back there again."

"Ya, me mooma."

"I remember her gasp when the blade crossed her throat. That pathetic whimper she gave."

"You be mah true kin."

"Indeed. We only have each other."

"Let's go and check on our guest. Da agent mon," Edjewale declared as he rose, putting on his black leather jacket.

"I have a knight ready to possess him. It has been waiting in the layers."

"Ya, I pick up on it. Tis naa gun be an easy ting ta break an agent."

"We will find a way to succeed. We always do."

Finley's eyes cracked open. They wanted to close despite his attempts to fight the weariness gripping his mind and body. The acidic stench of urine clung to the stagnant air. His hands grew cold and blue. They ached with a dull compounding pain, as the rusty iron shackles chaining him to the wall cut into his skin.

He writhed as the pain resurfaced in his consciousness. The sting from bite marks across his hands and face sent memories flooding back to him. Each breath drew more suffering from the swelling contusions over his chest and wincing from the sharp pain of bruised ribs.

Candles surrounded him, lining the ground in a circle. They illuminated the room just enough so he could see the layer of dirt and broken chunks of what used to be a floor. His sight rose from a jagged stone to a pair of gator skin boots. When he looked up, dark brown eyes peered through long dreadlocks. The wrinkles from the man's gaunt face compressed together as he grinned at Finley.

"Ya awake, boy. How ya be?"

Heavy steps pounded the floor along the perimeter. The outline of someone enormous moved amongst the shadows avoiding the light. Finley's attention was drawn to it, his breathing picking up pace as it halted for a moment. Two spheres sat on broad shoulders that could rival the width of a car.

"Don't let Roje over there scare ya, Agent. He naa gunna do a ting, lest ya upset us."

"Wh-ho are you?"

"I be Edjewale."

"You're the one that started all of this, huh?"

"Me, naa mon. I ansah to da Baron."

"Liar! You're that powerful voodoo priest we've been after."

"Oh, ya been aftah me, eh? Ya, I be da one." Edjewale held up the piece of quartz that was hidden away in his uniform. "I see ya come prepared. Good ting we stripped ya naked. Tis can't help ya now." He tossed the quartz into the darkness.

"You don't scare me. If that's what you're trying to do. You're the same as every other nefarious lowlife sorcerer we've combated."

"I don't tink so. Ya see agent mon, I be raised by a Haitian voodoo mother, and mah Jamaican father also be powerful with the voodoo. I know da secrets uv both sides and I has someone who be watching my back."

"Who?"

Edjewale rolled his eyes and chuckled. "So wuts ya name?"

"I'm not telling you shit!" Finley squirted a line of spit between his teeth and into the face of his captor.

Edjewale grinned, his long purple tongue licking it away. "I see we gunna do tings da 'ard way. Gud."

He reached out, seizing Finley's head with long craggy fingers. The agent tried to rear back, turn away, thrashing about in his shackles. When Edjewale's hands grabbed him, he felt like an action figure, helpless and pliable to the man's vast strength.

A flickering started in the mind's eye. The skeletal visage glared at him. Its blackened aura crackled and flared, drifting, and rising to the ceiling like steam. A coldness settled around Finley's body.

Let me in. The thoughts in Finley's mind weren't his own. *I am not here to hurt you. I can help you. We can make it all go away, if only you'd be my friend.*

Someone else was there. A presence his shifting eyes could not see, but his instincts felt drawn toward. The agent wanted to fight, but as he struggled with his mind to resist, the cold ushered it away.

"Your predecessors knew when to kneel before a deity. Here you are spitting upon one. I have plans for you, impudent ape." The hateful whispers of Baron carried like a breeze.

"You are no deity, demonic filth. There is only one God."

"Interesting. We shall see who shows you mercy first. Your God, or me."

"Just get it over with, demon. I'm tired of hearing your ramblings."

"You will be praising all glories to my name when this is over, righteous one."

The long claws reached out, scratching at his soul. Finley screamed, jerking in his restraints. His blue hands came to life as fingers curled into a tight fist. Baron plunged his hooks inward, ripping away at the light.

You're only hurting us and what can be. There's no need to fight. Just rest.

"Break, slave of El. You are pitiful. That is why your team left you behind. That is why no one is looking for you. They assumed you are dead. Because they know you are weak."

The agent's eyes widened. Images flickered in his mind, first seeing the withered face of Edjewale, then the rancorous glare of Baron. They alternated, until he was seeing both at the same time. The deep cackle of Edjewale drowned out his cries. It grew louder, until he couldn't hear his own thoughts. Finley saw the aura around them, flooding his vision with only the dark.

"We gun break ya, agent mon."

"Yes, shatter his essence."

Something shone just below his peripheral vision. A sharp pain followed along his abdomen, slicing through skin and muscle. Lines of blood streaked out, traveling down his bare thighs, until blood dripped from his toes. Another slash followed, the blade swinging like a pendulum. Finley screamed into the ceiling.

Crimson dripped down the agent's body. Edjewale stepped back with a smug grin as he followed the markings of his handiwork. Finley bit his lip, furrowed his brow, and glared back. He spat into Edjewale's face again.

"Naa ya be makin me angry, child."

"This one is tenacious."

"Ya, dis be no druggie or crazy."

"His will remains strong. My knight cannot penetrate his essence. Remove the source of his virility and his demeanor will weaken."

"Ya be a cold one, Baron. So be it. Gunna need da stuff ta keep 'im awake." Edjewale wandered off into the darkness.

You could avoid all of this suffering. We could avoid all of this. I do not want to harm you. I do not want to see you harmed. We can work together.

"Shut up!" Finley snapped. "You think I don't know your tricks? You will never possess me, you fiend! Never!"

The voodoo priest returned with a syringe in hand. He stuck the agent, injecting the contents in one smooth squeeze. The man's calloused fingers reached for Finley's member.

"No!"

"Gotsta. Baron is right. Ya not gunna break, so we gotsta take ya pride."

"You vile bastard!"

"Shh. It be over soon. I promise."

The blade made its mark. Finley hollered and thrashed about. Tears flowed. Edjewale sawed as the gore spilled over his hands. He fidgeted with the remainder of the extremity as the knife drove through. The last bit of meat attaching it was sliced away. It now rested in Edjewale's blood covered grip.

"Don't tink I be takin pleasure in tis. I only do what I 'aff ta. Ya made dis 'arda on yerself ten ya needed. I'm no crazy. Erreting I do be for a reason. The shadow makes these tings 'appen. Ya left us no choice."

Finley's body went limp.

Let me in.

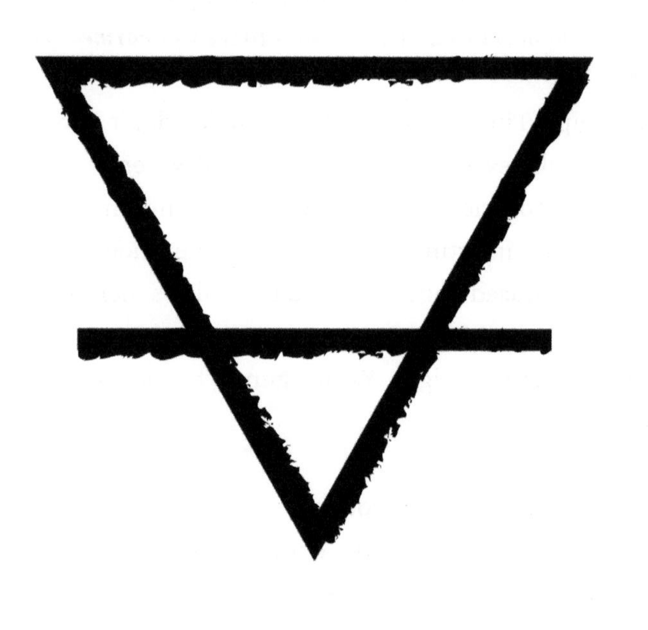

CHAPTER 14
THE DESCENT

Cobwebs draped from the ceiling of the basement, coated in a gray layer of dust along with everything else. The agents added to the myriad of footprints in the filth covered floor as they walked around the large boxes and sprawling furniture. Calvin gasped, his head dropping back before launching forward. A cloud of mist escaped his nose and mouth as he belted out a loud sneeze.

"Bless you, Calvin," Elizabeth said.

"Bless you, Rook." Fredrick patted him on the back.

"Thanks. Damn allergies."

"The Madam said she discovered the entrance around here when she probed the demon's mind," Curtis informed them.

"Keep your eyes open, team. Look for anything, a manhole, some stairs, a lever," Emmerich instructed.

"Yeah, these scumbags always have some kind of secret in their lairs," Callisto agreed. "We should move some stuff around if there's nothing obvious sticking out."

"Thanks for coming with us on this, Curtis," Emmerich said. "We appreciate the augment."

"Well, Badrick was my friend, too. Remember when the four of us were just recruits, hating life and trying to survive training?"

Emmerich chuckled, smirked, then nodded. "I thought Howler hated me back then."

"Turns out she just hated Freddy," Callisto chuckled.

"Hey," Fredrick snapped.

"My squad leaders are capable of locking down the asylum without me. They need some time to branch out on their own to develop as leaders. Besides, this duke sounds like one tough customer," Curtis continued.

"Too bad we couldn't bring all of Monarch." Fredrick chuckled. "Just hose the place down with hate and call it a day."

"That's too many bodies in what we're expecting to be a tight space, Freddy," Emmerich corrected. "That would cause so much chaos and probably end up with more casualties than we need. The grunts can lock down the asylum."

"Yep, there's still plenty of things that need killin' up there," Curtis agreed. "We will be augmented again after infil into the undercity."

"Yeah, we sure could use it." Freddy smirked.

"We're getting one operator from Muskrat," Emmerich said.

"I guess that makes sense. Send the tunnel rats to help us with the underground fighting. Just one though? You're the king. Howler loves you. Try to push for some more from Muskrat."

"Tunnel rats normally don't operate in groups, Freddy," Callisto said. "Think about when they were created back in Vietnam. It was just one lone gunman lowered into a hole to kill an entire underground base of enemies."

“Damn! Wish I could get that kind of training.”

“You’re too damn big and clumsy.” She smirked.

“They’re infiltrating into the sector by themselves, Actual?” Calvin asked.

“I know, right,” Fredrick added. “Talk about having a huge pair!”

“Yep. They prefer it that way. Besides, we don’t have enough time to wait for them. We have to push in now, try to apprehend or destroy the target while we have the initiative.”

“Here,” Callisto called out. “I found something.”

Dust flowed throughout the room as she flipped over half of a large rug. Hands waved away the cloud of particles. When it dispersed, Callisto stomped, rattling the hinges and flex handle of a wooden lid just below her feet.

“Yep, I thought the rug felt a bit uneven.”

“Good work,” Emmerich said.

“Good eye there, Agent Dukas,” Curtis said.

“It’s been used recently. Look at these footsteps leading to it. Someone wearing boots. The layer of dust on the lid looks disturbed, unlike the rest of this toilet.”

Emmerich raised the trapdoor, revealing a pathway of spiraling stairs cascading into darkness. He nodded to the others, before leading with the barrel of his weapon and descending. With soft steps, they continued down the narrowing path. Emmerich and Curtis scraped their shoulders against the jagged and uneven walls as the team followed in single file.

Callisto's vision faded as she began to pause. Warm liquid of iron and salt flowed into her mouth, the redness of which stained her teeth. The aching returned, throbbing from the purple regions swelling over her face and body.

I'm here again. The place of my birth and tempering. Where it all began. The Farm.

A bright light beamed in her face, blinding her vision, save for the glowing outline of the assailants that surrounded her. Blood continued to gush from her nose, bubbling out of her mouth as she struggled for air laced with stale cigarette smoke and the reek of chewing tobacco.

"Dukas, I'm not letting some self-righteous feminist bitch pass through my pipeline," the voice taunted.

They tried so hard to break me. They couldn't. At least that's what I wanted them to believe.

"First female candidate the CIA ever put through their Deep Black program," another mocked in a high pitch.

I was the first.

A fist flew into her vision, rocking her body in the confines of the chair she was imposed on. Strands of her dark hair grew taut with pain as it rolled into an assailant's fist. Callisto's head cocked back from the strain. The hot breath and spit of her assailant collided with the side of her face as he continued to mock her.

"You thought SERE school was tough. Four weeks, Dukas. I have your ass for four weeks. This is just day one. No woman has ever passed the Advance Interrogation Survival Course and no woman ever will. Now be a good girl and tell me what we want to know. Then this nightmare ends and you're back on a plane with the rest of the washouts."

"You're only a few sentences from heading back home to

pumpkin spice lattes and hair salons," the other jeered. "Tell us, Dukas. What's the code word?"

Through strain and coughing she answered, "Dukas, Callisto SSN 512-39—"

The physical pain I couldn't hide. No one could. But I never gave them the satisfaction of witnessing beyond that. I couldn't live with myself if I had.

"Bitch thinks she's funny," his partner cackled. "That's not what we wanted to hear."

"Break some fingers and dislocate the rib now. Get the hammer," he ordered as he uncapped the bottle where they had both spat their chew.

"I thought we didn't start breaking fingers until day fourteen? And isn't it just a pinky finger?"

"We're accelerating her training," he said, dumping the bottle on Callisto's head. "Break the pinky and the middle finger."

The longest month of my life...

The slimy brown liquid soaked through her hair, cascading down the side of her face, trailing down her neck and drenching the undershirt of her uniform. The blinding light faded, with the farm pulling away from her mind. The haze lifted until there was only the darkness of the underground once more. Emmerich appeared with his hand on Callisto's shoulder.

"It happened again, didn't it?" he wondered.

"I'm fine," Callisto answered.

"We all go through it. You're not alone."

"I know, babe. I've heard the lectures from the shrinks," she replied placing her hand on his. "You know how I—"

"Yeah, you deal with it differently. Never letting anyone see your weakness. It's not weakness to acknowledge pain. I'm also not just anyone either."

She nodded. "No, you're not."

"Together always," he whispered. "Just as we promised."

"In this adventure and the next."

Emmerich chuckled as her eyes shifted, making sure the rest of the team didn't spot their moment.

The four USA agents tracked down the hallway, weapon barrels pointing forward and at the ready. Their steps were slow, while their eyes scanned hard and fast through night optics devices, scrutinizing every dead body they passed, checking underneath, and behind each article of furniture they came across. After a sharp left turn down a new path, the agents stopped just short of a cell door, the first of many aligning the walls. The fireteam leader rose to the balls of her feet, peering into the thick window just above head level.

"You think we would've managed to get the power back on in this place by now. Catch anything, Anders?"

"No, Michaels. This place is disgusting. All I'm seeing is grime. You know what that means." Anders placed her hand on the doorknob.

"Pull and go. We're ready."

Anders turned the handle, before stepping back for a moment to deliver a powerful front kick to the door. It swung open, flying back, and crashing into someone behind it. The rest of the fireteam poured into the room. Michaels led the charge. A crouching figure staggered backward, it's mouth agape to let out a baleful scream. The ghoul's arms flailed as he fought to regain his footing.

Michaels spotted only a single bed and toilet, in the small box like area. "Short room," he called out.

"Mason, cordon with me," Anders ordered.

"Acknowledged," Mason replied as he spun around to monitor the corridor.

After scanning the corners, he peered ahead to see the inhabitant raise its curled fingers like claws and leap at him. Two shots snapped the ghoul's head back, spraying a warm mist into the air, staining into the padded walls. The assailant's body collapsed, lifeless before their boots.

"One tango down!"

"Let's hurry up clearing this wing and we'll link up with the rest of the squad," Anders ordered. "Cold ones on me after this is over, all you can drink."

"Now that's motivation," Murphy grinned. "Looks like the rest is cleared, boss."

A small patter along the floor receded around the corner of the hallway. Mason squeezed his buttstock into his shoulder, stepping sideways to pie off the corner. He peered down the corridor, seeing an entrance to another area nearby.

"Good work, Bravo," Anders continued. "Let's—"

"Andy, I had visual on something moving behind us," Mason called out.

"What is it?"

"I don't know, but it was quick, and I barely heard it."

"Sneaky zombs," Murphy slapped her knee with a giggle. "Maybe they know not to mess with the Bravo Fire Team." She gave Michaels a high five who nodded with a smirk.

"Regardless, we have to clear this place. Let's double back

real quick and see if we can track it," Anders ordered as she led their way around the corner again.

"There, Anders," Mason called out. "I saw it go into that door."

The fireteam leader nodded, acknowledging the words of her subordinate as they made their way to the wooden door. Anders halted looking back at Michaels.

"Ready two," she asked.

"Ready. On you, number one."

With a pull, the door opened revealing the game room they had arrived to earlier in the search. Michaels scanned the room from corner to corner, seeing only pool and foosball tables, a television mounted along the back wall, and a few couches. He pointed at the dead body.

"I remember this place, must've been an area Ghost encountered earlier," he stated. "The orderly was already dead when we arrived."

"Thankfully, we haven't engaged one of those yet," Anders added. "Hopefully, it stays that way."

A small thud took their attention, causing their eyes to rise in unison at the vents over the upper cabinets.

Michaels' weapon barrel followed the taps along the metal frame. The glowing crimson reticle of his close-quarter optic zeroed where it stopped by the darkness of an opening his NODs couldn't illuminate. "Something is slithering around in there."

"Another flesh grafted animal or something?" Mason gasped.

"I'm opening it," Murphy whispered as she climbed to the counter and reached up.

"We got you," Anders murmured. "Be careful."

The lid to the vents popped off without effort. Murphy

stared at the empty holes along the outline of it, devoid of any screws. "It was just sitting on there. Can't see inside, there's no light for the NODs to use."

"Moonbeam up," Anders ordered.

With a click, the flashlight on Mason's Kevlar helmet illuminated the opening as he peered into it. The light revealed gleaming blue eyes amongst wild strands of stringy blonde hair and a face grayed with filth.

"It's a little girl!"

"Can anyone tell if she's a ghoul," Anders asked.

"Come on, lighten up, Andy," Murphy replied. "Look at her, she's trembling in place. We've never seen a ghoul flee in fear before."

"N-no monster," the girl responded. "Only M-Madelyn."

"We're with the government, young lady. My fireteam is clearing this floor of any hostiles and civilians. Come with us and we can provide relief."

"Andy, I know you don't care for kids but sheesh," Murphy quipped.

"Where Badrick?" Madelyn asked.

"That's a member of Ghost," Murphy shook her head. "I think he's their medic. I heard he..."

"Yeah, Ghost Actual said something about a little girl being lost. This must be her. We're getting you out of here, Madelyn. Come with us."

She nodded, climbing down, before spring-boarding to Murphy.

"Tac-com this is Bravo Fire Team of third squad," Anders reported over comms. "We have rescued the little girl that Ghost briefed us about. We are making our way back to the vehicles with her ASAP."

"Finally, some good news," Tac-com replied. "I'll relay the information to Ghost Actual. I'm sure he'll be happy to hear it."

Murphy took Madelyn by the hand. "Don't mind Anders. She's just a serious by the book soldier. Stay with me, okay?"

Madelyn nodded. "O-okay. B-but where Badrick?"

Night optics devices snapped into place, illuminating their vision as they continued into the depths. The air became stale, each breath feeling heavier. A musty stench filled their nostrils with a lingering dryness that spread to their mouths.

"Beacons up?" Emmerich asked. "Give me a status report."

"Green to green," Ghost Team replied.

"Tac-com, this is Monarch Actual," Curtis transmitted over comms. "Ghost Team and I have located the entrance into old L.A. We are in process of descent. Over."

"Roger, Monarch Actual. We acknowledge your last. Queenbee wants a status every fifteen mikes."

"Affirmative. We will relay statuses."

"She also wants to know if you have the beacons for the DBMs."

"Roger, we are carrying three beacons for DBMs. Which are much appreciated."

"She confirms you are go for launch. Happy hunting and be safe down there."

"Will do." Curtis turned to Ghost. "Well, you heard the lady. We're launching mission. Let's get this asshole."

"We got some payback to dish out," Fredrick announced.

They stepped out of the pathway that led into an expansive

cavern. Their boots crunched against gravel and dirt, covering the tile of the floor and walls. As they continued, turnstiles appeared, stretching across the area. Emmerich tried pushing on the arms, but the device wouldn't budge. He leapt over it, the rest of the team following him.

Water dripped from above, splashing down into puddles. A few of the droplets pelted Calvin's head, causing the rookie to peer around before continuing to take up the rear. The pathway changed, dropping off into a shallow area with rusted tracks running through it and expanding deeper into the underground.

"Do we go left or right?" Emmerich pondered.

"Damn good question," Curtis said.

"This place is like a fucking maze!" Fredrick griped. "How the hell are we going to find our way around here?"

"Go right," Elizabeth whispered into Callisto's ear. *"Please, hear me, Cali. Go right. I can sense the negativity in that area. The darkness saturates the etheric layers in that direction."*

"Your whining isn't going to help Freddy," Emmerich scolded. "Any suggestions?"

"We should go right," Callisto said.

"Okay, I'm not opposed to that idea, but why?"

"I think Elizabeth is trying to tell me something. I can just feel it, like a thought popping in my head that isn't my own. If that makes sense."

"You ain't no trained scryer!" Fredrick snapped.

"Look, asshole! Madam Dupree told me that I should trust my instincts! So that's what I'm doing! I feel compelled to go right!"

Fredrick rolled his eyes while muttering under his breath.

"Don't make me punch you!"

"Calm down!"

“Freddy, shut up,” Emmerich said. “Cali, you feel that we should go right? This is Elizabeth saying this?”

“I think so. Asshole over there is right though. I’m not a trained scryer. But I’m feeling something.”

“I also think we should go right. I’m not just saying that to avoid getting punched by Agent Dukas,” Curtis chuckled. “I mean, the worse that can happen is we have to backtrack.”

“You did say Elizabeth was trying to warn us earlier in the op, right?” Calvin asked.

“Yeah. I could feel it.”

“I agree, then,” Emmerich concurred. “We’re going right.”

“Easy for you guys to say when you’re not lugging around the machine gun and twelve hundred rounds in your pack,” Fredrick scoffed.

“Shut up. Let’s go.”

They strode over the steel tracks, each step crunching down on the gravel, disintegrating underneath their boots as they continued their trek. Remnants of tile appeared in broken patches, serving as memories of a time when the location had a purpose.

“Actual, I have a question,” Calvin inquired.

“Shoot,” Emmerich and Curtis both replied.

“Standing down.” The later chuckled. “Sorry, force of habit.”

“All good, bud. So, what’s the question, Calvin?”

“Why would something so prestigious as this duke of hell, hide out in this dump? I mean, this guy is like a high-ranking officer amongst the scumbags, right? Wouldn’t he be quartered somewhere with comforts?”

“Only the chair-force goes to war with comforts,” Fredrick snickered.

“I’m not going to lie. I don’t have an answer for that,”

Emmerich replied. "Demons, Nephilim, whatever you want to call them, they all have different motivations and strategies. I wouldn't think about them in the same regard as you've been taught to hunt other forms of evil."

"Yeah, Rook," Fredrick chimed in. "I mean, we all know that werewolves and vamps have pretty much the same M.O. and weaknesses species-wide. But these demons are cut from a different cloth."

Emmerich nodded. "Agreed, we know little about their operations and personal motivations outside of what the scryers have taught us. My guess is this Andras or Baron that we're hunting is likely trying to distance himself from the main host in order to continue his work should things go awry. Even though we are removing the infestation from the asylum, a gifted sorcerer could easily restart this mess."

"Yup, and we'd be back to square one," Fredrick shook his head.

"That makes sense."

"I'm sure there're unseen factors involved," Emmerich continued. "These things aren't as simplistic as the others that we encounter."

"You're not alone. Focus, Cali."

"I have movement over here," Callisto called out.

Huddled amidst the piled stones, a man lounged, wearing an A-shirt and beanie. He leaned back, laying against the rocks scattered around him, arms draped out to his sides.

"Yyess..." the word was uttered between a whisper and a groan.

"Holy shit!" Fredrick gasped. "There's people living down here!"

Callisto approached, weapon at the ready, her finger poised on the trigger. The man didn't move. She studied his glazed over eyes as they stared into the dark expanse above them.

"Sir, we are with the United States government, here to help you," Emmerich announced. "Can you answer a few questions for us?"

The individual's head bobbed. His limbs spasmed. Callisto waved her hand in front of his face, only for his eyes to continue following the shadows above.

"He's gone, babe," Callisto announced. "Just look." She pointed at the drug needle resting in his lap.

"Whatever he's on must be some good shit, to not notice people with guns," Fredrick quipped.

"Should we help him, Actual?"

"No, Calvin. There's nothing we can do except focus on the mission."

"Agreed," Curtis said. "At least now we know we aren't the only ones down here."

"It... it..." The man murmured. "It's moving... all... around... us..."

"What's moving around us?" Callisto asked.

"It... peeling... me... away... where... I... the slivers... of... me... gone... run boy... run... tell... the... prophet..."

"What the fuck does that even mean?" Fredrick snapped. "This is just some strung out druggie shit."

"He can sense it. The negative reaches grow more intense with each step we take into the depths. Its energies are peeling away at us."

"Look, he's just a crazy bum. His mind is fried from the drugs—" he continued.

"Not just from the drugs... Is there someone else here?"

"—let's just keep moving. There's nothing we can get from him."

“We can’t help him either, team,” Emmerich announced. “Let’s Charlie Mike.”

As they stepped away, the man reached out with his trembling hand and groaned.

“Their... place... them... it... switches... washes our... world... gone...”

The shadow rifted in Callisto’s peripheral vision and the agent snapped her M4 into her shoulder. With her finger on the trigger, her eyes and weapon barrel scanned the piles of debris a few times before she turned away.

“The dark has a way of playing tricks,” she murmured.

“Cali, are you coming or staying with your new buddy?” Fredrick asked.

“I’m coming, asshole.”

The corridor outside of the war room echoed with the sounds of a screeching motor. The wheels of Madam Dupree’s chair squeaked on the polished floors, growing louder. When the elderly scryer arrived, Katherine opened the double doors and greeted her with a smile.

“I brought coffee.” Madam Dupree beamed, holding up two large iced cappuccinos. “I get tired of the hot sludge once in a while.”

“Caffeine is always appreciated, no matter the form.” Katherine hugged the old lady.

The Madam’s eyes shifted down the hall toward Katherine’s office. The Assistant Director nodded.

"Max, take the helm. I'm going to have lunch. You know what to do."

"Yes, ma'am. I'll find you if there's anything beyond my pay grade."

When Katherine entered her office, she held the door open for Dupree, who rode in and parked next to her desk.

"Thank you for augmenting the mission yourself, Simone. You didn't have to do that. It gave me great peace of mind knowing you were on the ground."

"It's good to stretch the old legs once in a while."

Katherine chuckled. "I'm glad you're doing well. You should be resting, though."

"So should you. You just lost the man you love."

The smile from her chuckle faded before Katherine took a sip from her coffee. "I'm trying not to think about it."

"I've noticed. Katherine, you have a mind like a fortress and you're not even a trained scryer. While impressive, that's not always a healthy thing. I'm not saying this as the spiritual head of the agency. I'm saying this as your concerned friend."

"I appreciate it, Simone. I'll grieve for him later. What brings you this way?"

"Well, I had to drop off my new pet at the vault and figured I'd have Rogue and Mustang teams codify the vessel. She's a mouthy one. Listen, there's something I wanted to talk with you about."

"I see. Something that couldn't have been said over comms or email?"

"Everything can be compromised. Radio waves are just another frequency, not much different from what we scryers use. The right individual could decode it."

"Good point."

"Kat, something big is happening. My new pet, Skid Mark—"

"You and those names." Katherine smirked and shook her head.

"— let something major slip in her thoughts. It goes deeper than the current task to stop the one that set this in motion. Don't get me wrong, we need to apprehend or terminate Andras."

"Ghost and Curt are already on it. As per your suggestion, I sent a member of Muskrat to augment them."

"Andras is a commander for a demonic invasion force. But I have a feeling this is all just a ruse."

"What do you mean?"

"There's something deeper here. When I was probing Paimon's mind, I discovered why that girl was murdered. We knew she was psychic, with a lot of potential. It's a shame really. She would've made an incredible scryer had we found her before the enemy did."

"Agreed. We have to start searching harder for the gifted. That's something you and I mentioned at the last meeting for the command staff."

"Her sacrifice caused a huge gaping wound in the etheric layers. Truth is these wounds are just a change in frequency, a drastic one. Andras and his vessel were bringing over something greater."

"How great?"

"Well, to create a wound like that, the Aztecs would sacrifice thousands of lives to bring over the serpent beings they thought were gods."

"So, you're saying—"

"I think all of this was to conjure a demon prince, Kat."

Katherine remained motionless, staring at the surface of her desk. The pace of her breathing increased.

"Kat, this is bigger than an extermination gig. All of this is just a setup, buying time for that prince to escape into our world. The army of possessed zombies, the flesh abominations, Metzger, the asylum, all of it—just a ruse to keep us off balance and unaware of their real goal."

"I was hoping we were just stamping out a typical menace before things escalated. My logical side was telling me to wait and see what the agents discovered before making any drastic claims, but my instincts have been hounding my thoughts about something more dire. Now we have confirmation. Andras and his vessel have been ten steps ahead of us this entire time. We've been strung along, reacting instead of attacking. They have the initiative."

"He still needs to die before we redirect our strengths. Wiping out the asylum infestation was a necessary move."

"Now I'm wondering..."

"Yeah, Kat. I've contemplated the same thing. Who is the demon prince that came through? More importantly, where is he?"

CHAPTER 15
APOCALYPSE RISING

I can barely hear his voice these days... Have I displeased our God? Maybe some blood offerings will appease him? The hunting parties... round up some more faithless during the next surface run. Children... yes, they must be children. Their purity will bring his favor back to us.

An eerie orange glow covered the room, flexing and shifting with the flames of candles lining the floor. Tiny feet tapped on the pavement just outside. When the boy arrived, he panted in haste with his heaving chest, pressing hard to enter through the squealing metal door.

He paused, taking in the sight of Malachi seated with his legs crossed amongst the drifting shadows. The doors to the stalls on his left were missing, revealing latrines congealed in black filth. Malachi's eyes opened, twitching and surrounded by streaking red veins. When he scowled, the young boy looked away, finding the floor. The man reached up with his long wart covered fingers, scratching at the heavy gray beard which hung to his legs. When he lowered his head, the wide brim of his straw hat covered his face.

"Whatchu want, boy?" Malachi growled the demand through his teeth. "Ya know I don't like being bothered when I'm feelin' the other side."

"I sorry, Prophet. But there's strangers comin'!"

"What they look like?"

"They had'ta be surface dwellers. They had guns. Smelt clean, too. Ya know, they reeked of soap. They had fancy get-ups and all kindsa stuff on 'em. They usin' some kind of face thing to see in the dark. So, they ain't got the sight like us."

"Did the intruders see you?"

"No, Prophet. They went right by us. We hid like you taught us."

"You did good, boy. Go fetch Hezekiah. Have him round up the rest of the Family. Let him know the time has come. I'm going to finish my meditation with the Lord. He'll know what to do."

"You can count on me, Prophet!" The boy exclaimed, running out the door.

Lord, hear my prayers. The beast has sent its forces to come for us. Give us strength in the times ahead as you have given us strength to survive thus far. I know that moments ahead are tough, as it says in the holy gospels, that your true believers will endure a time of tribulation. We have waited so long for the final battle with the beast. I beg of you, be with us in this time.

"I hear your call over time and space, my son," a whispery voice announced. *"I am with you. Destroy the interlopers. Face them with courage, and your salvation awaits. Hand over any survivors to my servant Edjewale the priest in the depths. Your tribulation is at its climax. Rise up. Show no mercy to those who would serve the beast. You are my prophet. Guide my righteous fury to those who would stand against my truth."*

Malachi reached down, grabbing his long wooden rod and

climbed to his feet. He raised the weapon into the air, belting out a guttural war cry.

"Yes! I hear you, oh Lord! I believe! I have faith! We cannot lose! Hallelujah!"

The team continued, weaving through the tall pillars of stone and piles of rubble. The tracks they followed disappeared underneath the clutter. They continued through, marching down a gradual slope into the shadowy depths. Fredrick sighed, pretending to lose his footing and bumping into Calvin. The rookie staggered a bit then glared back, socking him in the shoulder. Emmerich raised his fist, signaling the formation to halt. Yelling echoed in the distance, the garbled words fading into unintelligible noise before reaching them.

"Quit playing grab-ass back there, you two. I think I hear something."

"Yeah, same here," Curtis replied. "I think someone is screaming about the bible."

"I've been feeling something odd this entire time, babe. As if we're being watched."

"Cali, you're right. We're not alone. I can see faint signatures amongst the fog of darkness. I can't tell what they are, but they're stalking us."

The bellowing chant grew, with the faint clamor of a chorus following. The sloping horizon filled with outlines of a crowd, trudging toward their team. As they drew closer, the figures waved around baseball bats, axes, and torches. Dozens of their members shouldered rifles or shotguns, aiming down the tunnel.

"And remember!" the leader boomed. "The Book of Revelation! Thirteen-three! The head of the beast was slain, but its deadly wound healed! And those who dwelled on the Earth marveled at the beast! They asked who is like the beast! Who is able to make war with it?"

"We need to take cover," Emmerich whispered. "Now!"

"The beast that was wounded when their money towers were struck, has risen! It has sent its minions to wipe out those who still hold true to words of our Lord—"

"What... the... fuck..." Fredrick mouthed.

"—they have brought this time of tribulation! But we do not dwell on the Earth, for we stay inside of it! Therefore, we will not worship the false image, the unholy idol of their dollar! Give your lives on this earthly domain, for paradise awaits you in heaven! Seek out the deviant, the unbeliever, those that would not follow his voice!"

"There's so many of them," Callisto whispered.

"Cease your hiding, invaders," the prophet roared. "We know you are here! You face the Family and I am Malachi, Prophet who hears!"

"Blessed be," a chorus of voices followed.

"Em, I'm lookin on thermals from the M249, and they're armed," Fredrick warned. "All of them mean business."

The leader continued, "Let your true sight guide you, for without their instruments, they are blind in the domain of the faithful. Through the valley of the shadow of death, fear no evil! Thou art with me! Thy rod and thy staff shall comfort me!"

"Prophet!" a voice cried out several feet behind Ghost Team. "They're over here! They're hiding over here!"

"What the hell?" Fredrick snapped, turning to see a child climbing on top of a pile of stones. "Kid, shut the fuck up! What the hell is the matter with you?"

"Prophet! Over here!"

"As in Jeremiah! You are my hammer and weapon of war: with you, I break nations in pieces; with you I destroy kingdoms! Attack now, Nation of God's voice! Rise against the unbeliever!"

The loud roar of a shotgun blast echoed through the cavern. Buckshot ricocheted off the wide cement slab Ghost Team took cover behind. AR15 rifles spewed their bitter payloads, filling the area with glimmers of light.

"At least the kid shut up," Fredrick said. "How long was that little asshole following us? What an asinine move."

Calvin looked back, seeing the boy's body sprawled over the rubble. Blood streamed over his forehead, pouring out of a gaping wound from a stray bullet. "Sir, he was downed."

"That's not on us, Em. I don't want to get blamed for that shit back in the rear! The boy's own people smoked him!"

"Shut up and return fire!" Emmerich ordered.

The stones and dirt around Ghost Team erupted with minuscule explosions as enemy fire continued. Emmerich flipped a switch to the PEQ15 laser device on the rail of his M4 carbine. Through his NODs, he saw an infrared green laser streaking across the battlefield. The operator brought the line over the first of their enemies, marching toward them. A rapid pair of shots from his carbine struck, sending a green mist into the air as they ripped into the man's chest. Emmerich's target groaned as he buckled over and writhed on the floor.

"Have I not commanded you?" the prophet roared. "Be strong and courageous! Do not be afraid; do not be discouraged, for the Lord, your God will be with you wherever you go!"

Green lasers guided shots center mass into the attackers. Ghost Team continued returning fire, dropping the first line of the mob. The steady approach of their foes ground to a halt under the controlled salvo.

"I have to hand it to that crazy asshole," Fredrick said. "He knows his bible well. If I survive this, I'm going to start reading mine more than just once a month."

"He's an idiot!" Emmerich snapped. "From our limited bible studies, you should know he's using zero dispensationalism! The scripture is being completely taken out of context!"

Fredrick cocked back the charging handle of his M249. Flipping his NODs away, he angled the machine gun on its bi-pod, aiming through the PAS13 thermal sight on the largest cluster of foes. He placed his hand on the shouldered buttstock of his weapon for extra stability, letting a burst of fire rip.

"First Peter! Two-seven!" the prophet bellowed over his brethren, continuing to fire. "Honor everyone! Love the brotherhood! Fear God!"

Fredrick's machinegun spewed its wrath in three to six-round volleys. Flashes of lead bored through their foes, penetrating to those behind them as the storm of fire continued. The attention of the group turned to Fredrick's position along Ghost Team's flank. A concentration of shots ricocheted off the broken stone slab the machine gunner hid behind.

"There's so many!" Callisto said.

"Use pyro if you got them!" Emmerich ordered.

Calvin rolled to his side, unclipping one of the fat smaller pouches on his plate carrier vest. He withdrew a grenade, his fingers squeezing the safety lever and plump metallic body. Pulling out the pin, he hurled the device in a wide arcing toss, landing in the middle of the enemy ranks. Three seconds later, flame and smoke erupted in a massive explosion. Shrapnel darted from its epicenter, cleaving into more victims.

"Nice work, Rook!" Fredrick exclaimed.

"Grenade out!" Curtis tossed another.

Between exchanges of gunfire, the shrill cries of the wounded echoed through the tunnel. Their numbers continued to mass. Revolvers, hunting rifles, shotguns, and small caliber handguns fired back at the team.

High-pitched creaking entered the area. Emmerich gazed over as the ranks began to open, allowing a quartette to roll up with a stubby rusted cannon, on two large wheels. The crew grunted, pushing the weapon's large bore toward Ghost Team.

"Stand clear!" the prophet hollered. "Deliver them unto final justice!"

Emmerich filled one of the cannoneers with lead, but another approached from the rear holding a torch. The fuse was lit, and flames burned away, racing into the cannon's powder chamber. Emmerich gunned down the igniter and ducked behind cover.

"Incoming!" Emmerich screamed. "Get your asses down!"

The cannon's thunderous roar spewed carbon clouds. The muzzle of the weapon expelled a torrent of iron balls and nails, ripping apart the landscape. A storm of dust filled the air, with particles of stone and dirt raining down on Ghost Team.

"Everyone good?" Emmerich asked.

"Yeah!" Curtis replied.

"Those assholes are using grapeshot on us?" Fredrick hollered. "What the fuck is this? The Middle Ages?"

Emmerich peeked over, his attention caught by the

screams coming from the Family. A few of their members writhed on the ground, howling and pleading.

"I told y'all to stand clear!" Malachi reprimanded. "Your lack of discipline and faith has been your own undoing. The rest of you, forward!"

"Cleanse them! Cleanse them!" a voice screeched.

From the ranks of the Family, several individuals came sprinting. Through their NODs, Ghost Team spotted white rifting shapes fluctuating from bottles they held in each hand.

"Cocktails!" Emmerich screamed. "Fall back!"

The bottles hurled into the air, crashing into Ghost Team's cover. Glass shards and flame spread in a huge smoky mess as each collided with stone. The area swelled with a blazing inferno. Their vision clouded from the bright fire washing out their NODs.

"Shit!" Curtis patted the flames out of his sleeves. "We're in trouble!"

"Fall back, team! Put some room between us and them. I'm dropping the beacon!" Emmerich ordered.

"I got you covered, go!" Fredrick said.

The agent rose to his feet, shouldering his weapon and holding back the trigger. Bullets showered the mob's position. The flames grew around Fredrick. He looked back to see Ghost Team setting a point several yards behind him.

"Moving!"

"Freddy!" Elizabeth shrieked. *"No! Actual! Someone! Help him!"*

Fredrick began his sprint over to the others. His right leg wouldn't rise, only performing a jerking spastic step before the strength in it failed. A warm spot developed on his calf. Gritting his teeth, he clenched his fists, summoning his will to run harder. Fredrick only managed a slow limp. He dropped to a knee in the shadows. Pain coursed through his leg as he reached down. Senses vanished as his heart raced. The roar of the Family faded. The smell of gun smoke disappeared. Drawing his hand up, he observed lines of blood rolling down his fingers, disappearing into his sleeve.

"I'm hit! Damn it! I'm hit!"

"Freddy, take cover!" Emmerich ordered. "We're cut off! Just sit tight."

"Fuck! I can't feel my leg, Em!"

"I'm going after him!" Calvin hollered.

"You sit your ass there, Rook! Don't be a hero and get killed trying to save me! Listen to Em!" Fredrick looked to Ghost Team's position. "Damn, they seem so far away now..."

"We have wounded one of the interlopers!" Malachi roared. "After him, do not let him escape! The rest of you continue delivering justice to the damned!"

"Em, drop the beacon. Don't worry about me."

"What, no!"

"Do it!"

"No! Shut the fuck up and sit tight, Freddy! We're going to get you!"

The quick patter of steps drew closer. Fredrick hobbled behind cover, biting his lip and plopping down. From his seated position against a pile of stones, he unclipped the next ammunition drum from his vest, locked and loaded his machine gun.

"Punish them! Their greed! Their corruption! They bring it into our home! The surface dwellers must die! Only the faithful will inherit the Earth! Praise the voice of our Lord!"

"Come get some, assholes!" Fredrick roared. "Lead sandwiches for everyone! All you can eat!"

"Someone else is here!"

Fredrick snapped his NODs in place. An infrared beacon pulsed opposite of him, creeping from the shadows. Heavy shots rang out from an automatic weapon, bringing 7.62 millimeter rounds strafing into the family members outside of Fredrick's cover. He leaned over, spotting a petite figure holding a compact AKS47 carbine. She wore a black stained olive bandana and goggles on her head. There was no plate carrier on her chest. Instead, she wore an old fashion load-bearing vest over a black wet suit.

Her almond-shaped eyes came into view as she kneeled beside Fredrick. After slinging her weapon over her shoulder, the woman's tiny hands went into action, reaching into a large hip pouch, and rifling through plastic. The woman's hand slapped a compress against his thigh. The thick gritty sheet of plastic contained a layer that reacted with Fredrick's blood. He gasped as the gore around and in the wound began to thicken into gelatin, putting an immediate halt to his bleeding.

She grabbed his leg, straightening it, Fredrick's head rolled back as he groaned to the heavens. A sharp prickling pain followed. His head snapped down, gasping as she pressed a needle into his limb. In haste, she rolled the contents of her medical kit together, tucking it away.

"Are you an angel?" Fredrick asked.

"Shh, you talk too much," she whispered.

"Yeah, I hear that a lot."

The woman bounced to her feet, pulling her AK to her hands, giving a burst of fire as another foe came close. Dropping low, she sidestepped, a hail of bullets passed over her previous position. The woman returned fire, repeating the process, and moving along the shadows.

"Em, I'm stabilized. I think."

"You fixed yourself?"

"No, the agent from Muskrat is here! That's the second beacon you're seeing. She didn't turn it on until now!"

"Freddy, get the fuck out of there!"

"What do you think we're trying to do, Em? They got us pinned down!"

"Cleanse them!" Malachi screamed. "We have them two surrounded! Give them a taste of the fiery hell that awaits their souls!"

Fredrick started sliding, rocks scraping underneath his rear as the Muskrat agent tugged at his shoulder straps.

"You know I can hobble," Fredrick muttered.

"Then, up!"

Fredrick struggled to his feet. His entire frame quavering as he tried to put weight on his trembling right leg. He staggered forward, keeping his balance despite the debris tripping his feet. The woman pulled the release cord on his body armor. His ballistic plates fell out, both of them spilling with a loud thud.

"No! My armor, it's still good! Why'd you do that?"

She grabbed his M249 SAW and tossed it to the ground. Before he could swat her hand away, she unclipped his patrol pack, which stripped his communication buds from his ear.

"Woman! You're getting rid of all my gear! What the hell?"

With a stern gaze, she delivered a vicious slap to his face. She motioned her head to the right. Fredrick limped behind her, grumbling underneath his breath. His head swung to the shatter of glass usurping his attention. Shards and fire spread over the area they fled. The howling members of the Family came just around the corner with weapons firing into the shadows.

"Damn, it's a good thing we bailed," Fredrick whispered. "So, where the hell are we going? Em and the team are back that way."

"We're cut off. Have to maneuver around, taking the long way."

"You saved my ass. I'll follow you."

"Freddy, can you hear me," Emmerich asked, watching their enemies overrun the position with his brother's beacon. "Freddy!"

Emmerich lowered his weapon, gazing at the mayhem unfolding on Fredrick's position. The unruly flames and the cackling mob heralded what he was trying not to accept, hoping that his brother would pop up from the horror to fight his way out. As the rest of the mob collapsed on the position, one of their members raised Fredrick's helmet into the air with a triumphant and primal howl. The infrared beacon still attached to it was active in Emmerich's NODs.

He's gone... I've lost both my brothers...

The battlefield pulled away from his mind. Emmerich was standing on the hot pavement of the local basketball court on a summer's day. Freddy was across from him, dribbling and staring up at the basket that seemed so much taller than them.

"Flick the wrist and it curves the shot downward," Emmerich advised.

"I swear when I make it to the NBA, during my induction speech, I'm going to be like, 'this is for my big brothers that always looked out for me.'"

"Alright, Air Jordan," Badrick chuckled. "Let's just focus on the fundamentals before we start planning any draft pick speeches."

"Freshman year won't be easy, Freddy," Emmerich warned. "It's going to set the foundations for your high school career."

"Pssh, I got this. I balled around these same jokers during middle school."

When Fredrick took his shot, the ball bounced off the rim and into Emmerich's hands. The orange surrounded his vision, until it transformed into the fiery light around him, guiding the agent back to his reality.

Get it together. I have to guide the rest of the team out of this alive. They're counting on my leadership. Swallow the pain and grieve later.

Emmerich stopped firing, his vision glued to his little brother's beacon. Bullets whizzing overhead forced Ghost Team to lie low. He couldn't see beyond the slabs of rock and debris that choked the field. An ocean of flames seemed to rage between Fredrick and the rest of the team. Enemies poured into the area, tossing more cocktails and firing in every direction. Callisto patted his shoulder.

"I'm sorry, Em," Curtis said. "He was a good agent."

"What now, Actual?" Calvin asked. "Should we counter or withdraw?"

"Oh, we're countering all right. Tac-com this is Ghost8Actual. Requesting Close Air Support, DBM. How copy?"

"Ghost, this is Tac-com. We acknowledge your last. ETA on CAS is four mikes. Sit tight, over."

"Roger, we acknowledge your last. Deploying beacon now."

With a twist and a snap, the device locked together. Emmerich took one last look at the blinking red dot between the handles and nodded. "For Freddy."

A grunt escaped as he tossed the device with everything he

could muster. It bounced amongst the feet of the Family. Cronies of the ravenous mob looked down, and one picked up the DBM beacon, punching another who tried reaching for it.

"Must be one them surface dwellers' fancy weapons." The scavenger barked. "It's mine! I'm keeping it!"

The rest went back to scouring the area and taking random pop shots at anything they could find.

"Did the flames consume the infidels?" Malachi asked. "Find the remains! If they aren't burnt, that voodoo weirdo near the cart storage will barter for it!"

"Em, you heard that, right?" Callisto asked.

"Yeah. He's talking about our HVT."

"Spread out! Find the others, too! Slay them! Do not rest until the minions of the beast have been made to face justice!"

"Keep them busy, team," Emmerich ordered. "Try to shoot the ringleader."

"I'm trying, Em," Curtis acknowledged. "I don't have a shot. He's been hiding behind the others the entire time."

M4 carbines spewed rounds into the crowd. A few tracers lined the path of fire, downing several of the members. The Family returned with their own hail of bullets spraying across the area.

The roof of the tunnel rattled. The earth shuddered around them. Dirt and stone rained down on the mob as the ceiling gave way. Malachi looked up, as a long pointed metallic warhead spun through and bore down on their position.

Ghost Team wobbled, tucking their heads as the shockwave carried through the tunnel. The force of the explosion sent particles of dust flowing through the air. Smoldering body parts and debris sprinkled around them. When the quaking finished, Emmerich raised his head and weapon, waiting for the smoke to clear.

Fredrick bared his teeth as he groaned, dragging his foot over the uneven ground. The tunnel rat opened a nearby door that he hobbled toward and dived into. She slammed it shut. The room shook from the impact outside.

"Damn! They must've called in the Deep Burrowing Missiles!"

"That's good," she whispered. "Keep your voice down. We don't know if there could be any more tangoes around. The underground carries."

The woman tried to open the door. "It won't budge. There must've been a cave-in on the other side."

She looked down the long hall. "We won't be able to double back. Let's just push on through and find a way. Keep your eye out for cultists."

"Cultists, eh? I guess that's a good name for them. Speaking of names. What's yours?"

"Nhi."

"That's some kind of Asian, right?"

The tiny woman narrowed her eyes and raised her hand.

"Hey! Stop slapping me! We might as well get to know each other since we're stuck in the shit together!"

"My father was Green Beret U.S. Army. My mother was Viet Cong."

"What the fuck? That's a weird pairing. How did they—"

"You need a weapon. Here. And shut up. I move in silence. This is why I prefer to work alone." She handed him a pistol.

"What's this shit?" Fredrick scoffed. "Did you just give me a nasty Hi-Point nine mil?"

"Your fancy weapons wouldn't have lasted longer than a day or two in this filth. That's the best pistol on the market for surviving harsh conditions."

"Yeah, but it's a Hi-Point!"

She slapped him again.

"Ow!"

"Whispers only. Now shut up. We move."

CHAPTER 16
NON-GRATUM ANUS RODENTUM

Flames crackled along the scorched terrain. Pillars of smoke rose high into the ceiling of the tunnel. The passageways were silent, except for the crunching steps of Ghost Team as they advanced. Callisto patted Calvin's back as he coughed and gagged on the grainy warm air.

"Thanks, ma'am."

"Cali. Just call me Cali."

"The negative energies still radiate strongly in this place." Elizabeth sighed. *"I'm having trouble navigating the fog of darkness. Be wary, Cali."*

"We need to stay focused," Callisto said. "Mind your corners, and don't assume everyone or everything in the area is KIA."

"Agreed," Emmerich said. "We're not going to be able to find Freddy's body amongst this carnage. Let's Charlie Mike." *Am I growing numb to all this loss?*

Ghost Team walked between the charred portions of humanity decking the ground. A warmth swelled through the air, carrying the stench of roasted meat.

"Definitely one of the more interesting engagements I've had," Curtis noted. "You Ghost bubbas know how to zero in on trouble."

"No idea what that was all about," Emmerich replied. "It's hard to say if these individuals served Baron or not. My guess is they were a different faction we just happened to stumble across."

"Yeah, babe," Callisto added. "I don't think demons and Luciferians would be reciting biblical scripture in the middle of a firefight."

"It's another world down here," Curtis mentioned. "Who knows what we're going to encounter next."

Sunlight drew Calvin's attention, observing the hole left by the DBM. "Actual, won't the city wonder about all this destruction?"

"I'm sure Kat has a plan. I think it's going to be spun as a sinkhole problem to the public. Those DBMs leave a small entry point."

"Makes sense, Actual. I'm sorry for asking so many—"

"It's fine. You need to understand how things work. A thorough understanding will help your career in the long term."

"Actual, I'm sorry for your—"

"Let's keep moving, Calvin. We're about to bring this scumbag to justice, so he can't hurt anyone else."

"Roger, Actual."

Light shone from the small plastic LED lamp in the middle of the room, just enough for the men huddled around to see each other's faces. One smacked another's shoulder, prompting him to hand over the bottle they were sharing. Footsteps approached from the dark outskirts of the room. The bearded face of one of their comrades came into the light as he hunched over, adding a fourth to their number. He looked at the bottle then at his comrades.

"You gunna rat us out to the prophet, Lamech?" one asked with a smirk.

"No," he said, snatching the bottle and taking a swig. "I couldn't even if I wanted."

"What do you mean?"

"Fire hath rained from the heavens!" Lamech screeched. "I watched from a murder hole waiting for the forces of the beast to pass by. The prophet and many of our family have been claimed in the judgment!"

"What? So that's what all that noise was about. Good thing I didn't leave my post. Let the zealots handle that crap. They're the ones that cling to the promise. I'm just here for three hots and a cot."

"So, what's going to happen now?" another asked.

"Hezekiah is going to think of something. In the meantime, I was told to make sure all sentries remain vigilant and on post."

"We ain't goin nowhere."

"Yup," another agreed. "Just gonna sit here and milk this bottle a'shine."

The roar of gunfire caused one of the men to jolt, dropping the bottle as he struggled to unshoulder his rifle. A rapid series of flashes streaked out from the shadows. Lamech's body rattled, as rounds bored through his back. The front of his chest exploded when the shots exited his body. His comrades covered their faces from the gore splattering over them. The room went dark after he keeled over, crushing their lamp.

"Shit! I just bartered for that—"

More bullets rang out. The flashes came from five feet to the left of the initial barrage. Another of their members collapsed. They returned fire, hearing their shots ricocheting off the walls.

"It's an ambush!"

"Run! Let them know there's about ten of them moving in on our position! Go!"

As one of them turned to flee into the darkness, a burst of gunfire cleaved him down. The last remaining sentry fired, once again, his shots hitting only the walls. Illumination sparked out from a prone position. Empty shells collided with the ground, their smoke-filled hollowed bodies echoing in the room.

"You just killed four men at point blank range by yourself? Damn, you maneuver well," Fredrick said.

"Never stand still in the dark. The shadows are my armor," Nhi replied.

"That's some straight-up tunnel rat shit right there. You know I could've helped."

The outline of a hand went across his face. "Damn it, Nhi. Stop slapping me!"

"You talk too much. Stay close."

Fredrick listened for the faint patter of her steps, as she disappeared from view. While she moved, he followed the small gentle taps. *She's right. Something is going on here. I can... am I adapting to this tunnel rat stuff?*

The warm copper tang of blood and stale, dry smoke entered his lungs. The shadows around him formed Nhi's outline. He stepped over their downed foes and followed her into the next corridor.

When his boots hit the ground, he could feel his feet flatten, his toes gripping at the insoles. The warm air left his nostrils, pushing out of his mouth. After seeing the fog of his breath, he pressed his lips together, breathing through his nose instead. When his hands touched the walls, his fingers sensed every imperfect indentation along the layers of grime.

This isn't something you think about when you're focused on what you're seeing.

Nhi's gleaming dark eyes halted his tracks. She tapped his right shoulder. The patter of her tiny feet beat a path to the right. The outline of her frame in the shadows disappeared.

Some kind of noiseless, visionless movement drill instead of hand signals? I mean, I guess that would make sense because you can't really see shit down here.

Nhi crouched down at a break in the wall where several bricks were missing. She pointed at an area that expanded into a more extensive tunnel.

Fredrick nodded. Small lights were still functioning around the walking platforms along the side of the railings. Most of them were flickering, illuminating enough to reveal dozens of large carts lined through the vicinity.

"We could work our way from here and link up with the rest of the team. That is if they're still heading in this direction," he whispered.

Nhi tapped his arm twice.

"I don't understand."

She slapped him.

"Ow! Why?"

"It means yes."

"Okay, well, you have to teach me this tunnel rat shit. I don't know all the SOPs."

She raised her hand.

"Don't you dare!" he hissed. "I can't feel my face because of you!"

Nhi tapped his chest. "This means we're moving out."

"Oh, okay. Now we're getting somewhere."

Nhi went through the opening, crouching low with her weapon held in both hands. She took a knee after touching down on the walkway, scanning the area. Fredrick followed, crawling on his hands and knees. His uniform scraped against the exposed bricks, smearing dust over his body. He touched her back after climbing up to his feet and joining her. She tapped his left shoulder.

Okay, this one I know. We're heading left.

The tunnel rat began moving, her legs stepping high with slow placement each time she touched down. She kept her frame low and avoided any sections where the light touched.

When she steps, it's so that her feet never drag or accidentally kick anything. Each movement is so methodic and controlled.

Nhi halted, reaching back with a stiff arm to stop Fredrick's advance. She gazed at one of the carts. Motionless silhouettes stood inside the windows and opened doors.

Those carts are packed with people. This must be the housing area for those crazy cultists.

The duo continued, pushing along the outskirts amongst the shadows. Fredrick bumped into Nhi as she halted.

"What's goin on? Why did we stop?"

A breathy growl emerged from the darkness they observed. Choppy steps approached as something lurched in their direction. A figure draped in shadow drew closer. Glistening eyes bobbed with each step it took, coming to an abrupt halt and fixing on the two agents.

"You talk too much!" Nhi's snapped, raising her AK.

Her assault rifle roared. A burst rattled the man's body. He continued to move closer to them, staggering forward with his arms outstretched. The screaming began, churning from the man's gaped mouth and echoing throughout the shaft.

"Fuck! Nhi, I think it's a ghoul!"

The tunnel rat fired another burst into the skull of the creature. Assault rifle bullets punctured through his head, shredding apart the brain inside. It collapsed to the ground, spewing dust around them. The doors to the subway carts began to slide open. Shrill screams echoed into the darkness.

"Move with me!" Nhi ordered.

Fredrick followed the faint tapping of her steps as she scurried off. He maneuvered, pumping his legs to keep up while lifting his feet higher than usual. Each step made the dull pain of his wound resurge. Fredrick gritted his teeth and winced.

Not this crap again. I'm going to die here. Please don't let me die in this shithole.

Rapid plodding hounded them through the tunnel. Fredrick peered back to see several outlines treading through the darkness.

Nhi spun to her right, hopping up into the air and hurling a small canister. The metallic device clanged against the walkway on the other side. Miniature explosions popped off from it, filling the area with flickers of light.

That sounds like small arms fire.

Several of the pursuers broke off, charging into the direction of the noise. They stopped short, staring at the device that continued to hop across the ground, flaring and popping. Nhi banked hard left, pushing through a door. As Fredrick started to pass, she reached out, grabbing his arm and pulling him in.

"What was that you used?"

"Shh."

A cloud of stench engulfed them, stinging at their nostrils with the reek of ammonia from dried urine. Fredrick watched as Nhi took a position inside of a stall and climbed on top of a toilet. He scrambled past the grime-covered sinks and broken mirrors, taking residence in the one next to her and closed the door.

There's no way out from here. Did we just corner ourselves? Damn it, standing on this toilet hurts like hell.

The entrance to the restroom opened. Heavy breathing passed between clenched and bared teeth—dozens of steps past by the stalls. The door near Fredrick's creaked as one brushed against it. Shadowy forms passed between the break in the door, spotting glimpses of them as they scoured the area.

You can hear a pin drop. Hold my breath? No, that'll make it worse. If they stay here long, I'll gasp for air. Slow, relaxed breathing, Freddy. They'll hear anything else.

Gunshots rang from the tunnel. Wails erupted around them, the vibrations of shrill echoes carried throughout the restroom. Fredrick shut his eyes and rubbed his throbbing leg, trying to calm his breathing despite the relentless vigor of his pounding heart. The screaming left the room as the ghouls rushed back outside. More shots roared, loud and clear in the brief moment the doors opened again.

The team? "I think that was Em and the others," Fredrick said as they exited the stalls. "We need to push out and link up with them."

"Are you stupid? Did you happen to forget about the horde of demonically possessed zombies between them and us? You're stupid."

"Just do your tunnel rat shit and get us over there."

"If I'm going to do my 'tunnel rat shit,' then I'm staying put here, in the shadows, until it all dies down!" Nhi snapped.

"We have to link up with them. This could be our only chance—"

She slapped him.

"Ow!"

"No. We stay here. We don't even know if that's them."

"Stop slapping me! Who else could that be out there? That's sustained and controlled fire. From trained soldiers."

Nhi's eyes narrowed. She shook her head.

"Listen, I understand you Muskrats have different SOPs. But my strength comes from the team. Not skulking around in shadows. If we're going to complete this mission, we need to link up with the rest of Ghost."

"I can't believe I'm doing this." Nhi unslung her AK and handed it to him. "Switch with me."

"Wait. What does this mean?"

"You said your strength comes from the team. So, go be with them."

He nodded. "Thanks. We'll come back for you."

"If you make it to them." She handed him two banana-shaped magazines that he stuffed into his pockets.

"Thanks for the vote of confidence."

The frigid cold of the door caused a shiver as he leaned against it. Fredrick pulled the AK snug into his shoulder, taking a deep breath before slipping out of the room. Each step he took was slow, mindful of his actions. He continued along the walkway, brushing his elbow along the wall, guiding his way.

Shots chimed with tracers flying through the air. They seemed so far away. The ghouls belted out their jarring screams near Fredrick. He winced from the piercing ringing in his ears. The creatures began their sprint, heading right for him. Fredrick's heart thumped in his chest. His finger braced against the trigger. Vibrations from the noise pulsed against the goosebumps on his skin. Silhouettes raced past him, deeper into the tunnels.

Fredrick continued until the illumination of gunfire revealed mounds of bodies. Frenzied enemies bounded over piles of corpses, only to fall from the volley of fire. On the horizon, Ghost Team continued dishing out lethal hate to the oncoming hordes.

Jackpot! It's them! Gotta keep pushing!

"Grenade out!" Emmerich yelled.

Crap! That's right. I don't have my beacon! They can't see me!

A bright conflagration filled the center of the tunnel. Shrapnel darted in all directions, lodging into the bodies of horde members. Fredrick swayed. He gasped as his lungs took in a deep breath of smoke. An involuntary cough rushed from his lungs.

Oh shit!

Steps beat the ground near him, stopping close. Fredrick's ears rumbled from their primal growls. Tracer rounds flew by. In the brief illumination, the ghouls' empty eyes met with his.

I'm made! They see me!

The ghoul's scream bore down on Fredrick. They sped toward him. He fired. Liquid sprayed from the heads of outlines in the darkness. Fredrick's legs started pumping. The wound bit at him with a pain that climbed into his lower back and abdomen. He ran to the muzzle flashes.

"Em! Guys! It's me!"

"Freddy? Cover him, team!"

"He's calling off the horde. I can feel the corruption of their demonic essence falling back into the darkness."

Fredrick heard the rounds whizzing past, followed by bodies falling to the ground behind him. He ran up to the team, taking a position next to Calvin in the firing line.

"Sustain fire!" Emmerich ordered.

The last of the hordes' numbers fell to the relentless fire. Emmerich turned and hugged his brother.

"I thought you were KIA, knucklehead."

"Me, too. For a second. Then the agent from Muskrat saved my ass. She's incredible."

"Where is she?"

"In a bathroom up ahead. We took cover in it. She didn't want to chance going out while the horde was here, but I knew I had to link up with you."

"Okay—"

"I know it sounds weird, but these tunnel rats have a way of surviving in harsh conditions. I understand why she didn't want to go out."

"So be it. We'll link with her on the next push. You lost all your gear. Here take these extra NODs."

"I got nothing to mount it on."

"Use this," Callisto said, tossing him some duct tape.

"You always come prepared, Cali."

"Don't say I never give you anything," she snickered. "It's good to see you in one piece, asshole."

Fredrick nodded. "Likewise."

"It's good to see you again, sir," Calvin said.

"Yeah, Steiner," Curtis agreed. "I'm glad you're okay. Guess this means no boozing it up in your honor after we get back to the rear."

"Hey now, no need to get hasty, Curt. We can still booze it up." Fredrick taped the NODs to the rail of his weapon and handed the roll back to Cali. "Thanks, Rook. It's good to be back. But I'm far from okay. My leg is killing me... But, Em, I know where that asshole is hiding."

"What you have for us, Freddy?"

"Up ahead, not too far. After we grab Nhi, there's a series of subway cars that were housing all these bastards. I have a feeling he's somewhere around there."

"The negative energies are becoming more concentrated in these areas. That would make sense that a high-level demon would want this as their lair."

"He's right," Callisto said. "I can feel Elizabeth. I think she's saying that we're on the right track."

"Good," Emmerich declared. "Then, we finish this."

They moved through the darkness, with Freddy leading the way. He opened the bathroom door, poking his head in with a smile.

"Nhi, you can come out. It's Freddy. The gang's all here."

He waited a moment, before walking inside with Emmerich behind him.

"Freddy, where's your friend?"

Peering into the stalls, he shrugged. "I don't know. She's gone."

CHAPTER 17
TOUCH OF THE ABYSS

"These cars were filled with the zoms you just smoked," Fredrick explained.

Emmerich examined the dense layers of brown rust thickened over the wheels. The team maneuvered between the large vehicles, stepping over the double row of tracks as they passed through. Calvin peered inside of an open door.

"What the..." he gasped.

"You see something, Calvin?" Callisto asked.

"Yeah." He pointed inside.

A corpse lay with its arms strewn out on the floor. Gnarled stumps remained where the fingers and toes should have been. Withered strips of meat dangled from shredded genitalia. Blood stained the entire car from the seats lining the walls to the vigilant poles remaining erect amongst the carnage.

"I think we're losing your rookie, Ghost," Curtis announced.

Calvin gasped, spinning away and convulsing with dry heaves.

"Looks like they've been busy," Callisto murmured.

"Ahead. Focus Cali. The negative energies... grow heavier."

Around Elizabeth, a fog of darkness began to grow. The etheric layers thickened, her presence wading through the turbulent waves. Subway tracks vibrated, vanished, and reformed. A prickling cold settled over her, the intensity rising with each step. Whispers lashed out around her in vague unintelligible words fading from reality. Each voice laced with the sharp hostility of malign intent grew louder as Elizabeth followed. Her approach was halted by the calamity of rippling energies peeling away the foundations of the material realm.

"So much evil has been done here. The veil has been worn so thin."

"I think Elizabeth is telling me something."

"What you got, my love?" Emmerich asked.

"She's saying, it's over there."

Between two cars, a massive hole emerged into view, with the shattered remains of bricks scattered about the floor. Hair rose on their arms as they peered into the entrance leading into the unseen.

"Thank you, Elizabeth," Emmerich said. "That looks like the entrance to a lair."

"Every fiber of my being is telling me that asshole is in there," Fredrick said.

"Then let's go flush out a voodoo sorcerer and demon lord," Curtis announced.

"Tac-com, this is Ghost8Actual. Radio check, over."

"Anything?" Callisto asked.

"Nope. Same as when we were in Moorehouse."

"Charlie Mike?"

Emmerich looked to the others as they nodded.

"For Baddy," Fredrick declared.

"We Charlie Mike," Emmerich agreed.

Curtis took point as they stepped down into the blackness. The team descended for a while until the flexing light of a candle caught their eyes. The pathway expanded, turning into a large room. Tables were scattered throughout, a clammy body occupying each of them. The musty stench of mold and decay invaded their nostrils from the tepid air, buzzing with large flies.

Curtis stepped in first, making a sharp right turn. Emmerich followed, turning left. The rest of the team zipped right behind, alternating until they filled half the perimeter of the room.

"It's clear," Curtis called.

Fredrick gagged. "I wouldn't say that. Smells like shit in here."

"And sandalwood," Emmerich added. "The conjurer's incense."

"Look at these corpses," Calvin gasped.

Leather straps bound each of the cadavers to surgical tables. The eyes and mouths of the inhabitants were sewn shut. Black liquid oozed from the stitches, cascading down their faces. Roaches crawled over the skin, a number fluttering to the floor and vanishing into the shadows. Curtis applied two fingers, checking for a pulse on one. Looking at Emmerich with a long face, he shook his head.

Elizabeth saw the twisted expressions of those dwelling inside of the bodies. They released cackles of delight that morphed into bestial snarls the closer she drew. Their thoughts echoed through the layers, giving Elizabeth images of their screams projecting from the spent bodies. Reverberating wails flowed from them, through the etheric layers.

"It's the ritual sight. Demons inhabit these bodies now. They

wait for the time when their master can set them free. They want to warn their master. Kill them!"

"This is the breeding ground," Callisto uttered. "This is where he's turning them."

"The asylum is where he's housing them," Emmerich added.

"Poor saps." Fredrick shook his head.

"Yeah, this is some B.S." agreed Curtis. "I feel like a failure. We weren't able to save these folks in time."

"Elizabeth is saying something else." Callisto paused, taking a deep breath and closing her eyes. "She's saying we need to smoke them. Now."

Emmerich nodded. "Quietly, dispatch all of them. I don't want this asshole knowing we're here yet."

Curtis drew his OKC3S bayonet from his vest. With a click and snap, the six-inch blade locked into place at the end of his M4 carbine. He thrust forward with it, the weight of the carbine driving the knife with ease into his mark. The body of the first twitched as carbon steel punctured through the underside of its mandible. Curtis pushed it through, muscles and sinew gave way to its sharp edge, penetrating the brain. Ghost Team followed suit.

"The forces of EL approach!" screeched the voices dwelling within.

Cries stretched through the etheric layers. Elizabeth raised her hands. The darkness that surrounded her snuffed out the positive energies she tried to summon. With her etheric body trembling, she propelled it outward. A light flickered into her palms. She pushed back against the weight of the darkness, expanding it until flooding the room.

"Silence, devils! You will not warn your master today!" With luck, I wasn't too late.

Wailing permeated through the etheric layers, until death sent the demonic souls back to the void. A few ripples managed to escape, echoing into the recesses of the dark.

"The children of the usurpers have arrived," Baron declared.

"Yaa, I can feel dem, too. It's time."

"Make use of the preparations we have in place. I will deal with the agents myself. It will only last for a short time."

"As ya wish."

The candlelight heralded Edjewale's approach, illuminating the soaked cage floor. The woman inside leapt to her bare feet, grasping the iron bars. Her wide shaky eyes peered into his.

"Don't do this!" she pleaded. "Please! You don't have to do this!"

"Oh, but I do. Tis nahting personal. Jus' bizniz."

The bottom of the cage ignited. Yellow and orange flames raced across the iron, engulfing the hostage's feet and climbing up her legs. She howled and writhed. The woman bounced around until the fiery blaze swallowed her body.

"Oh my God, no!" Another voice cried out. "You monster!"

"Shh... everywun gun get their turn. Be patient."

Each throat strained, horrendous screams proceeded the eruption of misery from shattered minds. Negative energy spawned from their souls, submerging the area. The material realm wilted, peeling back until it blended with the lowest reaches of the etheric layers. Frigid cold pressed against Edjewale's skin, fluctuating into a sweltering heat that caused him to yelp. The voodoo priest focused his mind, easing away the shifting extremes. Whispering voices called out from the other side, their intent caressing his soul like lost lovers. Their wickedness beckoned through the layers, causing Edjewale to grin.

"It fades away. The abyss arrives. It heralds my final manifestation. Complete it."

Edjewale felt the immense strength he once carried flee from him. The embrace of his companion lifted. The lumbar ache came, followed by stinging arthritis in his hands. His vision blurred, and the conflagrations surrounding them blended until it appeared as an undulating mass of light.

"I dun like bein without ya."

"Finish it, my friend. The layers will stabilize in time, and I will not be able to sustain it for long. I must complete my manifestation. We will unite after I have finished with the lapdogs."

"As ya wish, Baron." Edjewale turned to a shadowy corner of the room. "Roje, go greet our guests. Baron needs some time."

A hulking figure rose from its squatted position—the gleaming visage of burning corpses reflected in his two sets of unblinking eyes.

Emmerich approached the door opposite the room. He pressed his ear against its cold wooden frame and looked back to the others. Callisto finished dispatching the last cadaver, nodding at him as she pulled the bayonet out and waved for the others to follow.

"I can feel so much anguish on the other side of the door. The negative energies are so dense. How is it worse than in here?"

"I hear someone's voice," Emmerich said. "I can't understand what they're saying though. You all ready?"

Each of them gave the thumbs up. Emmerich went through the door first. His steps slowed, and he gasped. His weapon barrel lowered. The strength in his broad shoulders gave, causing them to droop. He reached up at the body strewn in shackles placing his hand on the cheek of his friend.

"Finley!" Emmerich cried. "What did they do to you?"

"Egghead, no..." Fredrick's eyes shut as he looked away.

Blood saturated his legs, having rolled down and smearing the ground. His dangling toes left streaks from the small red pool beneath him. Deep crusted lacerations decorated his body like tiger stripes.

"The shackles aren't keyed, luckily," Curtis said. "They're like the ones used in the asylum. I'll get him down."

"I'm going to kill that bastard!"

"None of that cowboy shit today, Freddy!" Emmerich snapped. "You stay focused. I'm pissed off, too. But we're dealing with a high-level voodoo practitioner, one of the most powerful types of sorcerers. And this one is possessed by a greater demon. They'll kill the entire team if one of us slips up."

Fredrick felt a hand on his shoulder. He looked back to see Callisto. "We'll get him, Freddy. I promise."

"Oh, my goodness," Curtis exclaimed. "He's alive!"

Finley's eyelids twitched with the effort to open them. A whistle of heavy breathing escaped through his teeth. He rolled his head back gasping, then wilted again in his confines with a pathetic groan.

"Get him down, quick!" Emmerich urged.

Curtis worked at the straps, catching Finley as he fell over. "I got you. Hang in there."

"Egghead, you're a lot tougher than you look." Fredrick reached out to pat his head.

"I'm going to take him up to the surface, Em," Curtis announced. "You and Ghost Team should Charlie Mike without me."

"You sure you're good to make it up there?"

"Yeah, I'll double back the way we came. First, I'm going to get him on a table in the other room to stabilize his wounds. I don't want to lose him on the way back."

"Thank you, brother," Emmerich said, clasping his shoulder. "Please, get him away from this nightmare. I've already lost too many family members..."

Another entrance set amongst the shadows opened. Shrill and desperate screams filled the area, and the brightness from the next room blinded the team's sight in their NODs. Blaring whiteness washed over their vision, forcing their gazes away with an involuntary jerk. The door closed. When the shadows returned, a hulking figure appeared, its double set of eyes glaring with a primal rage.

A N D R A S

CHAPTER 18
WHERE IS YOUR GOD NOW?

Weapons raised at the monstrosity looming in the shadows. Its long arms dragged across the ground as it charged forward. Ghost Team spread out, forming a line on one side of the room. Their optics zeroed in on the abomination as it approached with pounding steps. Rushing into the candlelight, the first head appeared, canted to its bulging right side. A line of sutures traveled down its face, attaching its slanted head to the thick slabs of its muscular shoulder. As the shadows peeled off its stitch covered body, a second head roared, its quaking yellow eyes fixing on Emmerich.

"Not another damn Frankenstein!" Fredrick exclaimed. "How many of these fucking things does he have?"

"Open fire!" Emmerich ordered.

A barrage of gunfire pummeled the brute as it continued forward, reaching out for Emmerich with its ample six-fingered hands. The agent ducked beneath the wide swing, rolling on to his right side and tumbling away. Both heads opened their mouths, spewing wads of saliva as it roared. It turned, scanning for its prey.

Emmerich rebounded to his feet, stepping backward as he delivered accurate double tap bursts into the temple of the upright head. The rounds sank into flesh. A metallic rattle followed.

"This one has a metal forehead, too!"

"Aim for the backside of it!" Callisto ordered.

The abomination trudged for Emmerich with its heavy thumping steps. The monster's arms reached out, this time wide and low. Five weapons roared into action. A salvo of fire shook the back of the upright head as lead punched through the skull. The left side's leg buckled, he fell over, hitting the ground with a loud thud.

The remaining head wailed, searching for its foes but unable to pull its face away from the shoulder it was grafted on. Its arm struggled to hold up the body, but the weight of the other side kept it down. Emmerich walked around the monstrosity, pointing the barrel to the back of his skull and emptying the magazine.

"Who are you?" Emmerich raised his M4 to a corner of the room. "You have three seconds to identify yourself."

The team followed his line of sight. Fredrick smiled as Nhi stepped out. She approached with her hands risen.

"Whoa, easy, Em! That's my girl. The tunnel rat."

"I am Muskrat15Echo," Nhi acknowledged.

Emmerich sighed with relief, pulling the reticle of his optics away from their ally. "My apologies. It's been quite the ordeal. It's good to see you, and thanks for saving my brother back there."

"We have to get this one to the surface," Nhi said, pointing to Finley. "He's not going to last much longer. Some of those wounds look infected."

"Em, we should listen to her," Fredrick agreed. "She knows a lot about patching up folks."

"Anyone notice the screaming from the next room stopped while we were fighting that thing?" Calvin asked.

"Yeah, but we're not going to rush in and end up springing a trap," Callisto said. "Edjewale is cornered like a rat. That's usually when they're the most vicious."

"I don't like it," Emmerich said. "Prep yourselves before we go in there."

Nhi drew a small brown bottle from the fat medkit on her hip. She rubbed the liquid onto bandages and applied them around Finley's body.

"Here take mine, too." Callisto handed over her roll of medical tape and gauze.

"That's the best I can do for now." She pulled out a needle. "This is for the pain." Murmurs escaped Finley's mouth. His eyes rolled up into his head.

"Egghead? What did you say?" Fredrick asked. "We can't hear you."

"He's delirious," Nhi answered.

Curtis heaved their comrade over his shoulder. "Okay. I got him."

"Curt, don't go it alone," Emmerich said. "Take Nhi with you."

"Yeah, she'll be able to help you avoid engagements and if any complications occur with Egghead, you'll have a trained medic with you."

"Very well. Ghost Team, you all better get the evil bastard that did this to our boy," Curtis demanded.

“He’s already EKIA. He just doesn’t know it yet,” Callisto vowed.

“I’ll come back with augments from Monarch after we get Finley to safety. Lead the way, Ms. Nhi. Let’s get this man topside.”

“Yes, follow me! I’ll get us there safely.”

Emmerich bumped fists with Curtis as the large black man carried away their brethren. The tunnel rat and the leader of Monarch disappeared down the dusty corridor. Emmerich looked at the rest of Ghost Team.

“Green to green, Actual,” Calvin said.

“I’m with you, Actual.”

“Same.” Callisto popped a fresh magazine into her M4. She smiled. “And Elizabeth is ready, too.”

“Let’s get this sombitch,” Fredrick stated.

“For our friends,” Emmerich said. “And for all those that suffered. Let’s cleanse this filth.”

“For our family,” Calvin added.

When Emmerich opened the door, a wave of heat brushed against their faces. Blackened flakes drifted in the air, sticking to the skin of his cheeks. Fiery blazes around the immense room, stretched to the ceiling, filling it with thick clouds of smoke. Emmerich flipped his NODs away. He approached with the team filing in behind him, expanding the perimeter.

The shadows consumed Elizabeth’s vision. The prickling cold bit at her as the negative energies caressed her presence. She swallowed deep, focusing her mind, and filling it with resolve.

“I couldn’t hear their cries. The layers. They’ve been warped into another gaping hole. We’re looking into the abyss.”

The stench of burnt meat invaded their nostrils. It clung to their saliva, ensuring they tasted the spectacle. Emmerich and

Callisto approached the balefire at the center of the room. The shadows engulfed them as they pushed through the illumination. Callisto pointed at the charred hands clinging to the iron bars.

"What the fuck is that?" Fredrick exclaimed.

The team followed to where his AK was pointing. Amongst the light on the opposite end of the large room, sat a massive chair composed of human flesh. Calvin lowered his weapon, murmuring curses upon seeing the vista of wide empty eye sockets stretched over the headrest. Hair protruded in random patches, a mix of curly, straight, brown, blonde, and black. The blood stains that striped across it had long crusted over the dark and shriveled portions that were sutured together.

"That damned monster," Callisto snapped.

"I hear... people whispering," Calvin stated. "Does anyone else?"

"It's the demons within the darkness, just beyond the veil that separates them from our reality. They want to come over into our world, but something is keeping them at bay. Something they don't want to go near. He doesn't want to share with them..."

"Yeah. I hear it, too," Emmerich said. "Where the hell are they?"

"We be right 'ere, mon," Edjewale answered from across the room as he stepped out from a blanket of darkness. "I heard ya be lookin for meh."

You... Keep it together. If we take him alive, he could provide valuable intel. But... He killed my brother... Keep it together. "If you come peacefully, your life will be spared. You'll stand trial and spend the rest of your days locked away for your crimes against humanity," Emmerich declared.

Ghost Team put the voodoo priest in their sights.

"Ya not gunna shoot meh. Ya be soljahs, not murderers. I

gotta differ'int plan. 'ows bout I hav'a seat ober dere," he replied, pointing at his flesh throne. "Then I watch ya 'ave play time wiff da Baron."

"Don't be so confident about that, scumbag," Callisto snapped. "We are the Unholy Slaying Agency, after all."

The darkness gathered. Grim energies stretched through the room. A towering lithe figure stepped into reality. Part of him faded back into the hidden recesses. Serpentine pupils glared from beaming yellow eyes. A scaled brow arched over its draconic countenance. As Ghost Team raised their weapons, it unfurled lengthy blade-like claws.

"I can feel your anger," Baron rasped. "It is laced over the pathetic lament from your undisciplined minds. Come, children of El. Give in to your hatred. Claim your vengeance."

"You fall here, Andras!" Elizabeth yelled.

"Weapons free!" Emmerich roared. "Engage at will!"

Bullets raced through the air, sinking into the back walls. Baron moved across the ground in swift and noiseless steps, galloping toward the team. Calvin aimed at the demon. Seeing it zip out of sight, he shifted his weapon to the right, trying to retain his aim. Streaking pain slipped underneath his arms, piercing through the ballistic plate of his vest as if it were made from pudding. The warmth of his innards rushed out, soaking into his pants. Lines of blood streamed down Baron's arm as the demon raised the wailing rookie.

"Pathetic apes!" Baron snarled. "Mud people, from the dust whence you came, so shall you return!"

"I don't have a shot!" Callisto screamed.

"*But I do,*" Elizabeth said.

The scryer flexed her fingers as if she were clutching a ball. Her eyes shut. A slow rhythm took over her breath as thoughts cleared from her mind. A humming light began to gather.

Baron cocked back his arm, flinging Calvin's writhing body at Fredrick. The two agents toppled over. Fredrick managed to discard his rifle just in time to catch the junior team member. His head smacked on the hard floor, blurring his vision. The rookie's cries didn't register as he struggled to his feet. His head reeled back as the sensation of floating overcame him, and his shaking body fell over again, the aching from his head becoming unsurmountable.

No! Calvin! Freddy! Damn it! This isn't working. We're down to half strength and the fight has only just begun. We need something else... I got it! "Cali, do you still have those quartz rounds Madam Dupree gave us?"

Callisto nodded to Emmerich. She pressed the magazine release, reaching into the back of her vest pouches. "Good call."

"Bullets first, then we'll use the daggers."

A spark of light developed in Elizabeth's hands. It flexed and grew, forming into her clutches until shaping an orb. Her eyes met with the demon's hateful glare.

"Scryer!" Baron snarled. "I've sensed your presence in my kingdom since you arrived. You've been a thorn in my side long enough!"

She hurled the ball of light at the demon. Emmerich and Callisto watched as Baron staggered away, raising his claws in defense. The shadows withered. Small particles floated away from the demon's presence.

Callisto squeezed the trigger. Quartz pierced into the monstrosity, sending it vibrating and bellowing to the ceiling. She fired until her weapon was empty. The demon's shadowy essence peeled, with more portions breaking from its body.

"Malfunction! My weapon's down!" Emmerich yelled. "Damn it!" He slapped his M4, drew back the charging handle and punched in the forward assist.

Elizabeth focused, bringing her hands together again.

"Time to join your brother, Steiner!" Baron snarled as he rushed toward Emmerich.

Callisto hurled her M4 at the demon, then sprinted at him, reaching into her vest to draw her quartz dagger. She felt the breath from the demon's rumbling growl as he turned and raked his claws across her face and chest. The agent fell over, her vision filled with red.

"Stupid, bitch! You are out of tricks!"

Claws pierced her abdomen as Baron reached down and scooped her from the floor. Callisto buckled, her body folded over as the demon's fingers sank deep into her. The last bit of her fleeting strength called into her hands, clenching the dagger.

"What were you thinking, girl? I am forever."

"A queen always protects her king!" Callisto roared, plunging the dagger into Baron's left eye.

Baron screamed, anger fueling his resolve. The demon's grip tightened, heralding the snap of bones. The woman gasped as her frame went limp, the life fleeing from her body. Baron tossed her remains and staggered toward Emmerich.

"No!" Emmerich screamed. *My love... My life...*

"Yes... howl in grief!"

Quartz rounds ripped into the demon. Baron growled, wading through the hail of fire and raising his claws at the agent. Another globe of light smacked into Baron's back. Ripples of shadow escaped from his being, streaming into the air. The fading demon turned to see Elizabeth charging another.

"Andras!" Elizabeth screamed.

"You know my true name, puppet. It matters not. You haven't the necessities to exorcise me!"

"We're not here to exorcise you!"

"Bold words, little psychic gnat."

Emmerich pulled his quartz dagger from his vest, charging at the demon. Andras turned to meet the assault, his massive claws snatching the agent and squeezing. Emmerich gasped as his ribs collapsed, the breath forced from his lungs. With the last of his fleeting will, Emmerich raised the quartz dagger into the air, burying it into the demon's chest.

Andras bellowed, dropping the agent, and falling to his knees. Fragments of his body raced away. He clawed at the ground, his eyes widened, a screech escaped from his maw of dagger like teeth. The demon's essence withered.

"Break, fiend!"

Elizabeth pushed her will forward. A wave of light rippled through the etheric layers. Shadows streamed from Baron's presence, ripping the screaming fiend asunder. His cries echoed through the layers. The whispers stopped.

"Who's next?" Elizabeth thundered into the exposed abyss. She felt their auras receding from the wound, fleeing back into the depths of their prison.

The images cleared, as Fredrick struggled to gather himself from the throbbing headache. He held tight to Calvin. "It's... gunna be okay, Rook. Just... have to get... back on my feet."

After rising, he grabbed the AK from the ground and staggered forward. Sharp pain streaked through his back and down into his legs with each slow step.

"No..." he muttered.

Callisto's broken body lay in the fetal position on the ground. Unfurled strands of her chocolate brown hair wove into the blood pooling underneath her face. Fredrick lowered his head, his shaky eyes unable to hold the sight of his friend's corpse as the cold pain of loss began to swell from his core. His peripheral caught a faint movement in the corner. Emmerich's torso heaved with each shuddering breath he took.

"Em!" He limped over. "Em, say something!"

"Did we win?"

"Yeah." Fredrick knelt beside him. "He's dead. You guys did it. You killed that bastard."

"We did it..."

"Okay, I'm busted up pretty bad. Just give me a minute and we'll RTB—"

"I don't... have a minute, Freddy..."

"No! No! You can't leave me, Em! I can't do this shit without you and Baddy! You guys are the brave ones! You guys are the smart ones! You guys are—"

"You'll be... fine. You've worked... with the best... I need to be with... my queen in the next... adventure... I promised..."

Fredrick nodded.

"I can see... Elizabeth... She's well..."

"Goodbye, Actual, and thank you for everything."

"Em, fight it! Emmerich!" Fredrick leaned over. The tears flowed, soaking into his brother's uniform.

"He be one wiff da spirit world now," Edjewale declared as he stepped over.

The AK47 charging handle cocked back. A round chambered into place.

"Easy now, federal agent. I be unarmed and surrenderin'."

"Freddy, don't! It would be better to take him alive!" Elizabeth pleaded. *"He has valuable intel!"*

"Ya bruddahs fought well. Ya should be proud."

"You and that demon killed them!"

"Ya angray? I be upset, too. Ya slain mah only family. So, we be even."

"Freddy! No more killing. We've seen too much violence and blood. No more, please..."

The wrinkles on Edjewale's face rolled back, displaying a broad toothy grin. Fredrick aimed in. The muzzle of the AK47 rose to greet the voodoo priest.

B
A
E
L

CHAPTER 19
HONOR THE FALLEN

"Sacrifice," Howler spoke into the microphone as she gazed into the crowd. "That is a word that all agents and scryers have come to know and adhere to in their service to our world. Those that we honor today have made the ultimate sacrifice to assure that we do not lose the war to darkness. They were four of the best, and I had the privilege of working alongside three of them during my time as a team commander. We are safer today because of their tireless efforts to bring justice to the nefarious. Thanks to their dedication, less insidious threats plague humanity today. Agent Badrick Steiner, Agent Callisto Dukas, Agent Emmerich Steiner, and Agent Evan Smith will be missed, but honored in our memories as we persevere into the future they gave their lives to protect."

Rifles raised in white gloved hands. Blank rounds fired, spewing carbon from barrels and launching gray clouds into the air. The pallbearers marched two by two, carrying the caskets of their brethren. One wore the black and blue of the

Marine corps, with a blood stripe centered down the side of his legs. Another wore the Army uniform in all black, others dressed in the white Navy attire and Air Force blue.

The silence broke with grass crunching underneath their polished oxford shoes. Branches swayed in the distance from a light breeze that caressed them. The crowd watched from the rows of folding chairs as the small formation passed.

Katherine Howler walked to the forefront with Madam Dupree next to her. She turned to Fredrick, holding hands with Elizabeth and Madelyn. Calvin stood behind them. For a moment, the rookie's swollen red eyes connected with Howler's, before he turned his glistening face to observe the caskets positioned by their plots. Badrick's wife, Aisha, stood next to Elizabeth. Her hard stare beamed into Katherine, until she shook her head and lowered her gaze. The tears flowed from the woman, she lowered her hijab covered head, burying her face in her hands.

"Freddy, I'm not going to pretend like I can understand what you're going through," Howler lamented. "The agency—humanity, owes your family a debt that we can never repay. If there's anything your family needs, you just ask."

"Yes, ma'am."

"Kat. My team commanders call me Kat. All of you take as much time as you need to recover. We'll talk about restructuring Ghost Team later."

"Yes, ma'am."

"So, you'll be adopting Madelyn?"

"Yes, ma'am. It's a family tradition."

"I'm glad that Monarch was able to rescue her from the asylum after it was over."

The little blonde girl looked at Howler with her big green eyes. A weak smile was the best she could summon.

"What a pretty dress you have on."

Madelyn stared at the Assistant Director, unblinking in her statuesque state.

Three agents approached in solid black dress uniforms with white gloves. In their arms they held the triangle shaped, folded burial flags. Katherine handed two to Fredrick, a golden cross draped over each of them. The third, with a platinum crescent moon, was given to Aisha.

"I'll leave you to grieve." Howler lowered her gaze and walked away.

So much loss. Hundreds of civilian lives utterly ruined. The man I love is gone. I'll never be able to look up into his deep brown eyes again. My proteges gone. Along with the hopes I had for them. Despite their victory, I can't help but to feel we're losing the war. How do we stop the inevitable when our best couldn't survive?

Malin sat at the end of the long table, rolling her intense eyes at the banter of her peers. She glared at each of them, the darkness of her shadowy aura growing within the etheric layers. Her thick brows flared with disapproval, and she slammed her fist down on the table. A crack stretched through the polished wood as it shuddered. The room went silent.

"None of you are answering my question!" she snapped. "I don't care what happened at Moorehouse. I want to know where he is now! Anyone have anything other than what I've already been made aware of? If not, then for your sake, be silent. Now, it has been four days since he—"

The negative energies vibrated in the ether as the darkness

around them grew. The light of the sun didn't reach the building, leaving it in a shadowed tint. Malin felt her essence no longer anchored to her body, the layers erupting around her like a boiling cauldron. The sensation of her immediate presence was lost. Her fingers or toes lost their awareness. Gone was the pulse of breath that entered her nostrils despite the quickening pace. There was only the cold numbness that radiated a dull pain beginning to encompass her entire being. The meat suit she wore began to tremble, disregarding any attempt to collect herself. She shot up and out of her seat, her chair rolling backward.

"Never mind... he's here. Rise all of you, fools! Now!" she urged the others, scrambling to their feet.

The double doors of the room opened. A man in a suit stood before them. His angular face scanned each of them with a dour expression. His piercing scornful eyes connected with each of theirs, withering any contrary resolve that may have remained as he reprimanded the room with his glare. His hateful ire fell on to Malin. She dropped to her knees and pressed her face into the floor. The others followed her example.

"Prince Baal, my Master. We have been searching for you, ever since that fool Andras conjured you in such awful conditions."

"I wanted my arrival to remain as inconspicuous as possible," his sharp voice uttered, laced in a sinister eldritch tone. "I can sense the weakness radiating from all of you, like a foul odor. You've grown too accustomed to mortal comforts. It has clouded your judgment. Now tell me, where is my field commander? There's much we have to do."

"Slain, my Master." Malin trembled to the point of

convulsion. "His soul was disintegrated by the mortal forces, they—"

"Silence! It figures my best servant would be the one slain. That loss just hindered my plans." Baal hissed the words between his teeth. "Which one of you selected this vessel for me?"

"I did, my Master," she continued. "I thought you would want someone who was influential, young and psychically gifted."

"You did well."

Malin sighed with relief.

"Despite our recent taste of defeat, you will renew all efforts, continue everything I have devised."

"Yes, Master," they acknowledged in unison.

"Our setback was not a complete loss," Malin added. "We have finally managed to infiltrate the USA."

"This pleases me to hear. I will expect reports on that soon. I'm placing you in command of the mission. This is your priority."

"As you wish, Master. It'll be my pleasure."

"Where is my mother?"

"At the throne where Atlantis used to be," Malin answered. "The humans took to calling it Antarctica after the flood. She went there after being released from Sheol. We haven't heard much from her, except for the original instruction that was given."

"Very well."

"We will make arrangements for you to speak with her immediately, Master."

"Focus on your mission. My goal is to ensure our endeavors remain on course. Our time is short. The reclamation should be foremost in your thoughts. Let not your arrogance impede your better judgement. Humanity is asleep now. We have torn at the fabric of their faith, their government, their history, their reality. They must be kept off balance. Make no mistake, if they were to awaken to the truth of all things, we will be incapable of stopping them. Should any of you compromise our agenda, you will beg for the mercy of death."

THE HUNT CONTINUES:

AGENTS DEPLOYING TO JEFFERSON MOUNTAIN RANGE

Stay tuned for the next installment of the UNHOLY SLAYING AGENCY series, THE CANNIBAL PEAKS.

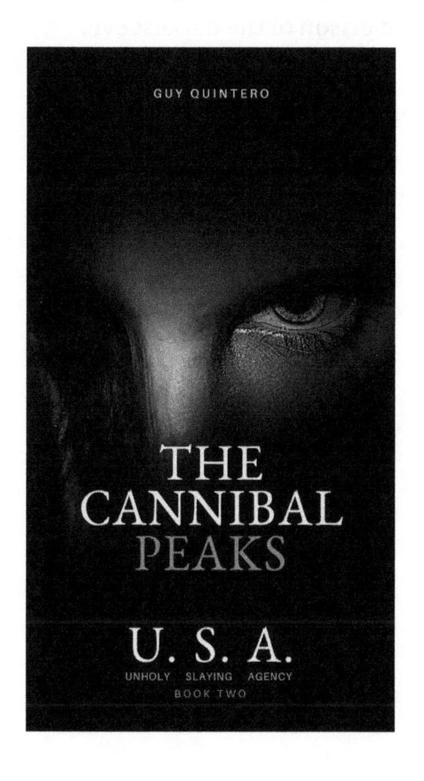

In the vast uncharted terrain of the Jefferson Mountain range, hikers go missing all the time. Within the dead of the night, deep in the most remote area, a young girl and her twin brother watch as their family is devoured by the things that move too fast. Now as adults, Artemis and Aristotle Coleman lead Raptor team into the heart of an underground kingdom in Jefferson, that was once the prison of the darkest evil.

Sign up for my newsletter to be notified when new books are released.

guyquintero.com/recruitment

ABOUT THE AUTHOR

Guy Quintero is a former reconnaissance soldier with three deployments under his belt. Quintero combines his military background and a life-long fascination with the occult, bringing a mix of bone-chilling horror and heart-pumping action. His inspirations are Stephen King and Tom Clancy. He hopes to follow in their footsteps someday.

GuyQuintero.com

instagram.com/guyquintero

facebook.com/GuyQuinteroAuthor

CPSIA information can be obtained
at www.ICGtesting.com
Printed in the USA
BVHW031753150822
644647BV00007B/95